The Law and Miss Mary

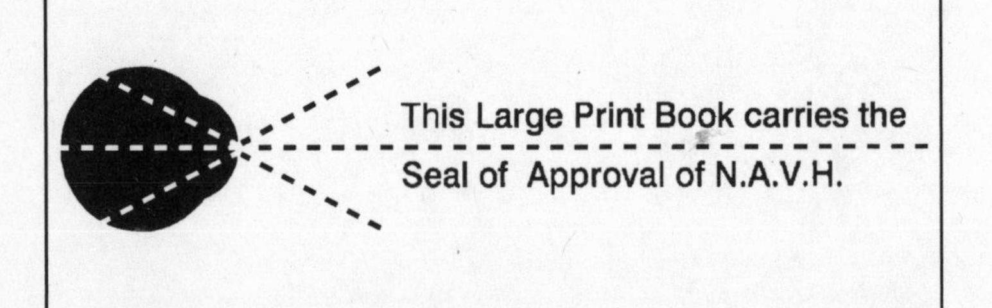
This Large Print Book carries the
Seal of Approval of N.A.V.H.

The Law and Miss Mary

Dorothy Clark

THORNDIKE PRESS
A part of Gale, Cengage Learning

Detroit • New York • San Francisco • New Haven, Conn • Waterville, Maine • London

This is a work of fiction. Names, characters, places, and incidents either are the product of the author's imagination or are used fictitiously, and any resemblance to actual persons, living or dead, business establishments, events, or locales is entirely coincidental.

Thorndike Press® Large Print Christian Historical Fiction.
The text of this Large Print edition is unabridged.
Other aspects of the book may vary from the original edition.
Set in 16 pt. Plantin.

LIBRARY OF CONGRESS CATALOGING-IN-PUBLICATION DATA

Clark, Dorothy.
The law and Miss Mary / by Dorothy Clark.
p. cm. — (Thorndike Press large print Christian historical fiction)
ISBN-13: 978-1-4104-2552-2
ISBN-10: 1-4104-2552-5
1. Large type books. I. Title.
PS3603.L359L39 2010
813'.6—dc22 2010006149

Published in 2010 by arrangement with Harlequin Books S.A.

Printed in the United States of America
1 2 3 4 5 6 7 14 13 12 11 10

For the Lord seeth not as man seeth;
for man
looketh on the outward appearance,
but the Lord looketh on the heart.

— 1 *Samuel* 16:7

This book is dedicated with
appreciation and
affection to my extremely talented
editor
Melissa Endlich, who knows how to
make each
book the very best it can be. Thank
you, Melissa. It
is a pleasure to know you, and an honor
to work with you.

And a special thank you to my
wonderful friend
Jean Mallery. It was Jean who first
learned, lo these
many years ago, that I was secretly
writing a book
and encouraged me to follow the Lord's
call. If it
hadn't been for you, Jean, I wouldn't be
working on

my seventh novel. Thank you for your faithfulness,
encouragement and love.

"Commit thy works unto the Lord,
and thy thoughts shall be established."

Your word is truth. Thank You, Jesus.
To You be the glory.

CHAPTER ONE

St. Louis, 1840

Mary Randolph shifted her gaze from the muddy waters of the Mississippi River flowing under the steamboat to the scratched and gouged promenade deck rocking gently beneath her feet. In spite of the sun shining overhead, both river and deck were dull, lusterless. The same as she. Tears flooded her eyes. She blinked them away and squared her shoulders, refusing the thought, determined that no remnant of the past would cloud this first glimpse of her future.

The tempo of the engines driving the paddle wheels slowed. A raucous blast from the boat's whistle split the air. Mary gripped the rail with both hands and peered out at the city of St. Louis, thankful for the sudden downdraft of wood smoke from the steamer's tall stacks that made her eyes smart and water, giving her an excuse for any betraying, glistening tears.

The *Fair Weather* gave another blast of her whistle, slipped into a berth and nosed up to the bank. Cobblestones paved the incline from the river's edge that leveled off in a street that formed the city's front door. Mary crowded closer to her brother in the sudden press of passengers along the rail and studied the area. Steamboats and other river craft of all descriptions lined the sloping bank, taking on or unloading passengers. Smokestacks belched plumes of acrid smoke into the warm, moist air. Whistles blew, announcing arrivals and departures. Ships' mates shouted orders to their crews. Chains rattled and ropes squeaked with tension as cargo was taken aboard or lowered to the dock. Hammers pounded as repairs were made. And beneath the din hummed the constant murmur of voices.

Mary blinked the moisture from her eyes and took a step back to use her brother as a windbreak while she adjusted her new hat. "I did not expect such a hustle and bustle of activity in a frontier city." She shook out the long tails of diaphanous fabric streaming from the base of her top hat down her back, and moved forward again to stand at the rail. "There must be at least twenty or twenty-five steamboats docked along this shore, James."

"I make it closer to thirty, perhaps more. It's difficult to tell." James leaned over the rail as far as he was able and looked up and down the shoreline. "There are so many smokestacks it looks like a forest growing out of the river." He pushed himself erect and placed his mouth close by her ear. "And only six of these steamers are ours — including this one. I shall write Father of the stiff competition immediately."

Mary released her hold on the rail, stared at the flecks of peeling paint on her gloves and lowered her voice to match his. "Do you suppose Father knew of the neglected, weather-beaten condition of the ships before he bought the line? If the *Fair Weather* is any indication, the vessels of the Mississippi and Missouri steamer line are in very poor condition."

"He knew. Wilson had all the information when he came to St. Louis to make the deal in Father's stead." James leaned closer to her. "And Father knows why. His agent had reported someone has been letting the ships fall into disrepair while they skimmed off the profits. I am to discover the culprit."

Mary stopped brushing her hands together to rid her gloves of the paint specks and looked up at him. "So *that* is the reason for our secrecy."

"Exactly." He turned his mouth back to her ear. "If anyone learns our father is the new owner, the thieves will cover their tracks and disappear. We must be cautious and trust no one with that information until I uncover the truth."

"You are warning *me* to silence?" Mary shot him a look of disbelief. "Surely you do not think anyone will learn our father purchased the line from *me?* Why, if I were a devout person, I would be on my knees this very moment giving thanks to God for our secrecy. This is the perfect situation for me." Her face tightened. "Of course, if it were not for God, I would not need anonymity from Father's wealth and status." The words came hissing out in a bitter whisper. She pressed her trembling lips together and turned away from the flash of sympathy in her brother's eyes.

"Mary, listen —"

She shook her head. Wind gusted over the rail, snatched the long, flowing tails of fabric on her hat and whipped them forward again. She brushed the filmy fabric from her face and swallowed the tears that threatened to expose her heart.

"Mr. Randolph?"

"Botheration!" James sucked in air and

held it. She glanced at him through her lowered lashes, saw his frown. The threat of tears fled. A smile tugged at her lips. She, Sarah and James all used the "hold and count" method to gain control when they were upset or annoyed. It was one of the gems of wisdom their mother had taught them. *Mother.* Homesickness washed over her like the river water whispering along the shore.

"We will discuss this later." James whispered the words into her ear and turned. "I am James Randolph."

Mary watched a heavy-set man, garbed in a black suit, shoulder his way through the milling crowd of passengers to stand beside them. She straightened as the man peered at her, his gray eyes magnified by the wire-rimmed glasses perched on his slightly bulbous nose. He dipped his head in a polite bow and looked back at her brother. Surprise — no doubt at James's youth — flickered across his face, quickly replaced by an expression of polite respect.

"Eli Goodwin at your service, Mr. Randolph. I am the bookkeeper of the Mississippi and Missouri steamer line. Captain Lewis sent word of your arrival, and I have come to escort you to the manager's residence. Mr. Thomas, the former manager, vacated the premises when he was dismissed from his position. You need not wait for your trunks. I have arranged for them to be delivered."

"How good of you, Mr. Goodwin. My sister and I have had a long journey and are most eager to get settled into our new home."

The man nodded. "I trust your accommodations aboard ship were comfortable and your journey a pleasant one. If you will follow me?" He turned toward the stairs leading down to the main deck.

James stepped back from the railing, creating a small space in the press of people. Mary gathered close the long, full skirt of her dark blue gown and stepped into the void he had created. Urged forward by her brother's hand at the small of her back, she followed in Eli Goodwin's wake.

Samuel Benton stood at the edge of the river, narrowed his eyes and drifted his gaze over the *Fair Weather*'s main deck. A few frowns, a few curt nods revealed that his purpose in coming to the levee had been accomplished — the crew knew the law was present and watching them. Perhaps it would be enough to discourage anyone who might intend to damage the ship. Though it could be that such danger no longer existed since the line had changed owners.

Sam scanned the deck again, paying particular attention to the firemen and engineer. He did not believe the mishaps on the three previously destroyed or heavily damaged boats of the Mississippi and Missouri steamer line were all accidental. Boiler explosions and shipboard fires were common occurrences on the river, but not to three of one line in such close succession. He had a hunch someone had helped the "accidents" along. And, after his talk with Thomas last week, it had seemed possible that the new owner of the line had a hand in it. It would not be the first time sabotage had been used to drive down the purchase price of a business. And the secrecy of the buyer's name was a possible indication of his involvement in the crimes. As Thomas said, what other reason could the new owner have for keeping his identity hidden? Of course, being replaced as manager of the line, that could be Thomas's anger talking.

Sam frowned and raised his gaze to the steamboat's promenade. He would have a clearer picture of the situation after he talked with James Randolph, the man taking Thomas's place as manager of the M and M line. Randolph was somewhere in that milling throng of people and he wanted to meet him, find out what sort of man he was. But first he wanted to ask Captain Lewis who, if any, of the crew Randolph may have met with during the trip. And it would be interesting to know who Randolph would speak with on his first afternoon in town.

Passengers began to file down the *Fair Weather*'s gangplank in a steady stream. Sam glanced their way, automatically checking faces for known criminals or gamblers with bad reputations. A flutter of blue on the promenade deck caught his attention. He looked up, saw a woman brush at the material adorning her hat. His policeman's mind registered facts — the woman was taller than average, and thinner, with dark hair. Not particularly pretty — at least not in a conventional way. But there was something arresting about the woman, about the way she held herself.

He watched her wend her way toward the stairs leading down to the main deck, noting her graceful, but purposeful way of moving. There was nothing simpering or clingy about her. And he guessed she did not need the protection of the man guiding her through the crowd. She looked quite able to manage without an escort. The way she followed in the wake of that man in front of her, bespoke —

Goodwin! Why was he here? To meet the new manager?

Sam scowled. He had been wondering if Goodwin had a hand in the M and M steamer disasters, though Thomas said no. He tracked the progress of the three of them with new purpose. Yes, the woman was definitely staying close to Goodwin. So the fellow with her must be the new manager. Thomas had not mentioned James Randolph was married. Sam shifted his focus to the man, catalogued the facts. Tall, dark, well-groomed. Fit, but on the slender side. He could not see his face. The three disappeared in the crush of people at the top of the stairs.

Sam pivoted and loped toward the gangplank. He would talk to Captain Lewis later. "Pardon me, sir." He gave a polite nod to the fellow coming off the walkway, stepped in front of him and held out his hand to stop the couple beside him. "Pardon me, please." He hurried past them, leaned against a wagon loaded with firewood and riveted his attention on the flow of people. It would be interesting to see if anyone other than Goodwin disembarked with the Randolphs. Or if someone was waiting to meet them.

Sam gave the area another quick scan, frowned. It was odd Thomas wouldn't meet his replacement. A twinge of unease reared. He quashed it. Thomas could be waiting at the office. Or he could be angry enough that he refused to meet Randolph and help him settle into his new position.

Three men and two more couples filed past. Sam glanced up. Eli Goodwin was at the top of the gangplank, the Randolphs at his heels. He studied James Randolph's face, looking for clues to the man's character, trying to decipher if he was expecting to meet someone. Randolph was young, very young, for such a responsible position. He looked to be no more than nineteen or twenty. Half Thomas's age. Sam shifted his gaze for a quick look at Randolph's wife and peered straight into her eyes. Brown eyes. Not dark. Medium — like her hair. And challenging.

Sam stiffened, told himself to look away — knew it was already too late. She had spotted him studying her husband. He watched them descend, let Eli Goodwin pass and stepped around the wagon into the path of the young couple.

"Mr. Randolph?"

"Yes?" The man stopped, looked up at him, dark blue eyes posing a question.

"I am Samuel Benton, Captain of the St. Louis police." He glanced at Randolph's wife, saw the coolness in her eyes, gave her a polite nod and looked back. "I bid you and your wife welcome to our fair city." He offered his hand, received a firm clasp in return. "I will be calling on you tomorrow. There are a few rules, regulations and other matters about running a steamboat line in St. Louis that I want to discuss with you."

James Randolph nodded. "I shall await your visit with interest, Captain." He turned to the woman and grinned. "Come, dearest, Mr. Goodwin is waiting to show us to our new home." He took hold of her elbow.

The woman laughed, changing her countenance from cool and austere to fond and amused. Her lips, which had been pressed into a firm line, curved upward in a soft smile. Honey-colored flecks sparkled warmth into her large, brown eyes fringed with long lashes. Sam stared, taken aback. How had he thought her not particularly pretty? She was —

"Stop it, James. Captain Benton cannot know you are teasing."

Her voice was low-pitched for a woman's, soft and easy on his ears. A bit husky.

Intriguing. She glanced up at him from beneath her hat's stiff brim and discovered him looking at her. The warmth in her eyes cooled.

"You have erred in your conclusion, Captain Benton. I am not James's wife. I am his sister."

"Forgive me, Miss Randolph, I assumed —"

"There is no apology or explanation needed, Captain. It was a natural assumption and of no import. I merely wanted to correct your error." The river breeze blew the fabric adorning her hat into her face. She frowned and pushed it back, looked up at him again, all trace of warmth and humor gone. "Now, if you will excuse us — I am weary from the journey and anxious to reach our new home. And to remove this ridiculous hat."

Her frosty demeanor killed his smile. "Of course, forgive my poor manners in detaining you." He glanced over at her brother. "Until tomorrow, Mr. Randolph." He gave them a polite nod and headed for the gangplank. If he hurried he could still catch Captain Lewis. James Randolph seemed open and friendly enough, but that did not mean he was above a little unscrupulous behavior. Perhaps on behalf of his boss? He would keep watch on his movements the next few days. As for his sister . . . what did that "ridiculous hat" comment mean? Women did not wear hats they considered ridiculous. Had she worn it by way of identification to Goodwin? Or as some sort of signal to someone else?

Sam frowned, stepped onto the *Fair Weather*'s main deck and turned to look out at the levee. Eli Goodwin was leading James Randolph and his sister up the incline to Front Street. No one had joined them. He scanned the area but could spot no one paying the Randolphs any particular attention.

He watched a moment longer, then satisfied he had missed nothing of importance, turned and strode toward the stairs leading to the captain's quarters on the hurricane deck. He would not only ask about James Randolph's activities on the journey, he would ask about Miss Randolph's activities, as well. It was quite possible — in spite of that forthright look in those beautiful, brown eyes of hers — that she would help her brother if he was involved in this steamboat sabotage business. He took another quick glance over his shoulder at the tall, slender figure in the dark blue gown, then gripped the railing and, bucking the flow of the departing passengers, started up the stairs.

Chapter Two

Mary walked beside James, taking in the hubbub of sound and motion around them. Workmen streamed in and out of warehouses, carrying filled burlap bags on burly shoulders or swarmed over huge stacks of crates or barrels. Laborers loaded carts with firewood and hauled it to their boats. Animals, in gated farm wagons, lowed and snorted. Others grunted and squealed as they were forced up gangplanks. Chickens squawked while barking dogs circled their cages. Mary had never seen or heard anything to compare with it. It was organized bedlam.

"That is our warehouse, Mr. Randolph." Eli Goodwin paused and pointed. "The one you see overtop the roofs of these smaller storage sheds. It was built on the higher ground because of flooding."

Mary's stomach flopped. She glanced from the large, brick building with "Mississippi and Missouri Steamer Line" sprawled in large, faded-white letters above the fourth-story windows to the muddy river, and was suddenly very thankful for the rising levee bank they were climbing.

"Does the river flood often?"

James's question brought a flash of the flat, rolling land along the river's banks into her head. Mary glanced at Mr. Goodwin.

The man nodded. "You can count on it in the spring. And if there are heavy rains upriver throughout the year, she will flood again. And there is no telling how high the river will rise. But business goes on. When floodwater covers the levee, the captains run their steamers in and moor them to the warehouses."

"You jest!"

James's challenge of the story gave her hope. It died when Eli Goodwin shook his head and started walking again. Mary tossed her brother a look of dismay, then followed the bookkeeper as he wove his way through the various piles of merchandise to the street at the top of the levee. Carriages, carts, drays and wagons of all sort rumbled over the cobblestones. Mounted men added to the traffic flow.

"This is Front Street. And that is Market Street across the way." Eli Goodwin indicated an intersecting road a short distance from them. "And there, on the near corner, is the company office."

Mary looked over at the narrow, two-story stone building. An oval sign bearing the company name held its place between a door and two mullioned windows painted red.

"A bank on one side, and an insurance company on the other corner. An excellent location."

Mary smiled at the satisfaction in James's voice. "And it is only a few steps away from the warehouse on the levee. Surely that is of benefit."

The bookkeeper nodded and shoved his glasses higher on his nose. "Do you wish to visit the office now?"

James shook his head. "No, tomorrow will be soon enough. For now, I want to get Mary settled in our new home. Is it far?"

"No, sir. It is only two streets away. We will cross here."

James's hand closed on her elbow. Mary pulled close her long skirts to avoid horse droppings as they followed Eli Goodwin across Front Street, dodging between a farm wagon full of produce and another loaded with squealing pigs to reach the walkway area in front of the stores. "Gracious me!" She jumped out of the path of a honking, wing-flapping goose being chased by a dog. "I have never witnessed such . . . such . . ."

"Pandemonium?"

She looked up at James and laughed. "The very word I was searching for."

"It is much quieter away from the levee, Miss Randolph. We go this way." Eli started walking up Market Street. The din of activity fell away as he led them past an intersecting dirt road, then turned right onto the next one and stopped. "This is it."

Mary stared at the small brick house sitting square on the corner lot. A porch across the face of the cottage shadowed the two mullioned windows, one on either side of a centered door painted white. Wood shingles, bleached and curled by the hot Missouri sun, covered the porch and house roof. Two brick chimney stacks stood at the cottage's gabled ends.

The chain supporting a dangling cannonball squeaked in protest as Eli Goodwin pulled open the gate in the lime-coated picket fence that enclosed the property. Mary dipped her head, thankful her hat was wide enough to hide her face, and stepped through the gate and up the short, brick walk. James would surely laugh if he saw her shock. Although, from his silence, she was quite certain he was as stunned as she. The cottage was charming, but so *small.* Why, you could set the whole of it into one end of the stables at home.

"Mrs. Dengler cleaned the place, made up the beds fresh for you and such. And I arranged for Mrs. Rawlins to leave a meal for you. She was cook for Mr. Thomas, the former manager, and has agreed to cook for you if you wish. They will both call on you tomorrow morning to learn if you want them to stay on, or if you prefer to set about finding other help." A frown drew Eli Goodwin's brows together. "I believe that is all. Here is the key to the house, Mr. Randolph." He handed James a skeleton key, gave a curt nod. "I wish you a good evening, sir. And you, Miss Randolph."

"And you, Mr. Goodwin." Mary offered the man a polite smile. "Your thoughtfulness will make our first evening in our new home a comfortable one. Thank you."

"And you have my gratitude as well, Goodwin. I will see you at the office tomorrow." Once inside, James closed the door, hung his hat on the hat tree and followed Mary as she moved out of the narrow entry into the room on the right. "I wonder if Mr.

Goodwin ever smiles?" He shrugged and glanced around the small parlor. "Well, here we are in St. Louis." His lips twisted in a wry grimace. "In a very *small* cottage. Are you sorry you came?"

Mary cast an assessing glance his way. "Now why was I certain you would ask me that very question as soon as the door closed behind Mr. Goodwin?" She lifted her hands and pulled out the pin holding her hat in place. "There! That is much better. I *told* Madame Duval these long ties would be annoying. But she insisted it was the latest style."

James frowned. "And why did *I* know you would avoid answering me? If you are disappointed, Mary — if St. Louis is less than you expected — it would be best for you to return home now." He flushed beneath her steady gaze. "I mean, rather than to unpack and have to go through all that work again."

"How very sensible and considerate. But I had no expectations, James. Only an intense desire to leave Winston Blackstone behind. *And* every other man living in Philadelphia who knows father is wealthy, as well." Her facial muscles went taut. She hated herself for believing Winston Blackstone's lies. For opening herself up to be hurt by his perfidy.

She turned and dropped her hat onto the

seat of a Windsor chair sitting beside the fireplace. It gave her a reason to turn her back on the sympathy in James's eyes. She should not have mentioned Winston. She hastened to change the subject. "And, in truth, I find St. Louis intriguing. Did you notice all those rough-looking, buckskin-clad men? And the Indians roaming about the levee mingling with the people? Do you suppose they are dangerous?"

"I am quite certain they can be."

She heard James move, listened to his footsteps draw close. She removed her gloves and tossed them down by her hat.

"Winston did not mean to hurt you, Mary. He did not mean for you to ever know about Victoria. He was doing the honorable thing and telling her goodbye."

Mary clenched her hands into fists. She had avoided talking about Winston ever since the night of the party. But James persisted. Perhaps if she explained he would stop trying to make her talk about what had happened. And perhaps it would cleanse her mind of the memories, free her to move on with her new life.

She turned around and studied her brother's face. "Why are you so determined to discuss Winston, James? You have been trying to do so our entire journey. Did Mother and Father charge you with the task?" She squared her shoulders and lifted her hand to stop his reply. "No matter. I will bow to your wishes and we shall discuss Winston and the entire sordid situation —" she pointed one long, tapering finger toward the ceiling "— *once.* But do not *dare* defend him to me. Do not stand before me and call his actions *honorable.*"

The word scorched her tongue, seared her heart. She took refuge from her pain in a sudden burst of anger. Allowed the heat of it to carry her words beyond the lump of hurt in her throat. "I saw Winston with Victoria in the gardens, James. And, I assure you, there was nothing lofty or honorable in their embrace. Nor did the ardor of his kisses speak goodbye — except to the announcement of our betrothal." She lifted her chin and hid her trembling hands in the deep folds of her long skirt. "At least I was spared the humiliation of a public betrayal. Although everyone present that evening did suspect the reason for the party was to announce our future marriage."

"Mary, I had no idea!" James hurried to her. "Why did you not tell us you had witnessed Winston and Victoria embracing in the gardens?" He reached to pull her close.

She stepped back and shook her head. If he put his arms around her, she would burst into tears. "And have all my family pity me even more? As you are doing now?" She turned away, brushed a stray lock of hair off her cheek. "It changed nothing that I saw Winston's betrayal with my own eyes."

"I suppose that is true. Though it may make it more difficult for you to forgive him."

"Forgive him?" She pivoted, stared up at him. "You are not serious, James?"

"Yes, I am." He stepped closer. "Listen, Mary. When you refused to see him before we left, Winston came to me and explained the entire situation. He confessed it was only after losing you that he realized how much he cared for you. He begged me to plead his case with you. Of course, I refused. But he convinced me that he is genuinely distraught at losing you." Warmth from his hands penetrated the fabric of her gown as he took hold of her shoulders. "Mary, Winston loves you and wants you back. He wants you to come home to Philadelphia and marry him. It is *that* which I have been trying to tell you the entire journey."

"He — He said — And you —" Her throat closed on the words. Mary dug her fingernails into the palms of her hands, fighting a sense of betrayal that was not fair to her brother. He did not know the entire story. She took a breath, held it, released it slowly. "I know you wish only what is best for me, James. And I thank you for that. Truly. But do not be swayed by Winston's persuasive powers. His only regret is in losing the generous dowry Father offered for me. It would have cleared all his debts. I know, for I not only *saw* Winston with Victoria, I *heard* him as well." She lifted her hand and tapped his chest. "Winston's pocketbook chose me, James. His heart chose Victoria." She made herself look at him and forced the rest of it out of her constricted throat. "And, as he said to her, 'What man would not choose her petite, blond beauty and sweet nature over my dark, angular plainness and bold, forthright ways were debt not an issue?' "

Anger darkened James's face. His chest swelled beneath her hand as he sucked in air. She blinked the sting of tears from her eyes and shook her head. "Do not say more, James. Please. Do not make useless protests. Winston's words only confirmed what I have known all my life. I am aware of how I appear in comparison to other women. It has always been so. Mother and Sarah shine like golden jewels. But it is only Father's wealth that gives me beauty and luster in men's eyes. And I, like every woman, want to — to be a jewel in the eyes of the man I love. Me — not Father's money. I want to marry a man who loves and values me for myself. And I will settle for no less."

"You are *wrong,* Mary!" James tightened his grip, gave her a gentle shake. "You are a lovely and desirable woman. And Winston Blackstone is a fool! As am I for believing him. He does not deserve you."

She touched her fingers to his lips, saw the hurt for her in his eyes, and forced a smile. "You are a wonderful, loyal brother, James. But please, do not be concerned for me. Perhaps somewhere there is a man — even here in St. Louis — who will see me as a jewel. And with no one here knowing who our father is, should such a man declare his love for me, I will be certain he cares for me alone. That is why it is so perfect that no one here knows of our father's wealth. And if that does not happen —" she took another breath "— I will yet be glad I came. For I would far rather be a spinster than a bargain. Now . . . we shall never mention Winston Blackstone again." She raised her face, kissed his cheek and spun away. "Shall we explore our new home?"

"That shan't take long."

The wry humor was forced. Mary sent

James a look of gratitude for accepting the change of subject and picked up her hat and gloves. “Shall we start with the upstairs? I want to put this ridiculous hat away.”

Chapter Three

Her first full day in her new home. Mary heaved a sigh and looked around her. What was she to do with her gowns? Her dressing room at home was larger than this bedroom. And her bedroom was — No. No complaints. Not even to herself. She had begged to come to St. Louis with James, and her parents had granted her wishes. She would not turn into a whining scold because of a few lost comforts.

She marched to the cupboard built into the niche on the left side of the fireplace and opened the door. There was room for five, perhaps six dresses, plus her nightgown and robe. She turned, fisted her hands on her hips and nibbled at the left inside corner of her top lip. She would need her plainest day dresses. And a finer one for church. The rest of her gowns would simply have to stay in the trunks. But where would she store them? Another dilemma.

"What is all this?"

Mary turned toward the door, took one look at James's baffled expression and burst into laughter. "I am choosing gowns to keep here in my room. The rest must stay in the trunks. I have no thought as to where — James! The office. Do you suppose there would be room in the back to store my trunks?"

"Perhaps. I will know after I see the place. I came to tell you that I am going there now." A frown crossed her brother's handsome face. "I have been thinking about those Indians we saw yesterday, Mary. I am concerned about leaving you here alone."

"Oh, poof!" She waved his concern away and lifted her rose-colored cotton gown from a pile on the bed. The matching embroidered jacket would come in handy for cooler days. "I will be fine. Mrs. Rawlins and Mrs. Dengler will be coming soon for their interviews. And, meanwhile, if any Indians come in with intent to do me harm, I shall simply hide myself in one of these stacks." She laughed and swept her hand through the air, indicating the dresses heaped on the floor, draped over the open trunks and spread out on the bed. "They would never find me."

James laughed, then sobered. "You are

certain?"

"Yes! Now go, and leave me to my work."

Mary sat on the settee, smoothed out her skirt and smiled at the women perched on the Windsor chairs. "I am impressed with the cleanliness of the house, Mrs. Dengler. I would very much like for you to continue to clean for us."

The German woman smiled and dipped her head. *"Dank."*

"And what is your given name, Mrs. Dengler?"

"I am called Edda."

Mary smiled at the older woman. "Are you prepared to begin work today, Edda?"

"I can do work today, *ja.*"

"Wonderful." Mary held back a sigh of relief. "There are gowns in my bedroom that must be packed away in my trunks for storage. When you finish with them, I would like you to make the beds."

"*Ja,* Miss Randolph."

Edda walked to the stairs and Mary turned to the woman on the other chair. "The stew you prepared for me and my brother last night was delicious, Mrs. Rawlins. As were the rolls that accompanied it. Do you always do your own baking?"

"Yes, I do."

"And are you available to cook for us every day?"

"I am." The woman nodded. "I am a recent widow with children full grown and gone from home. I have no call on my time."

Mary's heart contracted at the sorrow on the woman's face. "I am sorry for your loss, Mrs. Rawlins."

The woman dipped her head.

"Are you able to take up your duties today?"

Relief spread across the woman's face. "Yes, Miss Randolph. And my name is Ivy."

Mary smiled and rose to her feet. "I have paper and pen waiting in the kitchen, Ivy. If you will tell me what stores you require and what foods you wish for today's meals, I will see to their purchase."

The sun overhead was bright in her eyes. Mary dipped her head slightly, using the shirred brim of her coal-scuttle bonnet to shade her face. The deep flounce running around the bottom of the long, full skirt of her green gown brushed against the cobblestones as she walked down Market Street toward the river, the basket she had found in the kitchen swinging back and forth in her hand.

The sounds of activity on the levee became

louder and more distinct as she neared the river. Wind gusted, picked up dust and flung it about. She ducked her head against the onslaught, hurried around the corner toward the Mississippi and Missouri steamer line office building and ran full tilt into a muscular, lean body. "Oh!" She staggered backward. Strong hands gripped her upper arms, steadied her. She looked up to thank her rescuer.

"Captain Benton!"

"At your service." He released her arms. "Are you all right, Miss Randolph?"

The heat of a blush crawled across her cheeks. "I should ask you that question, Captain. Please forgive me. I assure you I am not in the habit of knocking into people. I was . . . well . . . I was hurrying to reach my brother." She gave a little laugh and straightened her bonnet that had slipped backward when she had bumped into him. "Our cook has given me a list and I am on my way to purchase needed stores and food for dinner. And, I confess, I am a little hesitant to brave the levee area without an escort."

She glanced up at him from under her hat brim. *Gracious, he was tall!* She was not accustomed to men tilting their heads to look down at her. "I am unfamiliar with Indians or mountain men, and I am not eager to meet any of them on my own. At least, not yet. Thus, I was on my way to ask James to accompany me to the grocer's." She was prattling like a silly schoolgirl in the presence of a handsome boy! Mary clenched her teeth together and tightened her grip on the empty basket.

"Very wise of you, Miss Randolph."

His calm answer restored her aplomb. "And why is that, Captain?"

"There are some rough and unsavory elements on the waterfront. We are working to clean up our city. But there is much left to do."

"I see." Mary hid the tingle of apprehension that slipped along her nerves and turned toward the office door. "Thank you for the information, Captain. Now I *know* I need James to accompany me."

A frown lowered his straight, dark brown brows. "I just called to speak with your brother, Miss Randolph. He is in a meeting."

"But Mrs. Rawlins needs —" Mary stopped, glanced at Front Street and took a deep breath. "Would you please direct me to the grocer's, Captain?"

"I will do better than that, Miss Randolph. I will escort you there."

"You?" Mary jerked her gaze to him.

He grinned, no doubt at her response. A slow, lopsided sort of grin that did queer things to her stomach. She took a step back, suddenly uneasy at the prospect of being in his company. The man was overwhelming. And why would he offer to escort her? "It is most kind of you to offer aid, Captain. But it would not be right for me to take you from your duties." She glanced up and down the street to choose her direction.

"The well-being and safety of the citizens of St. Louis *is* my duty, Miss Randolph. Allow me." He reached out and took hold of the basket. "If you are ready?"

His answer left her without argument, but did little to allay her unease. Mary glanced at him, then looked down at his hand gripping the handle. Unless she wanted to engage in a tug-of-war for the basket — a contest she was sure to lose since the man was twice her size — she had no choice. She released her grip on the basket.

"We need to cross Market Street." He held her elbow.

Mary forced herself to relax. She was being ridiculous. He had not offered to help her from some nefarious motive. It was a simple politeness. A duty. Not every man had a hidden agenda like Winston Blackstone. She walked to the curb beside him, tried not to feel delicate and protected as he guided her through the carriage traffic. But it was difficult not to feel that way with his tall, lean body shielding her, and his hand holding her so protectively. She gave a quiet sigh of relief when they reached the other side and he released her arm. She glanced around as they started down the walkway.

"Are you recovered from your journey, Miss Randolph?"

She nodded, gave him a polite smile. "Yes. Quite recovered, thank you."

"You are fortunate. Steamboats are a vast improvement on other river craft, but still, long trips can be exhausting." He smiled down at her. "If you don't mind my asking, where are you and your brother from, Miss Randolph?"

"Philadelphia" sprang to her tongue, but was quashed by another spurt of caution and suspicion. Why did he want to know? Did it have something to do with being a police officer? Well, she had no intention of telling him. That information might lead to her father's identity. The Randolph shipping line was well-known in Philadelphia. She glanced up, gave a graceful little shrug. "Why ever would I mind your asking,

Captain? We are from Pennsylvania." She shifted her gaze. "Oh, look! A bookstore. How lovely." She gave him another polite smile. "Do you enjoy reading, Captain?"

"I do. Though I seldom have time."

Some subtle change in the timbre of his deep voice warned her that he was aware of her evasion. She turned her head toward the two-story brick, stone and wood frame storefronts to hide her face from him. Those blue eyes were too observant.

A half-naked Indian, a pile of animal pelts folded over one arm, exited a leather goods store, then mingled with the people on the walkway and strode straight toward them. Mary froze, staring at the shocking sight of the Indian's bare torso. She had heard so many stories . . . His eyes, black as a night sky, bored into hers. She lifted her chin and crowded closer to Captain Benton, suddenly thankful for his presence. The Indian went on by.

"There's no danger, Miss Randolph. We've been at peace with the local Indians for many years. They come into town often to conduct business." He smiled down at her. "I know it is a shock to you Easterners at first, but their presence is a sight you will soon become accustomed to."

His smile and the calm in his deep voice

eased her nervousness. She nodded, looked away from his disturbing, penetrating gaze. "I am certain I shall, Captain Benton." She started walking again. He fell into step beside her.

"The plains tribes are a different matter, of course. But you are safe in town."

A shiver slithered down her spine. She glanced at him, uncertain of how to respond. Up to now, hers had been a pampered life. She was not used to feeling afraid.

"Stop, you little thief!"

Mary jerked her gaze forward. A young boy, panic on his face, was running toward them, a large man wearing a stained white apron in hot pursuit.

Samuel Benton leaped into the boy's path.

The boy tried to swerve, but the man behind him thrust out his hand, caught the boy's shoulder and yanked him to a halt. "Got ya! Now, you'll find out what thievin' gets ya!" He nodded at Samuel Benton and shoved the boy forward. "Throw 'im in jail with the rest of the thievin' jackanapes, Captain."

"Surely not!" Mary rushed forward, lifted her chin as both men looked her way. "He is only a boy."

"He's a *thief!* An' here's yer proof." The man grabbed the boy's right arm and jerked it upward. There was a crushed roll in his hand. A bony hand, attached to a pitifully thin arm.

Mary gasped. "Why, the boy's half-starved!" She glanced up at Samuel Benton. "He is hungry, Captain. Surely you will not arrest him?"

The captain's blue eyes darkened. "That is my job, Miss Randolph. He broke the law. The reason does not matter." He reached for the boy.

Mary stepped between them. "It matters to me, Captain." She stared up at him, at his darkened eyes, his set jaw and drew herself to her full height. "But I can see there is no room in your St. Louis law for mercy." She pivoted to face the vendor. "Unhand the boy, sir. I will pay for his roll."

Hope leaped into the boy's eyes. But the man in the apron let out a growl, tightened his grip on the boy's skinny shoulders and looked over her head. "You do yer job an' throw 'im in jail, Captain. There's too many of the rapscallions roamin' the streets an' stealin' from hard workin', decent people now. Y' let this 'un go, an' the rest of 'em'll be swarmin' around our stores like bees o'er clover."

"There is no theft if Miss Randolph pays for the roll, Simpson." Samuel Benton's deep voice rolled over her shoulder. "Release the boy."

"Wait!" Mary winced inwardly as the hope faded from the boy's eyes, but he was going to run the moment he was free, she could see it on his face. And she saw something else written there, as well. Shame. And defiance. She fastened her gaze on him. "I need someone to carry my purchases home, and I thought perhaps you would do that for me, young man. In exchange for your services, I will buy you a thick slab of cheese to go with that roll. Is that agreeable to you?"

Pride replaced the shame. The defiance gave way to caution. The boy drew himself up straight and nodded.

"Very well." She handed the man behind the boy a coin. "You may release him now."

The man scowled, lifted his hands from the boy's shoulders and walked away, grumbling beneath his breath.

The boy stayed.

Mary let out a breath of relief and turned to Samuel Benton. "Thank you for your help, Captain. But I no longer require your aid." She did not bother to hide her disgust at his treatment of the boy. "If you will please give this young man my basket and tell me where the grocer is located, we shall be on our way."

He stared down at her for a moment, then dipped his head. "As you wish, Miss Randolph." He handed the basket to the boy, then returned his gaze to her and made a slight bow. "Good day, Miss Randolph. You have no need of my direction. The boy knows the location of the store. Mr. Simpson is the grocer." He turned and walked away.

Mary watched his lean, broad-shouldered figure disappear into a nearby store, chiding herself for the disappointment weighting her stomach. What did it matter what sort of man Samuel Benton was? The captain was nothing to her.

Chapter Four

Mary looked down at the young boy clutching her basket and smiled. "And thus, we are left on our own. Where is Mr. Simpson's store —" She shook her head and gave a little laugh. "I cannot keep calling you 'young man.' What is your name?"

The boy stiffened, his nostrils pinched slightly, his eyes narrowed and his mouth firmed as he stared up at her. Had she looked that wary when Captain Benton questioned her? No wonder he knew her answer was an evasion. She kept silent as the boy studied her. After a few moments, he relaxed a little, gave a small shrug. "Name's Ben." He pointed a bony finger down the street. "Yonder is the grocer's." He lowered his hand and gripped the basket handle. Probably to hide his trembling.

Mary started walking, letting out a quiet sigh of relief when Ben fell into step beside her. He had looked poised to run, and if he decided to do so, she could not stop him. Her lips twitched at the idea of her raising her long skirts and darting among the shoppers on the walkway chasing after the boy.

A puff of wind swirled up from the river, lifting a sour odor from Ben. She held her breath, waiting for the gust to cease, and glanced down. Tears filmed her eyes at the close sight of Ben's grimy skin, the clumps of dirt and straw in his matted hair, his dirty and torn clothes. She guessed him to be nine, perhaps ten years old. So young. And so horribly thin. Had he no one to care for him?

Thoughts of the homeless children brought to her aunt Laina's orphanage in Philadelphia crowded into her head. The tears in her eyes threatened to overflow. Was Ben an orphan? She blinked the tears back, released her breath and focused on the situation. Ben needed help, not pity. And she needed information. It was possible he had parents — though his unkempt, half-starved condition made it seem unlikely.

She stole another look at the silent boy. He was so easily frightened, so ready to run. How should she start? *I always mask my questions with friendly conversation.* Of course! How many times had she heard her aunt Laina say that? Mary smiled, looked down. "I like the name Benjamin." She made her tone of voice light, friendly. "Is it a family name? Perhaps your father's?"

No answer.

She tilted her head to get a better view of the boy's face. His lips were pressed together and he was blinking rapidly. Her heart seized. "Ben —"

"This is the store." He shot across the walkway, stopped by a store's open door and looked back at her.

"Go away, you *ragamuffin!*" A woman loomed out of the darkness of the store, pausing in the doorway. "Urchins like you are not welcome around decent people! Go away, I say!" She made shooing motions with her hands, then drew her long skirts close so they wouldn't touch Ben before she started out of the store.

Ben cringed away from the entrance.

If that woman makes Ben run . . . Mary rushed forward, placed her hand on Ben's shoulder and pulled him to her side. She could feel his bones through his shirt. And his shaking. She straightened to her full height and gave the shorter woman her haughtiest look. "Ben is with me, madam. And he is very welcome." She ignored the older woman's gasp and, holding tight to Ben, brushed by her into the store.

The interior was cool and dark. Mary halted to allow her eyes to adjust to the loss of sunlight and to get her bearings. Silence fell. She swept her gaze around the room, met varying degrees of shock or disgust on the faces of the store's patrons and lifted her chin. "Come along, Ben." The click of the heels of her shoes against the wide plank floor echoed through the hush as they crossed the room. She stopped in front of the grocer cutting meat on a chopping block at the far end of a long counter in front of the back wall.

"Good day, Mr. Simpson." She gave him a cool nod. Gave another to the waiting customer who had backed away at their approach.

A scowl drew the grocer's thick, black brows together. "Get that thief outta here. I don't —"

"Ben is here to carry my purchases, Mr. Simpson." There were startled gasps behind her. The grocer's scowl deepened. She ignored a flurry of whispers and stared straight into the man's angry eyes. "And I am here to open an account. My brother and I are new in town and must establish our trade somewhere." She watched his scowl dissolve to the level of a frown. "My brother is the new manager of the Mississippi and Missouri steamer line. Of course, if you would prefer we take our custom elsewhere . . ." She turned away.

"No need fer that. My wife'll serve ya."

The words were low, reluctant. Mary turned back. The grocer inclined his head at a stout woman behind the middle of the counter and went back to his work.

Mary headed toward the woman, another spate of whispers accompanying her as customers moved out of her path. She didn't have to urge Ben to come with her, he matched her step for step, his head bowed, his gaze darting about the room like a trapped animal.

"Come again, Mrs. Turner."

Mrs. Simpson's customer glanced at Ben, snatched up her parcel and rushed away. Mary stepped forward. "I should like to open an account, please."

"Of course." Mrs. Simpson smiled at Ben, looked back to give her a welcoming smile. "And the name?" She dipped her pen and poised it over a book.

Mary stared, taken aback by the cheerful attitude. She returned the woman's friendly smile and let the hauteur slide from her voice. "James Randolph." She placed the list Ivy had given her on the counter. "These are the items I need today. And also —" she took her basket from Ben, placed it beside the list and indicated the crushed bun in the bottom "— this bun and a thick slab of cheese." She glanced down, caught Ben eyeing a large barrel, and looked up. "And two pickles from your brine barrel."

Mrs. Simpson nodded, turned and began selecting the items on the list from the shelves on the wall. Mary took the opportunity to look around the store. She caught the customers staring at her and Ben and gave them each a sweet smile. There was a sudden bustle of activity as they returned to their business.

"Will there be anything more, Miss Randolph?"

Mary turned, looked down at the filled basket and shook her head. "Not today, Mrs. Simpson."

The woman glanced toward her husband — who was wrapping a cut of beef in paper — then looked down at Ben, slipped her hand into a crock to pull out a piece of taffy. "I heard you tell Mr. Simpson that you and your brother are new in town, Miss Randolph. Welcome to St. Louis." She dropped the piece of candy beside the roll and the piece of cheese and slid the basket across the counter. "I look forward to serving you again."

"And so you shall, Mrs. Simpson. Thank you for the welcome, and for . . . everything." Mary smiled, met the woman's gaze in silent understanding, then handed the basket to Ben and headed for the door.

Sam turned the key in the lock, pulled the door open and stepped back. So did the man beside him.

"C'mon, Captain. It was only a little scrap."

Sam shook his head. "You pulled a knife, Hogan." He jabbed his thumb through the air in the direction of the cell.

"Yeah, but —"

"No buts. You know the rules here in St. Louis. You pull a weapon during a fight, you go to jail." Sam placed his hand on the laborer's beefy shoulder and applied enough pressure to move the man into the cell. He swung the door shut and shoved the key into the lock.

Hogan grabbed the bars. "C'mon, Captain. My boat leaves tonight. I gotta get to the levee and load cargo or Captain Rolls'll have my job."

"You should have thought of that before you pulled that knife." Sam turned the key, yanked it from the lock and started for the outer room.

"How about we make a deal?"

"No deal, Hogan."

"Not even to find out what happened to the *Swift Water*?"

Sam stopped, turned and stared into the bloodshot eyes in the scrubby, whiskered face pressed against the bars. "What do you know about the *Swift Water*?"

Hogan grinned. "You gonna let me outta here?"

Sam walked to the cell. "That depends on what you know and how reliable your information is."

"I know one of the crew was paid to blow her up."

"Sorry. Everyone has heard that rumor." He turned toward the door.

"But they don't know who."

There was certainty behind the words. Sam looked back. "Who?"

Thick lips pushed a curved line through the grizzled beard.

Sam nodded. "All right, fair enough. How do you know? I'm not interested in rumors."

"It ain't no rumor. I seen him flashin' money and braggin' about it in a tavern. Tellin' around what a big man he was an' all."

"Who paid him?"

Hogan scowled. "Don't know. You'll have

to ask him that yerself."

Sam nodded. The story had the ring of truth. "Do you know anything about the other destroyed M and M line boats? The *Clear Water* or the *Mississippi Princess*?"

"The *Princess* was an accident. Sawyer got her. Don't know about the *Clear Water*."

"All right." He stuck the key in the lock, paused. "But the deal is this — if you ever pull a knife in a fight again, you'll do double time for it. Understood?"

Hogan nodded. "Yeah." He glanced down at the ring of keys. "The name's Duffy. He's a stoker."

"I know him. Do you know what boat he's working?"

"Last I knew he was up the Missouri on the *Adventure*."

Sam twisted the key and opened the cell door. "All right, Hogan. Get back to the levee. And don't forget — no more knives or I'll put you back in here and throw away the key."

Hogan nodded and hurried down the hall. Sam followed him to the other room, tossed his keys into the drawer, then grabbed his hat and dogged the man's heels outside. Now all he had to do was locate Duffy. And find out if the man had any connection to James Randolph, or the new owner of the

M and M line. Maybe he could do that through Thomas, and not tip his hand.

He cut across lots to Olive Street, where Thomas had lived since vacating the manager's cottage, and knocked on the door of Emily Stanton's boardinghouse. He waited, wondering about the sudden sense of disquiet in his gut.

The door opened. He smiled and touched the brim of his hat. "Good afternoon, Mrs. Stanton."

"Why, Captain Benton!" Surprise widened the round eyes looking up at him. "What brings you here?"

"I need to talk with Mr. Thomas. If I could —" He stopped, staring down at her shaking head.

"You're too late, Captain. He ain't here."

The disquiet grew. "Did he tell you where he was going? I can catch up with him if —" The gray head was shaking again.

"He didn't tell me where he was going. Only packed up and left three days ago." A frown deepened the wrinkles in the plump face. "Late at night, it was. I heard someone on the stairs, peeked out my door and saw him leave. Sort of odd. Most times when someone goes sneakin' out the door in the middle of the night, it's 'cause they can't pay their bill. But he didn't owe me nothing."

"I see." Sam nodded, touched his hat brim again. "Thank you for the information, Mrs. Stanton. Good afternoon."

"Good afternoon, Captain." She started to close the door, then pulled it open and stuck her head out. "If you hear of somebody decent that needs a room, tell them I've got one empty."

"I'll do that, Mrs. Stanton." Sam trotted down the steps and headed for the levee. Now he had two men to track down. Duffy and Thomas. Queer, Thomas leaving like that. Could there be a connection between that and James Randolph's arrival? Seemed as if there might be. But why did Thomas *sneak* off? There was no reason for that, unless it was to keep his leaving a secret. And if that was so, who was he —

Sam's face tightened. Could it be *him?* Could it be Thomas didn't want *him* to know he was leaving town? Now why would that be? He tugged his hat down snug and let his mind play with that thought while he ate up the distance to the levee with his long strides.

"What is going on in here?"

Mary spun around, and gaped at her

brother standing in the washroom doorway. "James! You are home."

He nodded. "Yes. That is what I do when it is time to eat. I come home. Why the surprise?"

She laughed and hurried toward him. "I did not hear you come in the house is all. As small as it is, I was certain I would. I am sorry. I should have been waiting to greet you." She touched his arm, gave a little push — a signal for him to leave.

He stood his ground, riveting his gaze on the scene behind her. *Botheration!* She had wanted a chance to explain before he saw Ben. Especially since the boy was wearing a shirt that had been in James's dresser drawer when he left the house that morning. Her heart sank as he frowned at her.

"Mary, what —"

She squeezed his arm, sent him the silent "don't ask questions" command with her eyes that she had perfected during their childhood years. Of course, that was when her demand usually involved keeping a secret from their parents. It was different now. He would probably ignore her signal. "I am finished here, James." She gave him another tiny push, then looked over her shoulder. "Edda, if you will launder Ben's clothes, please."

"Ja." The plump woman turned, lifted the small pile of filthy garments off the floor and plunged them into the tub of Ben's bathwater.

James's frown deepened to a scowl. Mary gave him another pinch. "Shall we go into the parlor and chat while Ivy prepares our dinner, James?"

His gaze fastened on hers. "That is an excellent suggestion."

This time he yielded to her pressure against his arm and stepped back. She sailed past him, hurried to the small parlor and turned to face him. The scowl was still on his face.

"All right, Mary. Why is our cook's son wearing one of my shirts?"

"Our cook's *son?*" She laughed and relaxed into one of the Windsor chairs. "Ben is not Ivy's son, James. He is a boy from the streets who carried my basket home from the market. And as for your shirt . . . what else had I to dress him in while his clothes are being laundered? I could hardly give him one of my gowns."

"An unknown, dirty boy from the streets is wear—"

"Hush, James! He will hear you." Mary surged to her feet, then closed the parlor door and whirled to face him. "And Ben is not *dirty.* I had him bathe as soon as we fed him and he agreed to stay awhile — Ivy even scrubbed his hair clean." She glared up at him. "And shame on you for your lack of compassion! What —"

"Whoa! Hold on." James held his hand up palm forward. "Before you castigate me for my attitude, I think you should at least tell me what is going on. How that boy got into our house and —"

"I *have* told you, James."

"No, you have not. You told me that he carried your basket home." He frowned at her. "I cannot believe the grocer would have a boy that dirty and unkempt working for —"

"James!" Mary launched herself through the intervening space into his arms. "James, you are a genius! What a wonderful idea."

She planted a kiss on his cheek and spun out of his grasp. "I have been trying to think of what to do to help Ben. He is such a proud young boy, and you —" She stopped, frowned. "Of course, Mr. Simpson will not care for your idea. At least, not at first." She paced the short distance across the room, turned and headed back. "But Mrs. Simpson . . . Yes, I am almost certain she —"

He reached out and caught her by the shoulders. "Mary, what you are talking about? What idea? And who are Mr. and Mrs. Simpson? What have they to do with this boy from the streets? And what has he to do with us?"

"Nothing. And everything." She locked her gaze with his. "Ben is an *orphan,* James. And half-starved. Would *you* have let him be arrested and taken to jail for stealing bread to eat?"

Her words were soft, but challenging. James released his grip on her shoulders and straightened.

"You ask that question of *me,* Mary? You *know* I would not."

She placed her hand on his arm. "I *do* know, James. And I meant no offense. I asked only so you would place yourself in my position." She gave him a wry smile. "Neither one of us would be able to face Aunt Laina again if we allowed such a thing to happen in our presence."

He nodded, and his lips curved in a smile that matched her own. "True. Nor Mother and Father, either." His smile faded. "But you still have not told me how you met Ben. Or —"

"Or what?"

He shook his head. "My questions will wait until after I hear your story." He draped his arm around her shoulders, then led her to the settee and sat down beside her. "I am all 'at sea.' Begin."

"Yes, of course." She tucked a wayward strand of hair in the loose knot on the crown of her head and looked over at him. "You know I had marketing to do this morning — food stores and such?"

He nodded, then grinned at her. "It will take some time for me to get used to the idea of *you* doing household tasks, but . . . yes, we discussed that last night, *Miss Housekeeper.*" His grin widened.

She gave him her "big sister" look. "If you wish to hear the story, James, be serious!"

He tamed his grin to a smile and dipped his head in agreement. "I shall be."

"Very well, then." She angled her body toward him. "I was nervous about going to the levee alone — because of the Indians and mountain men — so I decided to go to your office and ask you to accompany me."

His levity fell away. He frowned. "Goodwin did not tell me that you came to see me."

"Because I did not." The memory of Captain Benton's grinning face flashed. Warmth crept across her cheekbones.

James stared.

Bother! Mary lifted her chin and gave him a look that dared him to comment about her blush.

He passed on the challenge. "Go on."

"At the front door, I chanced upon Captain Benton, who had called and found you busy in a meeting with some other gentlemen." She looked down at her hands. "He inquired as to my dismay at your unavailability and, when I explained, offered to accompany me to the grocer's." In spite of her effort, there was a tinge of defensiveness in her voice. She looked up.

James grinned. "So the *captain* is the cause of that heightened color in your cheeks. I shall have to remember to thank him for his kindness to you when next I see him."

She gave a little huff. "Stop teasing, James! It was duty, not kindness that prompted the captain's actions. Now . . . as I was saying. The captain and I were walking along Front Street when Ben came running toward us, with the grocer giving chase. He caught the boy and told Captain Benton to throw him in jail with the rest of the thieves." She paused, taking a breath.

"And you intervened?"

"Well, of course I did! It was obvious the boy was half-starved and frightened out of his wits. I thought surely the captain would show mercy, but when I protested the arrest, he said the boy was guilty of theft and he had no choice but to take him to jail." She jutted her chin into the air. "So I told him I would pay for the roll, struck a bargain with Ben to carry my basket and informed Captain Benton I had no further need of his services!"

She expelled her breath in another huff, then gave him a smile of pure satisfaction. "And that is how I met Ben and enticed him to come home with me. I suspected from his condition he was an orphan. On the way home I managed to get him to talk about his past." She sprang to her feet.

James rose. "And did you find out about his parents? Is he an orphan?"

"Yes. Ben's mother died two years ago. And last fall his father sold their farm and made plans to come west in the company of some friends. They started their journey this spring. Ben's father was killed fighting river pirates on their way down the Ohio."

"Poor Ben!"

"Yes. Poor Ben. The friends brought him downriver with them to St. Louis, took his father's possessions as payment, then told him there was no room for him in their wagon." Anger surging, she paced across the room, then headed back. "They left him here with no one to care for him while they joined a wagon train and traveled on." She stopped in front of him. "How could they *do* that, James? How could they rob a child, then simply leave him like that?"

He shook his head. "I have no answer for such unconscionable behavior, Mary. But I know Aunt Laina would be very proud of you. As would Mother and Father. As am I."

"But?" She gave him a quizzical look.

"But . . . I see some difficulties we must find solutions for. What do we do with Ben now?" He lifted a hand and rubbed the back of his neck, peering down at her. "Have you given thought to that? Is there an orphanage —"

Mary threw her arms around his neck and squeezed with all her might.

He returned the squeeze, giving her a puzzled look when she stepped away. "Thank you. But what was that for?"

"The 'we.' " She smiled up at him. "There is no orphanage, James. But the most wonderful thing has happened! Ivy is going to take Ben home to live with her. She is recently widowed and her children are grown and gone from home. It is perfect. Ben will be well cared for, and Ivy will not be lonely."

"That *is* a happy solution."

"Yes. And now you have solved the other

problem." She whirled away, turned back and clasped his hands. "I have been concerned over the cost to Ivy for Ben's care. *And* over Ben's feelings. He is a very honorable and proud little boy who wants to earn his way. Why, hungry as he was, he would not eat the roll and cheese I promised him as payment for his help until he had carried my basket home, for that was our agreement. Anyway . . ." She squeezed his hands. "Oh, James, I am certain your idea will work!"

"*What* idea?"

"Why for Ben to work at Mr. Simpson's store." She let go of his hands and whisked away again, her long skirts whispering as she moved across the floor. "Marketing baskets can become very heavy when you carry them for any distance. And I am certain ladies would be willing to pay for Ben to carry their baskets home. Oh, it is a lovely idea!"

"So is dinner." James laughed and slapped his growling stomach. "And I believe I hear Ivy carrying our meal in from the kitchen." He made a formal bow and offered Mary his arm. "Shall we discuss this situation further while we partake of whatever it is that is creating such a delicious smell?"

"La, it shall be as you wish, good sir."

Mary lifted her skirts slightly, made him a deep curtsy, then laughed and slipped her arm through his.

James chuckled and opened the door. "I do not know if I have Ben or the captain to thank, Mary. But it is good to see you so animated again."

Chapter Five

"We are in agreement, gentlemen?"

Sam glanced around the table, noting the response to the mayor's question. All nine of the aldermen nodded.

"Excellent!" The mayor smiled his satisfaction. "Let the record show that final plans for the addition to the courthouse have been unanimously approved and we hereby direct the work move forward with all dispatch. Now then, on to the next piece of business. It is for this that I invited Captain Benton's attendance on our assembly this afternoon."

Sam gave a brief nod as the aldermen glanced his way.

The mayor cleared his throat. "Captain Benton, all of us here are aware that our city has enjoyed significant growth in the past two years. We now have a theater, a hotel, banks. A water company is in the works. And the long-delayed plans for a public school are being drawn. The vast numbers of new buildings and the cobblestone paving of many of our streets have changed the complexion of our city from that of a wilderness town. And the increased safety of our citizens is also a factor in achieving that goal. I wish to commend you, Captain Benton, on the excellent job you are doing in taming the wilder elements among us."

There was a general murmur of agreement.

"Thank you, Mr. Mayor." Sam acknowledged the commendation and waited. He had not been called to this meeting only to receive a compliment.

"Because of all this, there is much to recommend St. Louis to men and women of substance and refinement who are considering moving west, not to the frontier, but to an established place. We want to attract those prosperous elite to our city."

There was another murmur of agreement.

"However . . ."

Sam braced himself.

"There is a problem that must be addressed if we are to be successful in our pursuit of that objective." A frown drew the mayor's thick brows together. "The lowborn and penurious people pouring into our city in the hopes of joining a train heading west are becoming greater in number every year. And while the monies they spend to buy wagons and supplies, or for repairing or restocking their wagons, are prospering our businessmen, the orphans and runaways they leave behind are becoming a plague, a *blight* on our fair city's image. You can scarcely walk down the streets without seeing the dirty ragamuffins skulking around. Why yesterday, one of them made so bold as to walk right past my wife into Simpson's grocer!"

Sam stiffened. *The boy the Randolph woman had saved from arrest!* It had to be him. Most youngsters were too frightened to go into a store alone.

"The experience was too much for my wife's sensitive nature. She was quite undone when she reached home. Levinia had a time calming her." The mayor scowled down the table at him. "This cannot be permitted to go on, Captain Benton! No person of wealth and culture will wish to set up business and make his home in a city that cannot keep its streets clean of such an ugly blemish. You do an excellent job of controlling the gamblers, drunks, mountain men, boatmen and others who frequent the more disreputable establishments on the levee. Yet these . . . these *street urchins* run amok among their betters. Have you an explanation for this deplorable situation, Captain?"

"I do, Mr. Mayor." Sam glanced around the table at each of the aldermen, trying to get a sense of where they stood on the issue. "The explanation is a simple one. I arrest law-breakers. And there is no law against children walking the streets of St. Louis. Thus, unless one of these 'urchins' is caught stealing, or otherwise breaking the law, there is nothing I can do about their presence on our streets."

The mayor scowled, drumming his fingers on the table. "That is a most distressing answer, Captain."

Sam held his face impassive, tightening the grip on his hat that rested on his knee. *If this ruined his chance to court Levinia —*

The mayor stopped his drumming, glanced around. "Gentlemen, we must find a way to get these ragamuffins off our streets. We can hardly pass a law denying all children that right — we have children of our own. And the people we are trying to attract for permanent settlement must be made to feel St. Louis is an ideal place for them to rear their children. They must feel we welcome their children as future productive citizens of St. Louis society. Have any of you a solution to offer?"

The aldermen shifted in their chairs, knit their brows and studied the table. Silence fell.

Sam held back a scowl. It seemed Miss Randolph's interference with that boy's arrest had stirred up a pile of trouble. He turned his hat in his hands and waited.

Alderman Field cleared his throat, leaned forward and looked toward the mayor at the head of the table. "What if we pass a law to the effect that any child under the age of twelve who is not a citizen of St. Louis must be accompanied by an adult when in town?"

The mayor leaned back in his chair, rested the heels of his hands on the table and drummed his fingers. After a moment he nodded. "That might work, Arthur. If any outsider questions the law, we will explain it is for the children's safety. Yes. That might work." The mayor's gaze shifted.

Sam straightened.

"Would that law give you the authority you need to get these dirty, unkempt jackanapes off our streets, Captain?"

"It would. As long as they are not accompanied by an adult, Mr. Mayor."

"Excellent! *Excellent!* All in favor of such a law?" The mayor smiled at the affirmative chorus. "Let the record show the law passed by unanimous vote. Captain Benton, you are hereby instructed to procure posters giving notice of the new law and post them in plain sight at the fields outside of town where these wagon trains form. And that, gentlemen, should settle our problem."

"And create another, Mr. Mayor."

The mayor's smile dissolved into another frown. "And what problem is that, Captain?"

"What do I do with the children I arrest? Our jail is meant for adults. There are no provisions for young —" Sam stopped, stared at the mayor's uplifted hand and held his silence.

"Your concern is misplaced, Captain. Those urchins are accustomed to rough conditions. They need no special provisions. Jail will likely be an improvement on their present living conditions. Now . . . you have heard the law, and you have your instructions. I am certain you will carry them out in your usual exemplary fashion. And that concludes our business. This meeting is adjourned."

Sam unlocked the cell door and pulled it open. "All right, Larkin, time's up. You're free to go. And stay sober. You cut up another man and I'll lock you up and throw away the key."

The large, bearded man rose from the cot and swaggered toward him. "Your threat don't scare me, Captain."

"That's a shame. Because it should." Sam smiled, a quiet smile that carried a promise, and stepped back to let Larkin pass. The big man's boots thudded against the plank floor, fading as he crossed the outer room. The outside door opened, then slammed shut.

The jail was empty again. But for how long? Sam glanced into the vacant cells. Thanks to the mayor's ridiculous law they would soon be filled with children. And what would he do with them? Grown men he could handle. But youngsters?

He frowned, strode to the outer room and dropped into his chair. One of those cells would already be occupied by a boy if Miss Randolph had not interfered.

He scrubbed his hand over the back of his neck, then shoved his heels against the floor and rocked back on the chair's hind legs. The look in those brown eyes of hers when he had been about to arrest that little thief had made him feel lower than a worm's belly. But when she had looked at the boy . . .

Sam shook his head, laced his hands behind his neck and stared up at the crack in the ceiling. Why had she been so concerned about a boy she didn't even know? And what was she hiding? Why didn't she want him to know where she was from? Not that that was rare on the frontier. Plenty of people who came west didn't want their past known. Still, if it had anything to do with her brother and the M and M line . . .

Sam shifted his weight, rode the chair forward till the front legs hit the floor. It was time to pay that call on James Randolph. Maybe he would be more forthcoming than his sister.

Mary stepped back toward the edge of the street and scanned the storefronts. Shoes . . . candles . . . cigars . . .

"You look a little lost, Miss Randolph."

She gasped, and spun around to stare at a blue shirt. One with a badge pinned to it. She lifted her gaze to Samuel Benton's face. Blue eyes gazed down at her.

"I did not mean to startle you, Miss Randolph. Only to assist you — if I am able to do so." He smiled and indicated the package in her basket. "I see you are doing some shopping. I hope you are finding our stores compare favorably with the ones you left behind in . . ."

"I have only been in one shop thus far, Captain Benton. That is hardly enough to make any comparisons." Mary looked again at the storefronts. The man's presence scattered her wits, and she needed to keep her senses about her. That was the second time he had tried to find out where she had lived back east. "I was searching for an emporium. Or a haberdasher." She glanced up at him. "I need to buy some items for Ben. Suspenders and such. If you would be so kind as to direct me?"

"Miss Mayfield's Emporium is five stores down, just before the corner." He stepped out of the way of shoppers passing by. "I'm glad I happened upon you, Miss Randolph. You have saved me an embarrassment. I'm on my way to speak with your brother and I thought his name was James, not Ben."

"My brother's name *is* James, Captain Benton. Ben is the young boy I took home yesterday." She gave him a cool look. "The boy you wanted to arrest."

"You took that boy *home* with you?"

Mary stiffened. "You need not look so *shocked*, Captain. Indeed, I find it offensive that you deem me the sort of person who would leave a child to roam the streets starving and uncared for." She looked him straight in the eyes. "What else was I to do but take him home with me? Let him be jailed?" Her challenge hit the mark, judging from the darkening of his blue eyes.

"What *else* —" He stopped, stared at her and sucked in air.

A surge of satisfaction flooded her. The man looked quite nettled. Good. Perhaps he would not be so eager to arrest another helpless child. She peered at him and waited.

"I assure you, Miss Randolph, I meant no offense."

Her hope flattened. So he was not going to change his mind about arresting children. She gave him a curt nod. "If that is so, Captain, then I accept your apology. Good day." She whisked about with a swirl of her long skirts and started down the street, focusing her attention on the storefronts. She refused to acknowledge her disappointment or to look back in spite of the tense feeling between her shoulder blades that told her he was staring after her.

Sam fisted his hand and rapped on the partially open door. This interview should be interesting if James Randolph was half as exasperating as his sister. That woman was undeniably the most sharp-tongued, irritating —

The door opened. Sam wiped the scowl from his face.

"Ah, Captain Benton. Come in."

"Mr. Randolph." Sam closed the door of James Randolph's office, shut all thought of the man's sister from his mind and extended his hand. Randolph's gaze was straightforward and friendly, his grip firm.

"How may I be of service, Captain?"

Sam shook his head. "There is nothing in particular, Mr. Randolph. I am sure Goodwin has informed you of all the regulations concerning businesses and steamboats in St. Louis. I am here because I make it a practice to call on new businessmen in town to let them know who I am, and that I am ready to assist them if they have any problems of a legal nature."

"An excellent idea, Captain. I appreciate the gesture. I shall certainly call on you should the need arise." James Randolph smiled and indicated the chair in front of his desk. "Please, have a seat."

Sam noted the openness in Randolph's face and gesture. It was not indicative of a man with something to hide from the law. But appearances could be deceiving. He removed his hat and folded his long frame into a Windsor chair. "I stopped by yesterday, but you were engaged in a meeting. You want to be careful who you deal with, Mr. Randolph. St. Louis sits on the edge of the frontier, and that creates problems unknown in the cities back east. It is easy for a man to cheat someone, then simply up and disappear — though we have ways of tracking them down eventually."

Sam watched James Randolph carefully, hoping to detect the slightest change in expression or demeanor as he talked. The veiled warning seemed to have no effect on the man. Randolph was either dense, honest — or a good actor. He pushed on. "We are doing our best to tame the less restrained who come to town to celebrate after months in the mountains or a long and successful journey upriver. And, also, to maintain some control over the establishments they frequent and the undesirable . . . er . . . shall we say, *residual effects* of those visits. And then, of course, there are the Indians. They are usually quite a shock to those who come to St. Louis from the eastern cities." He stared into James Randolph's eyes. "I assume you had no Indians freely roaming the streets of your city?"

"Nary a one, Captain. And you are right — they were quite a shock. Especially to my sister. Mary was reluctant to face them on her own. As was I, to have her do so." James Randolph rose, stepped around the desk toward him and extended his hand again. "Thank you, Captain Benton, for your kindness in escorting Mary to market yesterday. You have my deepest appreciation."

Sam rose and grasped the offered hand. "No thanks are needed, Mr. Randolph. It is my duty to see to the safety and comfort of St. Louis's citizens." He quirked his lips in a wry smile. "And I am not at all sure your sister shares your gratitude. My services as her escort were summarily dismissed after an encounter with a young thief."

"Yes, I heard of that." James Randolph's smile matched his own. "Mary can be a little autocratic when riled. And she has a soft heart for those who are downtrodden. Nonetheless, she is grateful for your assistance." The smile faded from Randolph's face. "Now, as you say there is nothing we need discuss, I must beg your pardon, Captain. The Mississippi and Missouri steamer line seems to have been run in a very slipshod manner by the previous owner and his manager, and I have much to do to set it aright."

Sam nodded. The disquiet was back. He filed away the two pieces of information he had learned from the visit. Thomas had run the steamer line in a careless manner, and James Randolph was hiding something. He had adroitly avoided the invitation to divulge the name of the eastern city of his origin — as had his sister. Perhaps it was time to tip his hand and shake Randolph up a bit, see what fell out into the open.

"I understand." Sam tugged on his hat and moved to the door. "Thank you for your time, Mr. Randolph. I make it my business to find out about the people who take up residence in St. Louis. And, if in the course of your familiarizing yourself with this business, you find that need for my services, do not hesitate to call upon me." He dipped his head and walked from the room, leaving James Randolph staring after him.

A steamship's horn pierced the silence. Another answered. Mary turned onto her back and sighed. She tossed the sheet aside, slipped her feet into her silk slippers and used the brilliant starlight to guide her to the window. Sleep was impossible. She was supposed to be in Philadelphia planning her wedding. Instead, she was at the edge of a wilderness in St. Louis, Missouri, facing an unknown future. How could she sleep when her whole life had gone topsy-turvy?

Her stomach cramped. She pressed her hands against her abdomen and took a long, slow breath to ease the pain of the nervous spasm. What would life hold for her? It was true she would rather be a spinster than some man's bargain. But that did not mean her desire to love and be loved, to marry and have children, to grow old with a beloved husband beside her was gone. It was all in her heart, and stronger than ever.

Tears welled. *Poor little Miss Mary. She'll have a hard time findin' herself a husband, bein' plain like she is. Now, if she was blessed with the beauty of Miss Sarah . . .* Oh, how true her nanny's words had proved to be.

Mary blinked the tears away and lifted her face toward the dark sky, the same questions that had plagued her all her growing-up years swirling in her mind. Why had God made her tall and thin and dark-haired? And, what was worse, given her the bold, forthright nature that was off-putting to men? Why had He not made *her* small and blond like her sister, with a golden beauty and gentle sweet nature that drew men the way nectar drew bees? The way Victoria drew Winston. Why did God not love her as much as He did others?

The familiar hurt squeezed her chest,

made it hard to draw her breath. She opened the sash, then went to her knees, crossed her arms on the sill and rested her chin on them to catch any movement of air. Muffled sounds of revelry, from the direction of the levee, floated in on a warm breeze. A steamboat blasted its whistle. Another answered. The noise of the levee continued day and night. And it was all so strange and new.

Fear nibbled at the last shreds of her composure. The tears she had held back slipped down her cheeks. What had she done? Was her decision to leave Philadelphia a right or wrong one? Should she have swallowed her hurt and her pride and accepted Winston as her husband even though she knew it was only her father's money he wanted? Was he her last chance for a family of her own? Was the pretense of love better than a life alone?

"Twelve o'clock and all is well."

The words came, muted but distinct. She grasped on to them like a lifeline. Twelve o'clock — the beginning of a new day. And all is well. Pray God it might be so.

Sam leaped back from the slashing blade, grabbed the mountain man's thick wrist and twisted. The double-edged skinning knife clattered to the floor. He grabbed a fistful of the cursing drunk's buckskin shirt and shoved him toward his deputy. "Take him to jail and let him sleep off his meanness. I'll run him out of town in the morning." He picked up the weapon and walked outside.

A roar of voices calling for whiskey or beer erupted behind him. Music started playing. The din mixed with the noise coming from the other saloons, the lapping of river water, the churning of paddle wheels and the blasting of steam whistles to make St. Louis's own peculiar sound of revelry.

"Twelve o'clock and all is well."

Twelve o'clock. Time to go home and let his lieutenant and the night guards take over.

Home. Sam snorted, adjusted his hat and started up the road. Home was a room in Mrs. Warren's boardinghouse on Walnut Street, handy to the jail and courthouse. True, it was a vast improvement over the broken-down hovels he had lived in as a kid. Or the open fields, hay mows and sheds that had been his only shelter after he had run away from his drunk of a father. But it was far from what he had planned. Still, he was getting close. He had made some smart investments that were swelling his bank account. And now, he was gaining entrance to

St. Louis society by courting the mayor's daughter. Yes, he was getting close.

He turned onto Walnut, glanced up at the dark, star-littered sky and smiled with grim satisfaction. *Remember when I was seven years old and I begged You for some warm clothes for Daniel and Ma and me, God? Remember how I begged You for a house without holes in the walls and roof so we could be warm and dry? For somebody to come and help us?* A hard knot of resentment twisted in his stomach. *Remember how Danny and Ma sickened and died from the cold? I told You then I would make it without You. That I would be "somebody" someday, and no one would sneer at me ever again. Remember, God? Well, keep watching, because I am almost there.*

He threw a last disdainful look at the sky, took the porch steps two at a time, pulled open the door and went inside.

Chapter Six

"My, it is warm!" Mary dabbed her damp forehead, tucked her handkerchief into her pocket and glanced toward James. "I keep thinking of how lovely and cool it always is at home, even on the hottest of days."

"Hmm . . ."

"An astute comment."

James lowered the newspaper he was reading and gave her a sheepish look over the top of it. "Sorry, Mary. I did not mean to ignore you." He set the paper aside. "I know what you are saying. I have thought of home a time or two myself today. I did not realize St. Louis was so much warmer than Philadelphia." His lips curved in a rueful smile of commiseration. "Randolph Court stays cool because of its large size. I fear there is no hope of that in this small cottage."

"How cheering you are."

He chuckled.

Mary stuck her tongue out at him like

when they were children and rose from the settee. "Do you suppose one gets used to the heat?" She lifted the strands of hair stuck to her moist neck, tucked them back into the loose knot on the crown of her head and sighed. "I think I will go outside and see if there is at least a breath of a breeze." She glanced his way. "Would you care to join me?"

"I would be delighted."

"Delighted?" She drifted by his chair and tapped his shoulder. "I think not. Agreeable perhaps. You would be *delighted* if I were a certain blond young lady named Charlotte Colburn." She threw him a smile over her shoulder and headed for the door. "But, alas, Charlotte is home in Philadelphia and you must content yourself with my company. At least for the nonce."

James grinned and shrugged into his jacket. "Charlotte is pleasant, but there was no understanding between us. And I am certain I shall meet equally pleasant girls here in St. Louis. And, while I do not deny I enjoy being with a young lady, my dear sister, I do not esteem their company more highly than yours. Only . . . differently."

"Indeed."

"Do I detect skepticism?" His grin widened. "For shame, Mary. I shall prove what

I say is true." He lifted her hat from the hook on the tree and held it out to her. "Shall we go explore our new town?"

"What a lovely idea!" Mary took the wide-brimmed straw hat, knotted the filmy ties beneath her chin and moved out onto the porch. She waited until he closed the door, then stepped down onto the brick path and walked to the gate. "Which way shall we go?"

James pushed opened the gate and motioned toward the cobblestone street forming the right border of their fenced-in corner lot. "I suggest we walk up Market Street, away from the river. It is coming on to evening, and I think it might be best to avoid the levee area."

"Yes. That might be wise. I have no desire to run into the 'unsavory elements' Captain Benton spoke of. Or the good captain, either, for that matter."

"Mary . . ."

She shot him a look. "Do not use that reproving tone, James. I know we are to be forgiving. But Ben is a *child.* The captain could have shown him mercy."

"He is a police officer. It is his job to arrest those who break the law."

"Yes, that is what he told me. And if the captain had had his way, that is exactly what would have happened to Ben." She stopped and faced her brother. "Do *you* think Ben belongs in jail?"

"Of course not, but you cannot hold it against the man for performing his duty."

Mary stared at him a moment, then turned with a swish of her long skirts and resumed walking. "My head tells me you are right, James. But my heart refuses to be sensible about the matter." She gave him a sidelong glance. "Homeless children do not belong in a jail. They belong in an orphanage — like Aunt Laina's. Alas, there is no orphanage in St. Louis. Nonetheless, the matter is well settled — despite the captain's lack of compassion."

They reached the corner and veered right. A steamboat's whistle blasted a strident note, then another. Mary glanced at James and laughed. "I believe I am becoming accustomed to the constant blare of those whistles. That time I only flinched instead of nearly jumping out of my skin."

He grinned down at her. "I am sure in a few more days we will not notice them at all. Or the Indians and mountain men. Though it is still something of a shock when one walks into the office and books passage on our ships. Particularly since they often pay their fare with *pelts*."

"Truly? I cannot imagine." Mary stopped and looked up at him. "How do you know what a pelt is worth?"

A frown creased his forehead. "I have no notion as to their value. I am learning to judge that. Meanwhile, I let Goodwin handle all such transactions while I watch. It is quite an art, bartering. The Indians are quite skilled at it."

Mary started walking again. "Have you found any information that points to whomever was skimming the profit from the line?"

"Not yet. Everything is too new — such as this trade in pelts. But I shall. I am watching Goodwin. There is something about the man I do not trust. It would not be hard for him to take advantage of my ignorance, so I am secretly keeping a careful accounting of all transactions, apart from the company records he keeps."

"And if you discover he is stealing from the line?"

"I shall have Captain Benton arrest him."

Mary snorted. "You mean if the good captain is not too busy arresting children." She turned her head and looked forward. The sun rode low in the sky, the bottom of the blazing orange orb hidden by the leafy canopy of a tree atop the rise they were climbing. She lifted her hand to shade her eyes from the glare of light and looked across the street at an imposing two-story brick building with a clock tower, topped by a pillared dome, in the center of the roof. A large park surrounded the building. Mary gave James a sidelong look. "Shall we cross over and see what that building is?"

He nodded and took hold of her elbow. They waited for a buggy to pass, then hurried across the street and walked up the wide brick pathway to climb the steps. The cooler air in the shade of the portico felt wonderful. Mary removed her hat, fanned herself with its wide brim and watched James stride over to a brass plaque on the wall beside the handsome double doors straight ahead.

"This is the courthouse, Mary. Rather small, I should think, for all —"

One of the doors opened and an elegantly dressed young woman stepped out onto the portico, almost running into James.

"Oh!" Light brown, delicately arched brows lifted and big, blue eyes opened wide as beautifully shaped lips parted in surprise. "Forgive me, sir. I was not paying attention to my path."

James smiled and made a polite bow. "Not at all, miss. The fault was mine. I should not have crowded the doorway."

"You are too kind, sir." Long lashes fluttered down over the blue eyes as the woman smiled, revealing dimples in cheeks tinged with a hint of pink.

Mary's chest tightened. The woman was petite, blond and beautiful. The same as Victoria. Everything *she* was not. She stopped fanning, raised her hat to her head and settled it a little forward to hide as much of her face as possible. The wide, gauzy ties she formed into a large bow to hide her small, square chin. There was nothing she could do about her height. Or her slenderness.

She glanced down, surreptitiously bunched the fabric of her long skirt at her narrow waist to make her frame look fuller, then looked back toward the woman and froze. So did the tall, blond man holding the door. Their gazes met. The heat of a blush spread across her cheeks, but Samuel Benton did not so much as flicker an eye. He only gave a polite nod, though she knew he did not miss the tiniest imperfection in her appearance, or her pathetic attempt to hide them.

Mary stood rooted in place, acutely aware of the sheen on her flushed face in comparison to the cool perfection of the beautiful, petite blonde. She felt like an ugly giant, but not for anything would she betray her discomfort to the woman giving her a keen, measuring look from under those ridiculously long lashes. Or to the captain, either. She squared her shoulders, lifted her chin and pasted a polite smile on her face.

Samuel Benton stepped forward. "Good evening, Miss Randolph . . . Mr. Randolph. May I present Miss Stewart." He looked down at the young woman. "Miss Stewart, Miss Randolph and her brother are two of St. Louis's newest citizens. Mr. Randolph has come to town to manage the Mississippi and Missouri steamer line."

James gave a polite bow. "Your servant, Miss Stewart."

Mary smiled and dipped her head, wishing she were seated. She was at least three inches taller than the woman. "Good evening."

Miss Stewart smiled in response, showing her dimples off to good advantage. "I shall have to tell my father of your arrival in our fair city, Mr. Randolph. I am certain he will want to meet with you. He is the mayor of St. Louis and very solicitous of its businesses." Her gaze shifted, chilled. "And my mother will want to make your acquaintance, Miss Randolph. She heads many of the charity and cultural events of St. Louis."

She turned to Samuel Benton and gave him a dazzling smile. "You were going to see me home, Captain Benton?"

"Of course, Miss Stewart." He glanced in their direction. "Good evening, Miss Randolph . . . Mr. Randolph." He offered Miss Stewart his arm, then escorted her down the stairs and out to Market Street.

Mary stared after them a moment, then reached up and yanked undone the huge bow hiding her chin, cross with herself for allowing Miss Stewart's beauty to upset her.

"Shall we go on with our exploring, Mary?"

She took a breath and retied the bow . . . smaller. "Yes, of course, James." She forced a smile and tried not to think of how her heart had faltered when the captain's gaze had met hers, or of how lovely Miss Stewart had looked beside the captain, as James took her elbow and they descended the steps together.

It was no use. Thoughts kept tumbling around in her head breaking her concentration. Mary sighed, put down her pen and lowered the wick in the oil lamp until the flame sputtered and died. She would finish the letter to her parents tomorrow.

The wood chair creaked softly as she rose

from the writing desk. A slight breeze rippled the fabric of her dressing gown as she walked to the open window. At least it had finally cooled off a little. That would make sleeping more pleasant. If only she could sleep.

Faint sounds of St. Louis's revelry drifting in the window were drowned out by the loud, persistent hum of a hungry mosquito hovering around her ear. She swatted the insect away and looked out into the moonlit night. Had Captain Benton spent the evening sitting on the mayor's front porch wooing Miss Stewart? Was he there still?

Mary frowned, leaned against the window frame and let the night breeze flow over her. Why was she unable to erase the couple from her mind? She was not normally so weak-willed. It must be the strong resemblance Miss Stewart bore to Victoria Dearborn that had her so . . . so . . . agitated. That, and the look of admiration in Captain Benton's eyes as he gazed down at the petite blonde. It was the same way Winston Blackstone had looked at Victoria.

Mary sighed, then shoved away from the window and walked to the four-poster bed. She longed to walk about, but the room was too small to pace. She sat on the edge of the bed, tugged a pillow from under the woven coverlet and reclined against it. The mosquito found her. Another joined it. She swatted them away, rose to her knees, yanked the gauzy bed hangings free of the bedposts and pulled them into place, making certain the edges lapped. That would keep the annoying insects away. If only there were a curtain she could pull across her mind to keep the unwelcome thoughts and images away.

She snorted and batted her eyelashes, dipped her head and looked up, ever so coyly, through them, as Miss Stewart had done while talking to the men. It was nauseating! Miss Stewart was an outrageous flirt, who was obviously dissatisfied lest she capture the admiration of every man she came in contact with. Why, Miss Stewart was flirting with James right under the captain's eyes! Why were men blind to such machinations?

Mary fluffed her pillow and sank down against it. *How would it feel to have a man look at you the way Winston looked at Victoria? The way Captain Benton looked at Miss Stewart? As if you were beautiful and delicate and precious? How would it feel to have a man love you?*

The stars shining beyond the filmy fabric blurred. Mary swiped the tears from her cheeks, grabbed another pillow and flopped over onto her side, hugging the fluffy softness close against her constricted chest. This loneliness was her portion in life. God had not seen fit to make her beautiful in the eyes of men. There was no sense in wishing for things that would never be.

Chapter Seven

Sam relaxed in the saddle, at ease with the powerful ripple and thrust of his horse's muscles, the solid thud of hooves against the hard-packed earth. It was a nice day for a ride, and it had been a long time since he had been astride Attila. He did not get out of St. Louis often.

He ducked under a low-hanging branch, rested his free hand on his thigh and glanced up at the cloud-dotted, blue expanse above. Too bad he could not have enjoyed this excursion more. But the trip's purpose was not to his liking. Still, posting notice of the new law concerning emigrant children under the age of twelve was part of his job, and he had done it. Now, he would have to enforce it.

His face tightened. So did his stomach. He blew out a breath easing the constraint and returned his attention to the trail ahead. The thick band of trees that hid the wagon train gathering site from the city was thinning. He would soon be back to town. He frowned and eased back on the reins, slowing Attila's pace.

At least it was late in the season. The wagon train forming now would probably be the last for this year. The influx of emigrants should stop soon. And perhaps by the time they began gathering again next spring, the situation concerning orphaned children would be different. Meanwhile, he would do what he must.

Sam set his jaw, clamped a firm lid on his unease and directed his thoughts toward his goals. He had worked with a view to them since he was old enough to muck out stalls and help farmers plant and harvest crops. He was not going to give them up now. He would do his job. And he would fulfill his plan.

He closed his eyes and summoned the vision he carried in his heart. His house would be perfect. There would be no soot, no faded fabric, no chipped paint in the wood trim or gouges in the wood floors. He would have carpets in every room, fancy furniture and real paintings on the walls. And it was going to be big. Three stories high with lots of windows and tall white pillars holding up the high porch roof.

He frowned and opened his eyes. He was close. Very close. The lead mine upriver he had invested in was proving very profitable. And his other interests were doing equally well. His finances were secure. What he needed now was the land.

He knew the piece he wanted. It had a knoll, the highest spot around, where he would build his house to look out over the river. It would be the first place seen by people coming down the river to St. Louis. A real showplace. All he had to do was wait for Charlie and Harry Banks to come back to town so he could make the old mountain men a generous offer for their property. Maybe then they would stop mining for silver and live an easier life in town. And then, when his house was built, he would marry Levinia Stewart and they would become the young leaders of St. Louis society.

Sam smiled, leaned forward and patted Attila's neck. He had it all worked out. All he had to do was court Levinia and wait for Charlie and Harry. He closed his eyes again, pictured the way it would be. But for some reason he could not see Levinia in the house. He frowned and stopped trying to place her there. It was too early. That was the problem. He had only begun to court her. But he intended to marry her. The mayor's daughter was everything he needed his wife to be. She was the most beautiful woman in St. Louis, a fitting mistress for his showplace house. And she was the key to his full acceptance into society.

Sam shifted his weight in the saddle and let his mind drift back to the way Levinia had looked last night. She had been agleam with beauty, clearly outshining Miss Randolph.

Miss Randolph.

Sam stirred, jolted by the same sense of guilt that had hit him when he had met her gaze last evening. It was clear, from the look in her brown eyes, that she still felt he was wrong about arresting that young boy. But that was his job!

Sam jerked his thoughts away from the condemnation in Miss Randolph's eyes. He knew the desperate acts hunger drove one to, but he could not afford to feel guilty for performing his duty. His job was providing him with the means to accomplish his goals, and he would not give that up for anyone. Certainly not for a woman with a pair of accusing brown eyes. No matter how beautiful those eyes were.

Danny had brown eyes.

Sam sucked in air, fought the pressure in

his chest. The approaching victory suddenly felt hollow. Danny and Ma would never know he was holding fast to the promise he made them to be so rich and important nobody would ever sneer at any of them again. At seven years old, he had thought that promise could take the place of the food and warmth God never sent in spite of his prayers. He had thought the promise was strong enough to keep them alive — the way it did him. But Danny was too small, and his ma too weak. Their sickness got worse until it killed them. He had tried to take care of them, but he could not save them.

Sam's face tightened. He glanced toward the sky. *I failed you and Danny then, Ma, but I will not fail you now. I will keep my promise to make you proud of me.*

He emerged from the trees and reined south, headed for Chestnut Street and the stables behind the jail.

The jail.

The tight ball of unease returned to his stomach. What sort of place was a jail for a kid?

"I am certain it would work out well for your store, Mrs. Simpson." Mary gave the grocer's wife a warm, encouraging smile.

"Marketing baskets can become very heavy before one reaches home, and I believe many of your customers would be willing to pay a small stipend for Ben to relieve them of that burden. I believe they would welcome such a service, and favor your store with their custom for offering it." She placed her hand on Ben's shoulder, drawing the stout woman's attention to the boy who was all shiny clean and dressed in clothes that had once belonged to Ivy's sons.

Mrs. Simpson glanced at her husband, who was stacking burlap bags in the corner, and shook her head. "You will have to gain Mr. Simpson's approval, Miss Randolph. And I am quite certain he will refuse you." There was commiseration in her eyes.

Mary thought it likely the woman was right, but she would not give up without a fight. Ben had been so happy when she had explained this idea to him. "Very well. Thank you, Mrs. Simpson." She lifted her chin, turned toward the corner to speak with Mr. Simpson and almost bumped into a small, elderly woman. "Oh! Forgive me, madam, I —"

"The fault is mine, dear." The woman placed a blotchy, thin-skinned hand on her arm. "I overheard a bit of your conversation and moved closer where I could shamelessly eavesdrop on the rest." The woman smiled, and the creases and wrinkles in her face deepened. "My hearing is not what it used to be. But I heard enough to know you have an excellent suggestion, young lady. If you will permit me to help, I believe the three of us —" another smile included Mrs. Simpson "— can convince Mr. Simpson it would prosper his store. Do you agree, Martha?"

Mrs. Simpson nodded.

Mary stared, stunned by the elderly woman's offer, and doubtful of its value. Still . . . Mr. Simpson held no fondness for *her.* And Mrs. Simpson had agreed. She smiled at the tiny woman. "I should be most appreciative of your help, madam."

"Good!" The woman returned her smile. "Now, ladies, let us see to Mr. Simpson."

Mary grinned. She could not help it. The woman's faded blue eyes were fairly twinkling. She was obviously delighted at the prospect of a challenge. But how could she help?

The woman sobered. She slid her basket off her arm and set it and a small piece of paper on the long wood counter. "Here is my list, Martha. But, as I shall not have to carry my basket myself, add a quart of molasses, a bag of tea and a good portion of honeycomb. Oh. And two of those lemons

— fresh ones, mind you. I must say, this is a most helpful idea. But tell me, what is the cost for this young man to carry my basket home for me?"

Cost? Mary took a closer look at the elderly woman beside her. How clever to persuade Mr. Simpson through his pocketbook. She should have considered that. But she had thought only in terms of a stipend for Ben. Mary held back a chuckle. The aged woman's face held an expression of pure innocence, yet she had raised her voice loud enough to be heard throughout the store, and was watching the result out of the corner of her eyes. Another good idea.

Mary wiped the smile from her face, lowered her lashes and shot a glance toward the corner. Mr. Simpson had straightened. He looked their way and a frown darkened his face. He brushed his hands together, sending some sort of dust flying into the air, and started toward them. Mary jerked her gaze back to the other women before he caught her watching him.

"You mistook my conversation with Miss Randolph, Mrs. Lucas." Mrs. Simpson lifted the hinged lid of a large wooden box and began to scoop tea into a small cloth bag. "Miss Randolph suggested that Mr. Simpson hire this young boy to carry baskets for our customers, but my husband has not agreed." She shook the bag down, dropped the scoop and tied the neck of the bag closed with a length of cord, then paused with the bag poised over Mrs. Lucas's filled basket. Her left eye closed in a quick wink. "Do you still wish these other items?"

The elderly woman sighed. "No, only the things on my list, Martha. Put the tea back and take the others out, for they will make the basket too heavy for me."

Heavy footfalls thudded across the plank floor and stopped. Mr. Simpson scowled at his wife, took the package of tea from her hand and placed it in the basket. "There's no need for that, Mrs. Lucas. I ain't heard nothing about this boy carrying customers' baskets, but it sounds all right." He placed the wrapped piece of honeycomb his wife handed him in the basket and added the lemons. "The cost'll be ten cents."

"Nonsense!" Mrs. Lucas's eyes narrowed. "I came to buy groceries, not to be robbed, Elijah Simpson! I shall pay five cents."

The grocer added the molasses to the filled basket, then crossed his thick arms over his burly chest and stared down at the diminutive woman. "Seven."

There was a rustle of movement behind her. Mary took a quick glance over her shoulder. The customers had stopped browsing and had drawn close.

"Stand your ground, Isobel!" A thickset woman with a jutting chin snapped out the words. "I should very much like someone to carry my basket, but I will pay no more than five cents. As you say, anything more is outright thievery!"

There was a chorus of agreement.

Mr. Simpson's scowl deepened. He raised his hands. "All right, ladies. All right. The cost'll be five cents."

Smiles spread over the faces of the assembled women at the grocer's growled words. They gave each other small nods of satisfaction and turned back to their shopping, chatting over their victory as they went.

Mary could have hugged Mrs. Lucas and Mrs. Simpson.

"Pick up that basket and get moving, boy!" The grocer snarled the words and turned away.

Mary's elation flew. "Wait, Ben." She took hold of Ben's arm as he reached for the basket, and pasted a polite smile on her face as the surly grocer pivoted around to glare at her. "I think you are forgetting that Ben is not yet in your employ, Mr. Simpson. Shall we discuss his wages?"

■ ■ ■ ■

Sam leaped off the gangway, turned and fastened his gaze on the steamboat as the *Independence* gave notice of its departure with three quick blasts of its whistle. He ignored the movement of the laborers around him, and held his place. The danger point would come when the *Independence* swung around to head upriver. She would be close to the *Washington* then, and an agile man could jump from the deck of one steamboat to another, if given enough reason to do so.

Sam tensed and focused his attention on the narrowing distance between the two boats. He figured the money Frank Gerard had been systematically winning from his victims at cards was reason enough for him to ignore the warning he had been given and try to make his way back to the table at the Broken Barge. But the gambler was trouble — he won too often, and by questionable means. He would not be allowed in St. Louis again.

The *Independence* finished the swing and straightened on its course. The muddy waves splashed lower on the cobblestones, then ceased and merged with the river on its way south to New Orleans. One more problem gone. But there still seemed to be an endless supply of them.

Sam tugged his hat brim lower and started up the slope. He stepped around a wagon loaded with crated shoats and angled toward the *Cincinnati.* She was leaving for parts north this afternoon and this would be the first departure of one of the boats of the M and M line since Randolph had taken over its management. It was likely he would be on hand. And that made this a perfect time for an "accidental" meeting with him. He knew the man and his sister were hiding something. And he intended to find out if it concerned the vandalism of the line. And he would look around to see if Duffy was among the crew.

"Thank you again, Mrs. Lucas."

"Hush, dear." The elderly woman patted Mary's arm and smiled at Ben, who was holding her basket. "The two of you have thanked me enough."

"But it was so *clever* the way you suggested Mr. Simpson hire Ben."

"Not clever, dear . . . necessary." The woman's faded blue eyes twinkled up at her. "I should be the one thanking you. I have not enjoyed myself so much in years. People look on you as useless when you get to be my age." A wistful look replaced the twinkle. "Now . . . I must get home. I am beginning to tire." She turned to go, then looked back. "You are a lovely young lady and I should like it very much if someday you have time to call upon me."

Mary smiled and nodded. "I shall come to call in a few days, Mrs. Lucas. After I am more settled."

The elderly face crinkled into a return smile. "I shall look forward to that, my dear. My home is on Chestnut. Ben will know the way. He can escort you and we shall have a proper tea!"

"Lovely."

Mary watched Mrs. Lucas walk away, Ben beside her carrying the grocery-laden basket. It did not seem too burdensome for him. Indeed, he looked proud and happy. They disappeared behind a group of women on the walkway and she turned to scan the storefronts. James had asked —

"Let me go!"

Mary snapped her gaze in the direction of the frightened wail. A young girl was crouched behind the rain barrel at the corner of Tanner's Ladies Shoe Store, trying to tug her arm out of the grip of a policeman. The officer bent over the barrel, grabbed the girl by the shoulder and hauled her out onto the walkway.

"Please!" The girl hung back, grabbing for the rim of the rain barrel. "I ain't done nothin' wrong. *Honest.*" Tears ran down her face, making tiny paths through the grime on her cheeks. Sobs shook her small, skinny body.

Mary's heart swelled.

"Another of those filthy emigrant children!"

"Something should be done about them, Clara. Can you not speak to Robert about the situation?"

"Indeed, Clara, you must! It is disgraceful the way they are let to roam about the streets disturbing good folks!"

Mary whipped around. Three women, their faces pinched in distaste, were giving a wide berth to the child and the policeman. And no other person in the area seemed to be paying any attention to the small girl's plight.

The unloved and unlovely of this world are often invisible to those of affluence. Her aunt Laina's words rang in her head. Anger stiffened her spine. Mary whirled back and marched forward. "What is the trouble, officer?"

The policeman looked up. "No trouble,

miss. Takin' this one off to jail."

The girl seemed to shrink before her eyes. The poor little thing was shaking like leaves in a windstorm. Mary began to shake herself — with growing anger. She fought to keep her voice pleasant. "And what has she done to warrant such treatment?"

"Nothin', miss. 'Tis the law now, is all."

A shadow fell over her. Mary turned and looked up, straight into the eyes of Samuel Benton.

The captain gave a polite dip of his head. "Have you a problem with one of my men, Miss Randolph?"

"I do indeed." Mary drew herself up to her full height. The man's size was intimidating. "This officer says he is taking this little girl to jail, though he admits she has done nothing wrong."

"I told her it was the law, Captain."

"All right, Jenkins. Continue your patrol, I will take over here."

"You want me to take this 'un to jail?"

Mary stepped closer.

"No. I will handle this." The captain grasped the sobbing girl's shoulder and the policeman strode down the walkway.

Mary lifted her chin and prepared to do battle.

"Have you ever been hungry, Miss Randolph?"

The question, posed in a conversational tone, stole the starch from her spine. She eyed him with suspicion. "Of course I have."

The captain fastened his gaze on hers. "I am talking about starvation hunger, such as these street urchins suffer."

Street urchins! Her anger came surging back. She drew breath.

He raised his hand. "You need not answer. Because if you had known such hunger, you would know that being fed every day would be a blessing to them."

"In jail, Captain?" Mary clenched her hands at her sides and looked him full in the eyes. "Is that what you tell yourself to soothe your conscience? That you are doing these *children* a favor by putting them in jail? Would *you* exchange *your* freedom for a meal?" His expression did not change one iota, but there was a tiny flicker in the depths of his blue eyes and she knew her words had stung him. She pressed her advantage. "There are other ways to feed a child, Captain Benton. And, as this child has done nothing wrong — by your own officer's admission — you have no right to jail her."

"You are wrong, Miss Randolph. Mayor

Stewart and the town council have passed a new law that went into effect today. It is now illegal for any child under the age of twelve, who is not a citizen of St. Louis, to be on the streets of the city unless accompanied by an adult."

She gaped up at him, held mute by astonishment. But only for a moment. "You are going to jail *children* because they are alone on the street?" Her voice was soft, lower and more husky than normal. "What of orphans like Ben? He is to be jailed, not for any wrongdoing, but because his parents had the bad fortune to *die?* That is absurd!" Her fingernails dug into her palms. "It is ludicrous. *Preposterous!* It is . . . it is . . ."

"The law, Miss Randolph."

The captain calmly inserted the words when she sputtered to a halt. She glared at him.

"And I am sworn to uphold it. Good day." He picked up the girl, eliciting a wail of terror.

"Wait!"

He tightened his grip on the struggling child and looked at her.

She cleared her throat. "You cannot take the girl to jail. She is with me."

"Miss Randolph —"

"You said children under twelve who are

not with an adult!" Mary lifted her chin and held out her hand. "I am an adult, and she is with me. Please put her down, Captain. I want to go home."

A frown pulled Samuel Benton's dark brown brows together. His blue eyes darkened. Mary squared her shoulders and lifted her chin a notch higher. Their gazes locked. And held. She refused to look away. She was right. And he knew it.

He looked down and lowered the child to the ground.

Mary released a shaky breath. *It has only been a moment. Surely it has only been a moment. It only felt like forever.* She leaned down and took the girl's small trembling hands, rough with scratches and ground in dirt, in hers. "It is all right, now. You have nothing to fear. You are going home with me. And we are going to get you something to eat." She glanced at the small, dirt-caked bare feet, then at the grimy little face and smiled. "You shall have a bath. And we shall get you a pretty new dress and some shoes to wear. Would you like that?"

The child stared up at her out of green eyes awash with tears. A sob broke from her throat and she threw herself against Mary's legs, buried her face in the fabric of her skirt and nodded.

Mary rubbed the little girl's bony back, blinked tears from her own eyes, then straightened and cleared the lump from her throat. "Come now, you cannot walk if you are crying. Take my hand." She gave the small hand that slipped into hers a reassuring squeeze and turned toward Market Street.

"You cannot save them all, Miss Randolph. There are too many of them."

The captain's soft words brought her to a halt. She turned back and looked up at him. "I would not be able to sleep at night if I did not try, Captain. But if what you say is true, then I shall need help. Would you care to join me?"

She left the challenge hanging there and walked off, shortening her stride so the child pressing close against her could keep pace. At the corner, she could resist no longer — she glanced back. Captain Benton was still there on the walkway, looking after her. No doubt wishing she had never come to St. Louis.

CHAPTER EIGHT

She felt him looking at her.

Mary lifted her head. Her brother was standing in the doorway, a grin on his face. "I amuse you, James?"

"Yes, indeed." The grin widened. "I never thought to see you mending clothes."

She wrinkled her nose at him. "I am not mending the dress. I am altering it. And it is about time all that instruction in fine needlework bore fruit." She looked down and took another stitch along the seam. "Callie is so thin, there were no dresses in the store to fit her. And I refuse to burden Ivy with this extra work. She is already doing so much, taking Ben and Callie in as she has. What a blessing it is that she was the cook for —" She stopped midstitch and gave a wry laugh. "Gracious. I sound like Mother — seeing God's hand in a *coincidence.*" She gave a little shake of her head, completed the stitch, then poised the needle for the next, using the thimble on her finger to push it through.

"Speaking of God . . ."

She slanted a look up at him. "Were we?"

"His name was mentioned."

She did not return James's smile, merely shrugged and worked the last few stitches of the seam as he walked to the chair opposite her.

"Do you realize tomorrow is Sunday, Mary?"

She did indeed. "And . . ." She jabbed the needle into the soft cotton fabric and tugged the thread through as she had countless times under Miss Spencer's tutelage.

"And . . ." James lowered himself into the Windsor, stretched out his long legs and crossed his ankles. "I went to the levee today when the *Cincinnati* departed. Captain Benton was there."

The needle stabbed into her finger. *Bother!* Mary yanked her pricked finger out from under the blue dress and stuck the tip of it in her mouth. "Captain Benton seems to be everywhere. Especially when innocent children are being arrested."

"I asked him about a church. He told me of several and gave me directions to their locations . . . though I got the distinct impression he did not himself attend any of them."

"That is not surprising. The man has no conscience!" She huffed, finished off the seam, then reached into the small sewing box her mother had insisted she bring along to the wilderness.

"I went to see the pastor of one of the churches. The service begins at nine o'clock, the same as at home."

She snipped off the thread and placed the scissors back into the box. "*There.* I am finished." She stuck the needle into the pincushion and tossed it after the scissors.

"Mary?"

She shot him a look as she shook out the small dress. "I heard you, James. I will be dressed in my finery and ready to go by half after eight in the morning. But I shan't like it." She flicked the lid of the box closed and secured the small latch. The little blue dress dangled from her other hand. She brushed the five narrow bands of darker blue fabric that circled the bottom of the skirt into place and sighed. "James . . . do you remember what Aunt Laina says, that 'the unloved and unlovely of this world are often invisible to those of affluence'?"

"Yes . . ."

She glanced at him, saw the question in

his eyes. "I never truly believed that until these past few days." She draped the dress over the arm of her chair, then rose and crossed to the window.

"Perhaps that is because you were never before confronted by situations that proved it to be true."

Mary nodded. "Yes. That must be the reason. Mother and Father and, of course, Aunt Laina and Uncle Thad care about the downtrodden. And they befriend those who share their feelings. I have never before seen people who . . . who are so selfish and uncaring."

There were soft footsteps on the carpet. James appeared beside her, leaned a shoulder against the window frame and looked at her. "We all played with the children at Aunt Laina's orphanage. And you and Sarah helped there when you got older. But none of us ever witnessed Aunt Laina's struggle to establish it. We only heard bits and pieces of the story as we were growing up."

A buggy rolled into view. She watched until it was out of sight, then turned to face him. "I never realized how courageous Aunt Laina is. I shall never forget the disdainful disgust on the faces of the customers at Simpson's market when they looked at Ben. Or the hard-heartedness of those three women on the street today. They looked at Callie as if she were some loathsome creature instead of a child. And everyone else on the walkway either glanced at her and the policeman and walked on or averted their gazes completely. They simply did not care about the child. And as for Captain Benton . . ." Her face tightened. "He does not bear speaking about."

"Mary —"

"Do not tell me again that the captain is only doing his duty, James. He is *wrong* to take those children to jail and he knows it. I saw it in his eyes. I do not know how the man sleeps at night. I hope it is poorly!" She gave another huff, walked to the small piecrust-edged table stand and picked up her sewing box to put it away in the corner cupboard. She turned to pick up the dress, gasped and spun about to face him.

He straightened. "What is it?"

"I only know of Ben and Callie, James! How many children do you suppose are already in jail? And how am I to prevent the arrest of more of them? I cannot patrol every street and watch every policeman." She stared at him, nibbling on the left inside corner of her upper lip while her mind circled the problem.

He pushed away from the window and

gave a little shrug. "True enough. Of course, if the law was revoked —"

"*James.* The law —" She laughed, rushed forward and threw her arms about him in a fierce hug. "Thank you, James. You are so very, *very* clever. That is the answer. I shall have that ridiculous law revoked!"

He had selected the right woman to be his bride. There was no doubt about it. Sam leaned against a pillar and let his gaze travel over Levinia Stewart as she spread the long, silk-flower-trimmed skirt of her yellow gown and seated herself on the swing. Yes, she was the perfect choice for his wife. That was exactly the way she would look gracing his porch. He would be able to picture her there now.

Levinia glanced up at him from under lowered lashes, gave him a dimpled smile and pushed one small, silk-slipper-clad foot against the floor to set the swing in motion. "You must not look at me so intently, Captain Benton. It is not seemly."

He rose to the coquettish cue. "Forgive me, Miss Stewart. But your beauty draws my eye as candlelight draws a moth. I find it impossible to resist looking at you. As, I believe, would any man."

The quick flash in her blue eyes before

she lowered her long lashes told him that she had been well pleased by his compliment.

"You flatter me excessively, Captain."

Her tone told him that she wanted more. He took the hint and fed her another morsel. "That would be impossible, Miss Stewart. My tongue cannot find words adequate to describe your beauty."

He was rewarded for his effort with another dimpled smile.

"I see you are not a man who accepts reproof, Captain Benton." Levinia's small foot peeked out from beneath her skirt to push against the porch floor again. The swing moved gently to and fro. "The evening is pleasant."

So the flirting was over for now. It was time for small talk. "Yes. The cloud cover has cooled things a bit. It will most likely rain tonight — and tomorrow."

"Oh, I hope not tomorrow. I have a lovely new dress to wear to church." A flirtatious, coaxing look came his way. "Shall I see you in church, Captain?"

Sam's face tightened. Church was the last place he wanted to be. But if he were to win Levinia and be accepted within the social elite of St. Louis, he would have to play the part. *Does this amuse You, God?*

He pasted a smile on his face. "I will be there, Miss Stewart. Though with you seated in the congregation, it will be hard for me to concentrate on the sermon."

Her small laugh rippled softly on the cool, evening air. "Gracious, Captain, you must desist from paying me so many compliments or you will quite turn my head!" She lifted her gloved hand and toyed with one of the blond curls dangling at her temples. "Mother is very pleased with this new law Father passed to clear our streets of those filthy urchins. She was quite undone the other day when one of them entered Simpson's market. He almost *touched* her gown!"

A delicate shudder. Planned, not real. And another of those feigned coaxing looks. *Does she practice?* He couldn't imagine Miss Randolph acting in such an affected way. He squelched a frown.

"I hope you will arrest them all soon and get them off our streets. They are a most unpleasant sight, and quite ruin a lovely day of shopping."

You are going to jail children because they are alone on the street? Because their parents had the bad fortune to die? Sam shook his head, studied Levinia's face to rid himself of Mary Randolph's voice in his head. "I shall uphold the law to the best of my ability, Miss Stewart."

"Oh, I did not mean to suggest you would do less, Captain. Father says he can always depend on you. He says you will go far." Levinia's pink cheeks dimpled in another smile that did not quite disguise the apprais-ing look in the widened blue eyes. "He says with his guidance and support you may even be mayor of St. Louis one day."

Sam dipped his head to hide his elation. "I am pleased to hear your father thinks well of me." He looked up and locked his gaze with hers. "And may I hope you feel the same, Miss Stewart?"

"Why, Captain —" Light flashed across the dark clouds on the horizon. Thunder rolled in the distance. "Oh!" Levinia placed a hand on her chest and rose from the swing. "I fear your prediction of inclement weather is coming true, Captain Benton." There was another flash of light, a low rumble. "I dislike storms. Forgive me, but I must go inside before the rain begins."

"I insist you do, Miss Stewart. I would not want you to take a chill. Please, allow me to assist you." Sam stepped forward and opened the door for her.

"Thank you, Captain Benton. I shall look forward to seeing you at church tomorrow." She gave him a quick smile and rushed inside. Sam tugged on his hat and trotted down the porch steps.

So the mayor thought he would go far. Maybe even be the mayor of St. Louis someday. Well . . . maybe he would. A smile split his lips. Levinia would be the perfect wife if he went into politics. And judging from her actions tonight, along with that measuring look she had given him, she was considering that possibility herself.

Rain pattered on his hat, splattered against his shoulders and danced on the hard, dry ground. Sam glanced up at the roiling clouds overhead and frowned. He was in for a good soaking before he reached home. But the courting call he had made on Levinia was worth it. He had found out his plan was going forward even better than he had anticipated.

The wind picked up. Rain pelted his back, plastering his shirt against his skin, but nothing could disturb the warm glow of satisfaction inside him. The only thing that could make this evening better was if he had ridden Attila. He smiled, pulled his hat brim lower and stretched his legs out into a ground-eating lope. Church tomorrow. It seemed God was going to help him achieve his goals after all.

■ ■ ■ ■

Was that thunder? Mary laid her book aside and crossed to the open window. Black clouds were tumbling across the sky. The ends of the branches of the elm tree in the backyard dipped and swayed in a rising wind. Light glinted across the horizon and her thoughts darted to her sister. She leaned on the windowsill and looked toward the northeast. Sarah was terrified of thunderstorms since she had seen lightning strike her fiancé dead aboard a ship they were sailing.

Mary shuddered and wrapped her arms about herself. If two sailors in a dingy had not spotted the skirt of Sarah's dress caught on a broken-off piece of the ship when she fell in the water, her sister would have drowned. Mary looked up, watched the black clouds filling the sky, shutting off the evening light. *Oh, Sarah, I hope the sun is shining on you in Cincinnati.*

The wind gusted, blowing the skirt of her dressing gown against her legs. Rain slapped against the raised window, coursed down the small panes and flowed off in rivulets. The candle on the washstand beside her bed guttered and died.

Mary shivered and stared out into the dark. How many young children were out there in the storm? Where did they take shelter? *You cannot save them all, Miss Randolph. There are too many of them.* Captain Benton's words flowed through her mind. They bore a frustrating truth. Doubt assailed her. She brushed the rainwater from the sill with her hand, closed the window and stared out into the stormy night.

Should she request an audience with Mayor Stewart? Or was Captain Benton right? If she was successful in presenting her petition to have this law removed from the city charter, what then? Who would feed, clothe and shelter these young, orphaned children? She had no room in this tiny cottage. And she could not ask Ivy to take in more of them.

The lightning flashed brighter. The thunder rumbled closer, and the rain drummed on the roof over her head. Mary sighed. It was too big a task for her alone. But she would do what she could. Tomorrow she would write and ask her father to increase her allowance. And to allow any more orphaned children she found to sleep in the warehouse. It was not enough, but it was a start. And she *would* call at Mayor Stewart's office on Monday. She could not help a child who was in jail.

Jail.

Her thoughts returned to her confrontation that afternoon with Captain Benton. *If what you say is true, then I shall need help. Would you care to join me?* Mary frowned and unfastened her dressing gown as she crossed to her bed. Anger had pushed her into challenging Captain Benton — but why did she get so angry with him? She knew he was only doing his job. It *was* his duty to uphold the law. And he had been gentle when holding Callie this afternoon, unlike the other policeman. But —

Mary shook her head and hung the damp dressing gown over the back of the desk chair to dry, then kicked off her slippers and crawled under the covers. She arranged her pillow, rested her head on the downy softness and closed her eyes. It did no good. The truth hovered in her heart, waiting to be confessed. She wanted him to be better than that. She wanted him to help the children instead of arresting them. She wanted to admire him.

The admission brought warmth rushing to her cheeks. She was attracted to Captain Samuel Benton, more than she had ever been to any man — including Winston Blackstone. Though why she should be was beyond her understanding. The man made her uncomfortable. Simply being in his presence was . . . disturbing. And today, when he had looked at her —

Mary snapped her thoughts away from the memory. She did not want to examine too closely how she had felt during that long, uneasy moment. That way led to more hurt. She was well aware of her shortcomings in men's eyes. Especially men like Captain Samuel Benton who courted petite, beautiful blondes like Miss Stewart.

Chapter Nine

Mary adjusted the long wrap that matched her amber, watered-silk gown and walked down the center aisle beside James, looking neither left nor right. Why did he always choose a pew close to the front of the church? She would much prefer to hide in the back, and he knew it.

James stopped beside a pew on their right and Mary slipped in, grateful for the opportunity to sit down. At least now her tallness would be disguised, not that anyone present could have failed to notice it as they had made that long walk! And thank goodness it was still overcast. The cool, stormy weather gave her an excuse to wear the dress with the high collar that hid her thin neck. And its matching bonnet, with the amber silk flowers clustered on both the inside and outside of the wide brim made her face look a little softer, less . . . angular.

Angular. How she hated that word! But it

had stuck in her head ever since she had overheard Winston use it to describe her to Victoria. It was unflattering . . . but true. Her cheekbones were — No! She would not think of her shortcomings.

Mary frowned and spread her skirt, then again arranged the lavish fabric of the wrap to make herself look a little heavier. It was the best she could do. She fixed her gaze on the pulpit, and by sheer dint of will, held Winston's words at bay. Soon she would have to rise to sing the chosen hymn and everyone would be able to see she was at least two or three inches taller than most of the other ladies assembled. That was enough to have to think about. Oh, why had God made her so —

The organist hit a chord.

Mary set her jaw and joined in the rustle and stir as the congregation rose. She knew the words to the hymn by heart, but her thoughts froze, arrested by the sight of the tall, blond, broad-shouldered man sliding into a pew across the aisle. Her pulse quickened. James was wrong. Samuel Benton did attend church.

She dipped her head to hide her face beneath the brim of her bonnet and watched the captain. He nodded and smiled at someone. She followed his gaze to see the object of his attention and looked straight at the mayor's daughter. The young woman's long lashes fluttered down over her blue eyes and two dimples appeared in her pink cheeks in a coy response to the captain's greeting.

Oh, my! Perfectly done. Mary let out a quiet sigh. The woman had flawless flirting abilities *and* beauty enough to draw any man's eyes — to turn any man's head. She dropped her gaze to the petite blonde's softly rounded shoulders and arms bared for all to see — and for the captain to admire. Not that *that* mattered. It was only the unfairness . . .

Mary yanked her gaze back to the front of the church, squared her shoulders and mouthed words, the familiar, acrid taste of bitterness in her mouth as she pretended to sing.

"I am reading today from the book of Isaiah." The pastor's voice rang out into the silence.

Mary sat erect in the pew and turned inward to think her own thoughts. God loved her less than those He blessed with beauty and charm; she did not owe His word her attention.

She rested her hand on the open Bible in

her lap and slanted another glance at Samuel Benton. He seemed at ease. But less than attentive. She frowned and tapped the toe of her shoe on the floor beneath the concealing hem of her skirts, the sound deadened by the multiple layers of fabric. Were young, helpless children being arrested and jailed while she sat here in church watching one of their captors stealing secret looks at Miss Stewart? And where had the woman bought that snippet of a hat that showed her blond curls to such advantage? She had never seen one quite like it. She would have to explore the shops of St. Louis this week and see what they had to offer. A hat like that would be a perfect birthday gift for Sarah. It would set off her delicate beauty the same as it did for Miss Stewart.

" '. . . he hath no form nor comeliness; and when we shall see him, there is no beauty that we should desire him.' "

No beauty? Mary glanced up at the pastor. Who —

" 'He is despised and rejected of men; a man of sorrows, and acquainted with grief: and we hid as it were our faces from him —' "

Mary stared, her attention riveted on the words. Why, the pastor could be speaking of the orphaned children. That is exactly the way the people in Simpson's grocer and on Front Street had treated Ben and Callie. They did not care that the children were alone and frightened and half-starved without parents to care for them. They despised and rejected them because they were dirty and unkempt. They would not even look at them. Or else they wanted to *jail* them.

Mary shot a look across the aisle at Samuel Benton. Did he see the similarity? Had he heard the pastor's words? It appeared not. The captain's gaze was fastened on Miss Stewart, not the pastor.

Mary drew in a long, slow breath and blinked her eyes to control a sudden rush of tears. She stared down at her folded hands, the words the pastor had read ringing in her head — *there is no beauty that we should desire him.* She bit down on her lower lip and blinked harder, furious that the words made her want to cry. Why should they? It was not anything new to her. She knew beauty made people desirable to others — and that a lack of beauty brought rejection. She should. Winston had rejected *her* for lack of beauty. That was a grim truth she carried in her heart. Carried and accepted. But . . .

She lifted her head and looked across the

aisle, unable to stop herself, though the sight of the mayor's daughter made the ache in her heart swell. Oh, why had God not loved her enough to make *her* petite and blond and beautiful? Rejection would never happen to Miss Stewart. A woman as lovely as she need never fear that. With her beauty, any man would desire her . . . as Captain Benton did.

The line of departing people ahead of them was barely crawling forward. *Another* reason she preferred the back of the church — one could exit quickly. And all she wanted was to go home and hide. She refused to cry — no matter how her chest ached. Mary inched ahead, stopped and tapped her foot, finding relief in venting her irritation. Did *everyone* have to shake the pastor's hand?

The short, plump, elderly woman in front of them, who had greeted them earlier, looked back over her shoulder. So did the woman's husband.

Mary pasted on a polite smile and stilled her foot.

James looked at her.

The pressure in her chest increased. They were too close — knew each other too well. She could read the silent "What is wrong?" in his eyes as clearly as if it were written on his forehead. She gave a slight shake of her head, mustered a smile she knew would not fool him and turned away from his close perusal. Her emotions were too raw at the moment for brotherly sympathy. It would break her down.

She stepped a bit to the side to see how close they were to the door and gave a soft sigh of relief. Only two more couples. The young man speaking with the pastor glanced her way and she looked down in maidenly modesty. A ridiculous subterfuge she affected upon such occurrences in order not to see the look of disappointment in the man's eyes when he got a good look at her face or realized her height and slenderness.

The line moved.

Mary stepped closer to James, adjusted her wrap to better cover her shoulders and waited.

The line moved again. The elderly couple spoke to the pastor, shook his hand and stepped through the door. A flash of sky, people drifting down the walk toward the street. *Finally!*

"Greetings, Mr. Randolph. I am so glad you joined us this morning." The pastor beamed a smile at James, then glanced her way. "And is this young lady the sister you spoke of?"

"Yes, she is." James's hand tightened on her elbow and drew her forward. She summoned another polite smile.

"Welcome, Miss Randolph. Thank you for coming to join us on this lackluster day." The pastor shifted his gaze to include James and offered his hand. "I hope you will both come again."

"We shall, Pastor Thornton." James released the pastor's hand and stepped back for her to precede him through the door.

At last! They could go home. The pressure in her chest eased. Mary took a deep breath, drew her wrap more closely about her and looked toward the street. She came to a dead halt, staring at the trio standing near the end of the brick walk. For one foolish moment she considered spinning about and running back inside the church. Instead, she moved forward. *Only nod a greeting and walk on by, James. Please walk on by. Do not make me stand there and be compared to* — He stopped. Had her hand been on his arm, she would have pinched him.

"Good day, Miss Stewart . . . Captain Benton." James dipped his head. Received a nod from the captain and a dimpled smile from Miss Stewart in return.

"And good day to you, Miss Randolph."

Samuel Benton rested his gaze on her briefly, then indicated the young woman standing beside Miss Stewart. "May I present Miss Stewart's cousin, Miss Green."

James bowed. "Your servant, Miss Green."

A farm wagon, with the faint smell of a barnyard about it, rolled to a stop on the road beside them and an older man tipped his hat their direction. "Afternoon, Levinia . . . Captain. Time to go, Rebecca."

The young woman gave them a friendly smile. "It was nice to make your acquaintance. Please forgive me for rushing off. But we have to hurry to reach home before dark." She turned to the others. "Do you want a ride, Levinia?"

"Gracious no!" There was the slightest crinkling of the small, narrow nose. "You go on, Rebecca. Captain Benton is escorting me home."

"Very well." Rebecca Green moved to the wagon.

James stepped forward and offered her a hand up. She took her seat, smiled and waved. "Good day, all."

"Good day." Mary returned Rebecca's wave and joined James on the walkway.

Levinia Stewart slipped her gloved hand through the captain's arm and dimpled up at him. "Shall we go, Captain Benton?" She turned the smile on James. "So nice to see you again, Mr. Randolph." The residue of the smile came her direction. "And you, Miss Randolph. Good day."

"Good day." Mary returned Miss Stewart's smile in kind.

The captain tossed a nod their direction and the two walked off, with the wagon lumbering its way up the road ahead of them.

Mary glanced up at James. He was staring after them, a bemused expression on his face. She gave a quick tug on his sleeve. "Shall we go home?"

"What? Oh. Yes, of course, Mary."

She turned and started off. He fell into step beside her. "Please try not to look as besotted as the captain, James. I know Levinia Stewart is beautiful, but —"

"Miss *Stewart?*" James looked over at her and shook his head. "Miss Stewart is pretty enough. But Rebecca Green is beautiful."

Mary gazed up at him, her mouth agape. "Rebecca Green? James, Rebecca Green has *freckles!*"

"I know. I saw them." He grinned. "Did you notice they look darker when she blushes?"

"No. I did not even —" Mary gave him a suspicious glance. "When did she blush?"

"When she put her hand in mine to climb into the wagon."

Mary laughed. "You sound very pleased that you caused that blush."

"I am." He leaned down and pushed open their gate. "I wonder where Miss Green lives. And if she goes to church every Sunday. I think I will ask the captain the next time I see him." He shoved his hands in his pockets and whistled his way up the walk.

Mary stared up at him. Had he lost his mind? How could he think Miss Green lovelier than Miss Stewart? Why, she could point out a dozen flaws that made her less attractive. But it was obvious James meant what he said. She stole another sidelong look at him and shook her head. Absolutely besotted!

"You'll be all right, boy. There's no reason to be afraid." Sam motioned the silent boy into the cell, locked the door and walked away. He had learned that was best. The kid was so scared he could hardly walk or talk, but the others would take care of him. There were four of them in there now. And a girl in the cell beside them. A little girl . . . seven, maybe eight years old.

The muscles in his face drew so taut his

skin hurt. He tossed the ring of keys in the desk drawer, grabbed his hat off the hook beside the door, then went outside and drew in a deep breath of air. Free air. All the prisoners he talked to said the air was not the same when you were locked in a cell. And for the first time, he understood what they meant. When he locked those kids in, they were so frightened they could not breathe right and his own lungs labored to draw in air for them. Air that was stale and thin and unsatisfying.

Sam tugged his hat into place and started down Chestnut Street toward the levee. A steamboat whistle blew news of its arrival. He quickened his steps. Maybe Duffy would be working this boat. Or perhaps there would be a gambler with a bad reputation, or some other unsavory character onboard he could arrest or continue out of town. *Something* that would make him feel like a law officer doing a worthwhile job again, instead of a bully picking on kids. If it were not for his goals . . .

Mary Randolph's face popped into his head. He gave a low growl. The woman was becoming a major annoyance. She made him feel like a criminal, though he was the one upholding the law. But all the same, he admired her spunk. The way she lifted that small, square chin, ready to defend a child she did not know. . . . Amusement tugged his scowl into a smile. He had no doubt she would fight *him* if she had to. She was a born she-bear, that one. The thing was — that was one fight he had no real heart to win.

Chapter Ten

"Excuse me, Miss Mary." Edda stood in the doorway, her eyes wide, her hands buried in her apron. "There is a policeman come to see you, *ja?*"

"A *policeman?*"

Edda's head bobbed. *"Ja."*

Captain Benton. "All right. Thank you, Edda. I will be right down." Why would the captain come to see her? Mary frowned, put away her pen, placed the stopper in the ink well and then rose to look in the mirror. As usual, wisps of hair were escaping at her temples and down her neck from the knot on the crown of her head. *Why could she not make them stay in place?* She lifted her hands to tuck them where they belonged, then shrugged and headed for the stairs. What did it matter? The captain was not paying a social call. All the same, she tugged the bodice of her gown more smoothly into place as she walked down the stairs.

"Good afternoon, Ca—" Mary halted, stared at the swarthy policeman standing beside the front door, then moved forward again. "I am Mary Randolph. You wished to speak with me, officer?"

"Yes, Miss Randolph." The policeman whipped off his hat and dipped his head. "Captain Benton sent me to bring you to the jail."

"To the *jail!*" Shock tingled through her.

"Yes, miss. I am to escort you."

"But . . ."

"And he bids you hurry."

Mary gaped at him, then gathered her wits and shook her head. "Officer, I do not know why the captain sent you to arrest me. But I have done nothing wrong, and I am not go —"

"Oh, no, miss, you have it wrong. I am not here to arrest you. It's about the child."

Relief turned her knees to jelly. She placed her hand against the door frame to brace herself. "The child?"

"Yes, miss. The young girl. She's took sick."

"Oh. I — A moment, officer."

Mary turned and headed for the kitchen. Why had the captain sent for her? She — Did it matter? A child was sick, and she was wasting time. She quickened her steps, pausing at the kitchen doorway. "Ivy, I am going to the jail to see about a sick child. Please explain to James if I am not home in time for dinner."

"The *jail?*" Ivy stared, then shook her head and nodded. "I will tell him."

Mary whirled about and rushed to the front of the house. When the policeman had broken the news to her, had she looked as shocked as Ivy? Her lips twitched. Probably so. She sobered, grabbed her straw hat off the hat tree and settled it on her head. "All right. I am ready, officer."

"Yes, miss."

The policeman opened the door. Mary stepped onto the porch, grabbed the long, gauzy ties of her hat and knotted them under her chin as she followed the policeman down the steps to the gate.

"Captain Benton is waiting inside, miss." The officer opened the door of the square, one-story, stone building and stepped aside for her to enter.

Mary took a deep breath and stepped into the dim interior. Gray stone walls supporting the room's dingy, plastered ceiling absorbed the light from the two front windows on either side of her. The door behind her clicked shut. Movement drew her eye and her stomach flopped as Samuel Benton rose from his desk chair and strode toward her.

"Thank you for coming, Miss Randolph. I apologize for bringing you here, but —"

"I prefer an explanation to an apology, Captain Benton. Why am I here?" Mary stared up at him, not caring about her rudeness in interrupting him. "I understand there is a sick child. But what do you expect from me?" His face flushed. He was no doubt angered by her tone, but she cared not a fig for Captain Benton's feelings. Any man who would arrest children was not worth polite consideration.

"I had Doc Patterson look at the girl. He says she needs nursing care, and the mayor refuses to —" He stopped and cleared his throat. "I thought perhaps you would be willing to —"

"Volunteer my services as a nurse?" Another flush. Was he embarrassed about the situation? Good! "Where is the child?"

"In a cell in the back. I'll take you to her." He grabbed a ring of keys from a desk drawer. "This way."

"A moment, Captain." It was obvious Samuel Benton was in a quandary. Mary squared her shoulders, looked him straight in the eyes and shamelessly took advantage of his dilemma. "If I nurse the child, it will be on my terms."

He stared down at her a moment, then nodded.

Mary followed him through the doorway on the inside wall and paused, taken aback at the sight of the barred cells that lined both sides of a short, dark corridor. She had never been in such a dismal, cheerless place. A raspy cough from one of the cells started her moving again. She hastened after the captain into the darker region, keeping her hand firmly anchored to her side, though she wanted to clamp it over her nose. A musty, sour smell mingled with the odor of human waste permeated the place. She took shorter breaths and regretted having to breathe at all.

The captain stopped. Keys jingled. Metal scraped against metal. There was a loud click as he unlocked one of the barred doors. "In here, Miss Randolph." He stepped back to allow her room to pass.

The cramped cell received light from a single barred window high in its outside stone wall. Mary swept a quick glance over the interior. A painted stand with a crockery wash bowl on its surface stood beneath the window. A metal pail covered with a wooden plank sat beside it on the slate floor. On either side, their heads jammed against the stone wall, were two narrow cots. In the cot on the right lay a little girl, her thin body barely causing a lump in the striped blanket that covered her.

Mary glanced at the captain, wanting to take the girl and lock *him* up in her place. "What is her name?"

"Katy Turner."

She brushed by him into the cell and knelt beside the girl's cot. The small, dirt-streaked face was flushed, the eyes closed. "Hello, Katy. My name is Mary, and I have come to take care of you. How do you feel?" She placed her hand on the small forehead. It was hot and dry. The girl's eyes opened at her touch. Tears rushed into the blue eyes bright with fever.

"M-my th-throat hurts." The girl's voice was thick, raspy. The tears overflowed onto her grimy, gaunt cheeks. Cheeks that should be round and pink.

Mary nodded, anger welling until it pushed the breath from her lungs. "You will feel better soon, Katy. I promise." She looked toward the cell entrance. "I shall need your help, Captain Benton." Her voice was as frigid as the girl's forehead was hot.

Samuel Benton's face tightened, but he made no protest, merely stepped to her side.

Mary tucked the blankets around the little girl, then stood, tipped her head back and looked up at him. "I am taking Katy home to care for her, and she will *not* be back, Captain. I will find her a home or she will live with me. Now, as she is too ill to walk, you must carry her for me. Please lift her carefully."

"Miss Randolph —"

"Those are my conditions, Captain." Her voice was quiet, her tone implacable. Mary set her jaw and met Samuel Benton's scrutiny without so much as a flicker of her eyes. Something flashed deep in his. She did not bother to try to define it, merely turned and strode to the door of the cell. Her heart jolted. Across the corridor, six young boys of various sizes, dressed in dirty, tattered clothes, clung to the bars of their cells, staring at her.

There was movement behind her. The captain's footsteps drew near. Mary blinked tears from her eyes, smiled at the boys and hurried down the corridor toward the doorway and freedom, with the faces of those small boys seared into her heart and mind.

Mary's hands shook so she could hardly hold her scissors. She could not remember ever being so angry. Not even when Winston had betrayed her with Victoria.

She cut a hole in the seamed end of her embroidered cotton pillow slip, cut two smaller holes high in the side seams, then grabbed a long piece of ribbon from her dresser drawer and headed toward the dressing room. She paused beside Edda, who was on her knees tucking the ends of a sheet under the pile of folded quilts on the floor beside the end wall of the bedroom. "Is the pallet ready, Edda?"

The housekeeper fluffed a pillow and placed it on top of the sheet. "*Ja.* 'Tis ready, Miss Mary." She spread her short, thick fingers wide and patted the pile. "And 'tis nice and soft, *ja?*"

"It is exactly what I wanted." Mary smiled her appreciation and hurried to the dressing room. "How is Katy doing?"

Ivy looked up. "I think she is feeling some stronger, thanks to that broth she managed to swallow before her bath."

"Good. I have her nightgown ready." Mary looked at the skinny little girl in the tub. Her eyes were closed. "Poor little thing, she looks exhausted. Help me get her out of the tub so I can dry her off and get her into bed." She hung the pillow slip over the edge of the washstand and slipped her hands under Katy's thin arms. Ivy slid hers under the child's skinny legs. Mary nodded and together they lifted the little girl from the tub.

"I — I'm c-cold."

"I know, but you will be warm soon." Mary grabbed a towel, wrapped it around Katy, then went to her knees and began to dry her. "Thank you for your help, Ivy. Please go finish that sage tea concoction now. And be sure to add the honey — it helps to hide the taste of the vinegar." Thank goodness she had helped at her aunt Laina's orphanage. At least she knew what to do for a sore throat.

She finished drying Katy and pulled the pillow slip over the child's damp hair. The little girl shivered. She tied the ribbon around the tiny waist, pulled her close, gave her a quick hug then took her by the hand. "Come along, Katy. Edda prepared a lovely bed for you so you can rest and get better." She led Katy to her bedroom, helped her onto the pallet and tucked a blanket around her fragile, shivering body. Katy's eyes closed.

Mary stood by the bed watching until she was certain the child was asleep, then stepped over to the writing desk they had shoved into the corner to make room for

Katy's pallet and took her seat. She pushed aside the letter she had been writing to her sister Sarah when the officer arrived and pulled a clean sheet of paper forward. There was a tiny *clink* as she removed the stopper from the ink well and dipped in the pen.

Katy moaned. Mary glanced down at the sleeping child. Soft, black curls tumbled around the bony face that was flushed with fever. *How could anyone jail such a child?* Mary's spine stiffened. She wiped the tip of the pen against the neck edge of the ink well. She needed help and she knew exactly where to find it. She touched the pen to the paper and began her letter.

Dearest Mother and Father,

"What are you going to do with her when she is well, Mary?" James looked from the child on the pallet to the furniture shoved close together along the walls of the cramped bedroom and shook his head. "She cannot stay here. There simply is no room."

"Shh, she might hear you, James." Mary motioned for him to follow her out of the room. She grasped the banister and started down the narrow stairs, then glanced over her shoulder at him. "There is no need for you to concern yourself over Katy. I have everything planned."

James gave a soft snort. "I have no doubt of that. You are a very resourceful young woman when you want something, Mary Randolph."

She stopped, turned to face him. "I could not leave Katy in jail with no one to tend her, James. And I cannot send her back there when she is well."

"I know that, Mary. And it seems Captain Benton knows it, also."

"He does now!" She gave a little huff and spun around to walk into the parlor.

"What is happening here, Mary?"

"What do you mean?" She walked to the settee and turned to face him.

"I mean you act awfully prickly whenever Captain Benton's name is mentioned." He fastened a brotherly gaze on her. "Do you really dislike the man that much? Or is the opposite true?"

"That is ridiculous!"

"Is it?"

"Yes. It is. And stop smiling."

"All right." He walked over beside her. "What is this plan of yours?"

"Well, Katy will stay here where I can tend to her until she is well. Then she will share Callie's bed at Ivy's house." She sighed. "That takes care of the sleeping arrangements. But it still leaves meals . . . and clothes . . . and schooling . . ." She shoved a strand of hair off her forehead, then smoothed her hands over her hair, which only resulted in more of her wild, dark hair falling free.

"And have you a solution for those, as well?"

She seated herself on the settee and looked up at him. "I believe so. Of course, Ivy cannot afford to provide for the children. And *I* am responsible for bringing them into her life — therefore, they shall take dinner and supper here. And my allowance is sufficient to provide the necessary clothing for them — at least for now. And I will school them while Ivy is cooking our meals."

"And if you save another child?"

She shook her head. "I have no idea what I will do if that happens. I shall have no trouble if, when Father reads my letter, he agrees to increase my allowance. If he does not . . . well . . ." She gave a tiny shrug.

James sat in a chair, leaned forward and looked her straight in the eyes. "Mary, you cannot spend every bit of your allowance on these children. You have needs, also."

"Yes, but —"

"There is no 'but,' Mary. I will help. But even with my help . . . Even if Father does increase your allowance . . . You will not be able to sustain the expense of three children for long." He took her hand in his. "*Think*, Mary. Children grow. Their needs increase. And if you save another, and another . . . It will be impossible for us to provide for their needs."

She gave another long sigh. "I know, James. I have thought of nothing else all afternoon. And I know what you say is true. But I cannot turn my face away and pretend I do not see their suffering. I cannot simply leave these children to their fate, which is to be jailed for no reason other than they have no parents to care for them! I cannot do that, James. I cannot!"

She pressed her lips together. Blinked. Blinked again. He squeezed her hand. She looked up at him. "When I was at the jail today, there were six boys —" She lifted her hands and wiped away the tears on her cheeks. "I know I cannot care for all of these children, James. I *know* that. But if you had seen them holding on to those bars and looking out . . ." She drew her hand from his, rose and then walked over to look out the window. "I shall simply have to think of something."

"Thank you for carrying my packages home for me, Captain."

"My pleasure, Miss Stewart."

She smiled up at him. "I am so glad you happened by Virginia's house as I was leaving. It gives me the chance to tell you how very pleased Father is that you have so quickly rid our streets of the disturbing presence of those filthy urchins. Mother and I are pleased, as well. It was most pleasant shopping today. I did not see *one* of those dirty creatures lurking about."

Sam nodded. "You won't see them from now on. They are afraid to be on the streets in the daytime for fear of being arrested. They come out at night, hoping the darkness will hide them." *Because of him.* He frowned. "And it may be that some of them are ill. A little girl I had in jail is sick. Doc Patterson said she needed care, but your father said there was no money for such expenses."

"Well, of course not. Gracious! That care would be very expensive. And all of Father's plans to improve and beautify St. Louis are costly." Levinia gave a toss of her head, bouncing the golden curls spilling from the back of her bonnet. "And why should the good citizens of St. Louis pay for the care of those disgusting urchins? If they were not so dirty, they would not be sick." She stopped, gasped. "Oh, my! I certainly hope they do not pass on their filthy diseases to the rest of us." She took a step back. "Are you quite well, Captain?"

Did the woman never think of anyone but herself? Sam squelched a bubble of irritation at her total lack of sympathy for the orphaned children's plight. "I enjoy excellent health, Miss Stewart. I would not allow myself the pleasure of your company did I not." The compliment soured on his tongue.

"But if you are around this sick . . ." She gave a helpless little wave of her hand.

"Girl," Sam supplied, keeping his tone pleasant. "You need not fear, Miss Stewart. The child is no longer at the jail. Miss Randolph has taken her to her home to care for her." The image of Mary Randolph leaning over the child in the jail swam before him. The concern on her face, the kindness in her voice. He pushed it away, bent down and opened the gate to the mayor's house with his free hand.

"Miss Randolph? Who — Oh, I recall her now. She is that tall, thin, *plain* woman we met on the steps of the courthouse last week. And again after church on Sunday." She gave him a coquettish glance from beneath her long lashes.

It was an invitation for him to pay her superior beauty a compliment. He knew it as surely as if she had spoken it out loud. Annoyance rippled. Something in him turned stubborn. He nodded. "That's right. That is Miss Randolph. Though I don't know as I would call her plain." *Not with those eyes, and that proud little chin.*

Anger flashed across Levinia's face. "You find her attractive, Captain Benton?"

Careful, Sam. He smiled down at her. "You know who I find attractive, Miss Stewart."

She tilted her head and sent another of her dimpled smiles his way.

She hands those smiles out like a reward. His annoyance surged again. Sam scowled. What was wrong with him? "Here we are." He took her elbow, helped her up the steps to the porch, then released her arm and handed her the packages. "Good evening, Miss Stewart."

She gave him a sharp look. He sucked in a draught of night air and pushed his vexation aside. "One could hope that Virginia Weller lived at a greater distance." He forced a smile. "Our walk would have been longer."

"Yes. That would have been pleasant, Captain." She flashed her dimples at him. "Good evening."

Sam opened the door, watched Levinia enter the house, then hurried to slip through the gate toward Chestnut Street, headed for the stables. He needed a ride. A long ride on Attila over the plains outside of town to clear his head and get his thinking straight before he sabotaged his own goals. But all the same . . .

Mary Randolph, plain? Sam snorted. Not to his way of thinking!

Chapter Eleven

Another steamship whistled its arrival. As a horse trotted down Front Street, Sam glanced over his shoulder, automatically taking note of the rider. A buggy rumbled over the cobblestones and he peered into the night, but it was too dark for him to see its occupants. He didn't recognize the horse or the rig. Probably someone come across the river from Illinois town on the ferry.

He faced front again as James Randolph tucked the key to the door of the Mississippi and Missouri steamer line office building into his pocket and opened the door. Sam followed Randolph inside and closed the door. The noise of the activity on the levee was reduced to a muffled din by the building's thick, stone walls.

"The ledger is over here." Randolph lit an oil lamp on the table by the window and crossed the room with it, splotches of yellow light bobbing across the plank floor as he walked.

Sam followed him around a table to the high bookkeeper's desk and pushed aside the stool.

"Here are my tallies." Randolph handed him a sheet of paper covered with neat columns of numbers, then held the lamp so the light fell over the desk.

Sam focused his attention on the figures, shifting his gaze between the company ledger and the paper in his hand. There was a sizable discrepancy between the totals. To the company's deficit, of course. He closed the ledger. "The bookings for passage recorded are certainly less than those you have written down, Mr. Randolph. And they can be easily proven. What about the pelts you have listed? Where are they?"

"In the back room." Randolph headed toward the rear of the office. "I apologize for bringing you here this late at night, Captain Benton. But the pelts are to be shipped to New Orleans tomorrow. Tonight was my only chance to prove my suspicions are correct."

Randolph opened the door to the back room and lifted the lamp high. "Over here." He moved forward and light splashed on bundles of pelts stacked at the end of a long table against the far wall.

Sam strode over to them, put the paper down on the table beside the first stack and began to count. He watched Randolph out of the corner of his eye. The young man was mad as a hungry bear, but handling it well. "You're short, all right."

Randolph nodded. "I figured if Goodwin was the one skimming the profits from the company, he would in some way take advantage of my ignorance of the value of pelts. I would not know the difference in value recorded in the ledger and true value. That is why I kept count of the ones he accepted as payment. And, as I suspected, he has made off with a portion of the pelts. That is another reason I brought you here at this late hour. I believe Goodwin may be leaving town tonight."

Sam studied the young man's face. "Goodwin has likely been stealing company profits for quite a while. Why do you think he is planning to run tonight?"

"Because of this." Randolph picked up the piece of paper on which he had carefully recorded all the transactions of the past week and started back to the front office. "I keep this in the top right drawer of my desk, hidden between two papers in a folder. When I went to get it tonight, it was between the wrong two papers."

An expression of disgust swept over Randolph's face. He closed the door of the back room. "I leave the door to my office ajar, so I can hear and record all the transactions. The hinge squeaked a bit this morning and when I looked up, the opening was a bit narrower. Someone had bumped the door. I believe it was Goodwin."

The young man shook his head and placed the oil lamp back on the table. "He must have seen me writing down information and suspected I was on to him. When I came back tonight to check on the pelts, I saw the list had been moved, which meant he must have searched my desk after I went home for the evening. So I counted the pelts, confirmed my suspicions were correct and set out to find you."

Sam moved to the front door. "It looks as if you have proof enough, Mr. Randolph. Do you want to press charges?"

"Yes."

Sam nodded. "All right. You hold on to that piece of paper — and I will go pay a call on Goodwin. If we get lucky, I may catch him with the pelts." Another steamship whistled news of its departure. He looked in the direction of the levee. "But my guess is — since he learned you now know — he has already left town." He opened the door. The sounds of activity and nighttime revelry poured in.

"I will come with —"

"No." Sam shook his head. "This is my job, Mr. Randolph, and I'll handle it. You have done your part. I'll be in touch." He stepped out into the night and turned north. Goodwin lived on Olive Street. Near the boardinghouse Thomas had stayed in. Sam frowned and hurried his steps, even though he was sure the man had already caught a steamboat out of town.

Mary stooped to feel Katy's forehead. The summer savory herb Ivy had given her seemed to have broken the fever. The little girl felt cooler. And she had stopped moaning and thrashing about in her sleep.

Mary let out a sigh of relief, and stepped over to the window. It was too warm in the bedroom for her comfort, but she did not dare open the window and expose Katy to the cooler air. She glanced back at Katy. The little girl was sleeping soundly. It would be all right to leave her for a few minutes.

Mary snatched up her dressing gown and tugged it on as she went downstairs and out onto the porch. The sounds of St. Louis's revelry drifted to her on the breeze flowing from the river. She lifted the thick, heavy braid off the back of her neck and moved to the steps. It was so late. Why did James not return? And why had he gone back to his office tonight? Had it something to do with his suspicions of Eli Goodwin?

She dropped the braid and placed her hand against the post beside her. Could James be in danger? She glanced up at the star-sprinkled sky. *Please, God, do not let any harm come to James.*

A steamboat whistle blew three short bursts.

Mary jerked her gaze down from the sky. Why had she prayed? It was useless. Her family believed that God loved them, watched over them and answered their prayers. But she was not one of God's favored. Why would He care enough to answer her prayers? Tears filmed her eyes. In spite of her mother's teachings, *her* prayer was simply an ingrained habit, not an exercise of faith.

Footsteps sounded. The gate creaked. Mary started, slipped behind the post and looked toward the street. The dark form took on shape and features. "James!"

Her brother stopped, looking up at the porch. "Mary? What are you doing awake and outside at this late hour?"

She smiled down at him. "Waiting for you

to come home. *And* catching a breath of cool air. It is warm upstairs and I did not want to open my bedroom window. I thought a breeze might harm Katy."

He nodded and started up the steps. "How is she doing?"

"Much better." Mary smiled at him as they crossed the porch. "Her fever has broken. And she is sleeping well."

"That is quite an improvement." He opened the door.

"Yes." Mary glanced up at him as she walked into the house. "What has kept you so late, James? Has it something to do with your suspicions of Mr. Goodwin?"

"Yes. I now have enough proof to press charges."

"Those secret records you have been keeping."

James scowled and nodded. "Yes. But Goodwin found them. That is why I had to take care of things tonight. Captain Benton has gone to arrest him — if Goodwin has not left town."

"I see. At least the matter is solved and you can now turn your full efforts into making the steamer line the best in St. Louis."

"I am not certain it is solved, Mary. I believe Captain Benton thinks there is someone other than Goodwin involved. I could be wrong, of course."

She watched him hang his hat on the tree. "Speaking of Captain Benton, James . . ."

"Were we?" He glanced down at her and grinned.

She knew immediately he was thinking of their conversation last Saturday evening. She wrinkled her nose at him. "His name was mentioned." Her dressing gown floated around her slippered feet as she moved into the parlor. "I have been thinking about those small boys Captain Benton has in his jail. Their faces are haunting me." She lifted her chin and turned to face him. "I cannot leave them there, James. I have to get that horrid law revoked, then go to the jail and bring them home." Her pose of bravado collapsed. "Will you come with me?"

James shook his head. "I cannot, Mary. With Goodwin gone, I have to stay at the office."

"Oh, of course. I had not thought . . ." She brushed at her hair and glanced around the small parlor. "If I bring those boys home, I have no idea where they will sleep . . ."

James stepped closer, draped his arm about her shoulder and squeezed. "You get those boys free, Mary. We will find a way to take care of them."

CHAPTER TWELVE

Mary made a slow pirouette and studied her reflection in the mirror. Today she wanted, *needed* the confidence of looking her best, and she had chosen to wear one of her finest gowns. The light, ecru pongee with cinnamon-colored lace trimming the collar, the puffed sleeves and long, three-tiered skirt flattered her dark hair and eyes. At least, that is what Madam Duval said. And it must be true, for her mother agreed.

Mary turned her back on her image, then picked up the matching gloves of cinnamon lace and pulled them on as she walked out of the dressing room.

Her only regret with her choice of gown was the matching hat. If one could call it that. Mary frowned and lifted her hand to touch the wide band of matching fabric, shirred to stiffness and trimmed with flowers made of the cinnamon lace. The band circled the thick, loose knot of hair at her crown. There were no bows to hide her neck or chin, only the narrow ribbons that slid alongside her coiled hair and tied in the back. And there was no wide brim to hide her face. She glanced at her everyday straw hat hanging on the hat tree, but rejected the idea of wearing it instead of the minute confection. The straw hat would not do today. Elegance suited her purpose.

She sighed and walked to the kitchen. "I am leaving now, Ivy."

Ben slipped off a stool at the table and gaped up at her. "You look pretty as a flower, Miss Mary!"

"Why, thank you, Ben." She laughed, leaned down and gave him a quick hug, then straightened, glanced at Ivy, who had paused from her work of kneading dough, and gave a little shrug. "It is the fancy dress." She looked down, ran a cinnamon-colored lace-gloved hand over her skirt, then glanced back up. "I wanted to tell you, Edda will stay upstairs with Katy. And that I told Callie she must come downstairs soon. I do not want Katy tired. Oh! And please make sure Katy has more of the sage tea concoction every hour for her throat. It does seem to be helping." She tapped the toe of her foot and nibbled at her lip. "I believe that is all. I will return as quickly as possible."

She turned with a swirl of her long skirts and started back through the dining room. "Wish me well!"

A chorus of well wishes from the kitchen and from upstairs followed her to the front of the house. She laughed at Ben's and Callie's exuberance as she stepped out onto the porch, and closed the door. With another swish of her long skirts she turned and hurried down the front steps.

"Good morning."

"Oh!" Mary jolted to a stop and looked up. Her breath caught at the sight of Samuel Benton. She pressed her hand to her chest and stared at him.

He stared back.

Warmth spread through her, heating her cheeks. She had no hat hiding her face. No wonder he was staring! Her fingers twitched. She wanted to lift her hands to hide her foolish blush, but refused to do anything that might call his attention to it. She could, however, do nothing to hide the deep breath she must take or swoon. She drew in air, expelled it, drew in more. It helped. She was less . . . shaky. She lowered her hand to her side, wished he would look away and when he did not, lifted her chin. Let him see her plainness! "Did you want something,

Captain Benton?" *Good!* Her voice was steady.

The captain nodded, then cleared his throat. "I had to speak with your brother this morning. I was on my way back to the jail and thought I would stop by and see how Katy Turner is doing."

"How *Katy* is doing?"

"Yes." The blue eyes looking down at her darkened. "In spite of your poor opinion of me, I am not a monster who hates children, Miss Randolph. I am a policeman doing his job. If I did not care about Katy Turner, I would not have sent for you when the doctor said she needed care."

Embarrassment sent the heat flowing into her cheeks again. And, once again, she refused to hide the flush. She deserved his poor opinion. "You are right, of course, Captain Benton. Please forgive me. I am grateful you sent for me when Katy became ill, and I hope you will do the same for any other children you may find in the same condition." She mustered a smile, then moved forward when he turned toward the street. "Katy is doing much better. Her fever broke last evening, and her throat is much less raspy and sore this morning. We have been giving her sage tea with honey and vinegar."

The gate squeaked. She looked down, uncertain as to what she should do. But he was holding it open for her. She smiled her thanks and stepped through.

"Which way?"

"I beg your pardon?" She looked up, but looked down again. The directness of his gaze was disconcerting. It was no wonder she felt discomposed! She reached up to pull the brim of her bonnet farther forward to hide her face, then remembered her hat had no brim. She brushed an imaginary hair off her temple and lowered her hand.

"Which way are you going? Toward the levee?"

Gracious, he had a deep voice! "No. I am going to the courthouse. To pay a call on Mayor Stewart." She shot a quick glance at him to see how he took that news. He merely nodded.

"I am headed that direction, if you would accept my escort?"

Poor man, trapped into offering because of good manners. And she could not refuse for the same reason. "That is most kind of you, Captain, thank you."

They walked the short distance to the corner and turned uphill. A slight breeze played with the dangling ends of the thin ribbon bow that held her hat in place. The sun warmed her back. She sighed, grateful that her features were now in the shade.

"Are you becoming accustomed to St. Louis, Miss Randolph? To the clamor and din of the steamboats and levee? To the sight of Indians and mountain men roaming the streets?"

There was a smile in his voice. Mary met his gaze. The memory of that moment when she had seen her first Indian and crowded close to him for his protection flashed between them. And then she remembered Ben, who she had also met that day, and looked away. "I am indeed, Captain Benton. I no longer jump every time a steamboat blows its whistle. And I am no longer wary of going shopping without escort. But I despair that I shall ever become accustomed to the sight of the Indians."

He chuckled, and the sound seemed to bounce around in her stomach, causing it to quiver and tighten. She took a breath to ease the sensation. "You said you had to speak with James this morning. Were you successful in arresting Mr. Goodwin?"

"You know of that?" He took her elbow. "We cross here. Mind the step down." He waited for a passing wagon, then guided her at an angle to the other corner. "I'm afraid Goodwin escaped. When I got to his boardinghouse, he was already gone. I made some inquiries on the levee and found he had taken passage on a steamboat headed downriver. There's no telling where he'll go from there. To join Thomas, likely."

She looked up at him. "The former manager of the line?"

He nodded, took her elbow again and guided her onto the brick path that led to the courthouse. "That's right. I figure they had to be working together. Otherwise Thomas would have turned Goodwin over to me, same as your brother did."

They reached the courthouse steps and he offered his arm. She stared at it, remembering the image of the petite Miss Stewart clinging to it. Comparing that to her own tall self soured her stomach. But there was no help for it. She slipped her hand through and rested it on his forearm, aware of the firm, muscular strength of it as they began to climb.

"I have come to know your brother quite well since you arrived in St. Louis. He's a fine man."

"On that we agree, Captain Benton." She drew her hand from his arm as they reached the portico and forced a smile. "Thank you for escorting me, Captain. I am grateful for your kindness."

He gazed down at her, and the heat crawled into her cheeks again. She had not meant it to sound like a dismissal. He crossed to the double doors, opened one and gave a polite little bow. "My pleasure, Miss Randolph. The mayor's office is the first door on the right."

"We have no money for an orphanage, Miss Randolph, and I will not have those *urchins* roaming our city, stealing from our shopkeepers and cluttering up our streets with their dirty, unkempt presence! They are offensive to our finer citizens!"

Finer citizens? Mary took a breath, held it, then slowly released it. Clearly appeals to the mayor's conscience would not work. Perhaps he would be moved by financial considerations? "Mayor Stewart, when these *children* are arrested and jailed, the city must provide them with meals and a place to sleep — the same as would be done in an orphanage. Surely there is a building available to the city where —"

"*Miss* Randolph —" The mayor's palms slapped against the top of his desk. He rose to his feet. "I have tried to be patient, but my patience is at an end. In an orphanage, the city would have to pay people to care for these urchins. In jail there are already keepers to —"

"*Jailers,* Mr. Mayor."

The man's face flushed an angry red. "Those ragamuffins stay in jail! As for meals and a place to sleep — they will *earn* their keep. There are jobs they can do on the additions to the courthouse, and on the public school we are to begin constructing."

Mary shot to her feet and looked him straight in the eyes. "And did your daughter help construct the private academy she attended, Mr. Mayor?" The words flowed from her mouth sweet as honey.

The mayor's eyes narrowed. He rested his palms on his desktop and leaned toward her. "You have a bold, sharp tongue, young woman."

"Better a bold, sharp tongue than no heart, sir! Good day!"

Mary whirled about, took two steps and faltered at the sight of Captain Benton standing beside the open door. She raised her chin, her back ramrod straight, and marched on. When she reached the door, she shot him a glance that told him what she thought of men who would treat helpless children in such a fashion and stormed out into the corridor.

"Miss Randolph, wait!"

She turned, her entire body quivering with

anger, and watched him walk to her. "You might have warned me of the mayor's plans to make laborers of the children, Captain. You might have warned me that my visit to his office would be futile."

His face flushed. But his gaze held steady on hers. "I did not know the purpose of your visit, Miss Randolph, or I *would* have told you. And I heard of his plans to use the children as laborers the same time as you, when I stepped in that office minutes ago. The mayor does not inform me of his plans."

"I see." Sadness swept over her. Unreasonable, unwelcome sadness. She believed him, but it made no difference. "Well, you know now, Captain. What are you going to do about it?"

She pivoted and walked to the front doors. And this time she did not look back.

Mary moved about the store, anger driving her steps. She may not be able to get those boys out of jail at the moment, but she could do something to make their lives a little brighter until she could think of a way. How anyone could be as heartless as the mayor when it came to children was beyond her. And Captain Benton was little better!

She frowned, picked up a ball, turning it

in her hand. That would not be a good choice, as the cell was far too small to allow for throwing a ball. And if it rolled out of the cell, who would retrieve it for the boys? She put the ball down and moved on.

To be fair, the captain *had* sent for her when Katy took sick. But he should not have jailed her in the first place! Of course, if Katy had been on her own on the streets, what would have happened to her when she became ill? She would have had no care.

Mary paused. How many other children on the streets were sick or injured in some way? The possibility of their suffering made her ill. And angrier. There had to be some way to provide a home for those children! And she would find it.

She glanced at the shelves in front of her. Smiled at the sight of a gaily painted kaleidoscope. That would be perfect. If it were light enough for them to see through it. It had been so dark and dank in that cell! She put the toy in her basket, added another for the children at home and moved on. What else? She needed six toys. One for each of those boys, so they could be busy, have something to do. Tops!

Mary added two of the wooden toys to the basket and wandered over to another table. A game of checkers caught her eye.

That would entertain two of the boys at once. She picked up the wooden box and a smile touched her face. She and James often challenged each other at checkers. Sarah was not as much fun to play with. She was not as competitive. What else? Jackstraws! Yes, they would do well. And perhaps one of those wooden cup-and-ball games. And paper dolls for Callie. There were several to choose from. She made her selections and went to the counter.

Sam sat deep in the saddle, the wind blowing in his face, the thunder of Attila's hoofbeats in his ears. The chestnut loved to run and Sam gave him his head, exalting in the power and strength of the horse's legs beneath him.

He needed this. He needed this wild gallop out here on the open plain to clear his head. He needed time alone. Only he and Attila . . . running.

Sam's face went taut. He leaned forward, patting the thrusting neck. "Ease up now, boy. Ease up."

The chestnut slowed. Sam held him to a canter and rode on trying to escape his own thoughts . . . his conscience . . . the memory of Mary Randolph's accusing eyes. Those *eyes!*

Sam glanced to his left. The sun was hanging low in the western sky. He reined Attila into a big sweep toward the right, and headed back toward town.

What *was* he going to do? Why did Simon Stewart have to come up with this scheme for using these kids for free labor? It was . . . it was *wrong*. Plain wrong. And there was no way to put a good face on it. What kind of life was that for kids? Up in the morning, marched to a job — And what sort of job would it be? Picking up rocks? Sifting sand? What? Then marched back to their cells, fed a supper of scraps from the restaurant — half of it not fit to be eaten — and then laying down their hurting bodies on hard cots and sleeping behind locked, barred doors until the morning when it would start all over again?

Sam swept his gaze over the waving grasses on the plain, on the band of trees he was approaching. He was free to go where he wanted — but not those kids. They were locked up in cold, dark cells away from the sunlight and fresh air. And they had done nothing wrong. Nothing to deserve such treatment. It was all because they had no parents. No one to care about them.

No one but Mary Randolph.

She had brought them toys. Things to

make their days a little brighter. And what a fighter, that woman! A smile tugged at his lips. Taking on the mayor of a city to fight for kids she didn't even know. The smile died unborn. Sam stared into the distance — saw the past. What would his life have been like if there had been someone like Mary Randolph to care enough to fight for him? And what of Daniel? Maybe Daniel would have lived if there had been someone like Mary Randolph to take him into her home and nurse him when he was so sick.

Sam's stomach knotted. He yanked his thoughts from that path. That was a dangerous, *costly* road to travel down. The past was dead. There was no help for the boy he had been, but there was plenty of help for the man he was determined to become. Help from the mayor and Levinia, to achieve all he'd dreamed of. He tried to summon her face but Mary Randolph stayed stubbornly in his thoughts.

She was a pretty woman. He had known that from the first time he saw her laugh, but he hadn't realized *how* pretty until today, when she came hurrying out of her house with her brown eyes sparkling, her lips curved in laughter and her dark hair shining in the sun. It was the first time he'd seen her without a bonnet. She was beautiful. And when she smiled . . .

Sam blew a long breath of air into the twilight and shook his head. He'd had all he could do to stop staring at her. And when she had taken his arm . . . She sure fit well at his side.

He scowled, turned Attila onto the path toward town and slowed him to a walk. He had no business thinking about Mary Randolph. He was going to marry Levinia Stewart — even if she seemed less admirable than he had thought. He could be wrong about her. But even if he wasn't, he was not going to give up his plans. All he needed was the deed to the land he wanted for his house. Then he would ask for her hand.

But what about those kids?

Sam reined in the horse at the stables and dismounted. He pulled open the door and led Attila inside, the comfortable sound of the horse's hooves thudding against the puncheon floor easing his tension. He undid the cinch strap, reached for the saddle and froze.

He narrowed his eyes and absently scratched under Attila's mane, examining the idea that had popped into his head from all sides. The argument might hold water. Maybe there *was* a way to help those kids.

CHAPTER THIRTEEN

Sam closed the door and turned to face the portly man behind the desk. "Thank you for seeing me, Mr. Mayor."

"Not at all, Captain Benton." The mayor waved him toward a chair. "What is this meeting about?"

"These street children." Sam winced inwardly as the mayor's eyes narrowed. If this cost him —

"What about them?"

"Well, sir. They present a problem I did not, at first, anticipate."

"And that problem is?"

"Sickness." Sam removed his hat and took a seat. "It has been worrying at me ever since Ka— the girl took ill a few days ago."

"She's worse?" A scowl darkened the mayor's face. "You told me you would handle the problem, Captain."

"I did, sir. When you refused money for the nursing care the doctor ordered, I had

Miss Randolph brought to the jail. She is nursing the girl." No need to tell him that he had allowed Mary Randolph to take the girl home.

The mayor's scowl deepened. "You would do well to keep that woman away from the jail, Captain. She is a busybody! Now, what is the problem?"

A *busybody?* Because she helped the children? Sam frowned. "Quarantine."

"What?" The mayor jerked forward in his chair. "The jail is under *quarantine?*"

That had got his attention. Sam shook his head. "No, sir, it is not. But I have been pondering what would happen if one of the street children we arrest has some sickness that would bring that about. Consider what would happen if the jail, and my men and myself, were all placed under quarantine."

"Unthinkable!" The mayor stared down at his desk. His short, fat fingers drummed against the smooth mahogany surface. "That would be an impossible situation."

Sam held his silence, let the mayor's imagination picture the situation and the resulting chaos in the city. The man lifted his head, looking at him.

"That cannot be allowed to happen, Captain."

"I agree, sir. That is why I came to you."

Sam tightened his grip on his hat. "The city must open an orphanage to house the children. There is a building on Spruce Street —"

"Nonsense! An orphanage costs money!" The mayor rose and strode to a window to look outside. "There are more roads to be paved. The city water works must be completed. And the courthouse is to be expanded. And the park." He pivoted, paced back to his chair. "These are the things the finer citizens of this city expect me to provide for them, Captain. Not an orphanage for the children of emigrants who die on their way west."

Sam's face tightened. It was becoming harder and harder to hold his tongue. To swallow the mayor's callous attitude. He drew a calming breath. "They also expect police to protect them from the wild and unsavory elements of this town, Mr. Mayor. And if the jail were under quarantine, that service would be halted. The boatmen and mountain men would make the levee unsafe."

"I am aware of that, Captain Benton!"

"Then, sir, you agree the children must —"

"Do not speak to me again of an orphanage, Captain! I will not be known to the fine citizens of St. Louis as the mayor who wasted their money!"

Wasted? Sam's hand clenched. His hat brim curled beneath his fingers. "Then what is your solution, sir?" The question came out sharper than he intended.

The mayor narrowed his eyes. "Do I detect a spirit of insubordination, Captain?"

"Only concern, sir." Sam rose and clapped on his hat, using the time to get his temper under control. "I am concerned that this practice of housing these street children in the jail may one day interfere with my ability to perform my job."

"I see. Well, concern yourself no more, Captain Benton." The mayor leaned back and smiled. "There is a simple solution that will prevent such a scenario as you present from ever happening. From this time on, you and your men shall not arrest any child that shows signs of sickness."

Mary wielded the eraser, then chalked different numbers on the slate she had bought that morning. A lock of hair fell onto her forehead. She brushed the hair back, held the slate up for the children to see and smiled encouragement. "Three plus three equals . . ."

Ben scowled.

Callie looked down, her lips moving silently as she pressed the tips of her small fingers one at a time on the table. Her right hand shot into the air. "I know, Miss Mary."

Ben's scowl deepened. "That's 'cause you cheated."

"Did not!"

"Did to! Countin' on your fingers is cheatin'. Ain't it, Miss Mary?"

"*Is it not.* We do not say 'ain't,' Ben." Mary looked across the table at Ben and Callie and struggled to keep a smile from her face. It had been such a short time since she had rescued them, silent and afraid, from the streets, and already they acted like brother and sister. "And we do not argue, children. It is impolite and —"

She stopped. Listened — heard Edda going to answer the knock on the door — and returned to her work with the children. "Callie, I know it is easier to count on your fingers —" Her pulse stuttered. Was that Captain Benton's voice? She chided herself for her foolishness and focused her thoughts back on the business at hand. "But it is better if you memorize the answers to —" She glanced up as the maid came to stand in the dining-room doorway. "Yes, Edda?"

"Captain Benton to see you, miss."

Her foolish pulse stuttered again. Picked

up speed. "Thank you, Edda." She put down the slate, then ran her hands over her hair. "I will be right back, children. You think about the answer to the problem while I am gone."

She hurried to the front door, paused to collect herself and then opened the door. Samuel Benton stood on the porch, his big hands resting on the shoulders of the small boy who stood in front of him. She swept her gaze from the boy's frightened, grimy face, to his scratched and dirty hands, over his ripped overalls and shirt to his dirty feet. Another arrest. Her anger flared. She looked up at the captain.

He gave a slight nod. "Forgive my intrusion, Miss Randolph. I don't mean to disturb you. But I think this boy may be ill."

"Oh." Concern overrode her anger. Mary leaned down and peered into the boy's blue eyes. They were shimmering with unshed tears, but clear. She smiled. "I am going to feel your forehead for fever, young man. All right?" She stretched out her hand.

The boy jerked his head back and glared defiance at her. "I ain't sick!"

The captain's hands tightened on the boy's scrawny shoulders. "Miss Randolph is only trying to help you. Let her feel your forehead, son."

Son? Mary shot her gaze to Samuel Benton's face. He looked . . . different. She pulled her thoughts back to the boy, slipped her hand under the matted lock of hair hanging down over his grimy forehead. It felt normal. She saw no sign of illness. "Captain, I do not know why you believe —"

"I know my bringing the boy to you is an imposition, Miss Randolph. And I apologize for it."

She glanced up, shocked by his interruption. She had never known the captain to be rude. Obstinate and heartless, but not rude.

"I had a meeting with the mayor this morning — about the possibility of an epidemic at the jail that would result in a quarantine."

"A quarantine!" Mary shot up straight. Stared at him. "But that's . . . that's . . ." *Ingenious.* Why had she not thought to use that argument? And why was he telling her about his meeting? Did he think she cared if his jail were shut down? She would rejoice!

"Yes. A terrible possibility." He shook his head. "As you can imagine, that would be an impossible situation for the city." He stared straight down into her eyes.

Something in her stirred — went on alert. He was telling her this for a reason. "Yes. Impossible." She struggled to follow. Where was this leading?

"Because of that possibility, the mayor decreed my men and I are *not* to arrest any children that may be sick. However, I am no judge of such things. So I brought the boy to you."

"Oh. *Oh!*" Understanding flashed between them. A smile birthed in Mary's heart, rose to her lips and eyes. She could have hugged the man! She leaned down and touched the boy's forehead again. "I do not believe the boy has a fever, Captain Benton. But his eyes *are* unnaturally bright." She straightened again, looked full into Samuel Benton's eyes. "Perhaps it would be best if you leave him here with me — in case." Something flickered in his eyes. Relief?

"Perhaps that would be best, Miss Randolph. With your permission I will take him inside."

The boy leaned back, dug in his heels. "I ain't goin' in there!"

Samuel Benton turned the boy around, held his skinny upper arms and then squatted on his heels in front of him. "Listen to me, son. It is this, or jail. Do you want to be locked in a cell?"

Mary stared at the captain, at the look of concern and compassion on his face — the firm but gentle way he held the boy as he talked with him — and her heart got caught in her throat. What had happened to the cold, heartless policeman that did his job without regard to its consequences?

The captain looked up. Their gazes met. And held.

The boy stirred.

The captain cleared his throat and rose. "The boy is ready to go in now."

Mary nodded and stepped aside — fought to regain her equilibrium as the captain herded the boy into the small entrance hall.

"The answer is six, Miss Mary. Three plus three is *six!*" Ben came running, slate in his hand, Callie on his heels. Both children came to a dead halt when they saw the captain . . . backed up a step . . . then another.

Mary stepped forward and placed her hand on the new boy's thin, bony shoulder. His wiry body tensed at her touch. "Ben, would you and Callie please take this young man to the kitchen and ask Ivy to feed him? I will be along in a minute."

Ben shot a wary glance at the captain, then nodded. "Sure, Miss Mary." He motioned to the boy. "C'mon. Ivy's making cookies." He headed toward the kitchen. The boy stole a glance at the door, glanced up at the captain, then followed after Ben. Callie trailed off in their wake.

Silence fell.

Mary glanced at the captain. He was looking at her. She dropped her gaze and smoothed at her skirt feeling crowded and knowing it was foolish. How could a room get smaller? "Thank you for bringing the boy to me, Captain." She made herself look at him and noticed he had removed his hat. "I will take good care of him."

"I know that." His voice was soft, low-pitched. His gaze held hers. "I've seen — Ben, is it? — carrying grocery baskets for the customers at Simpson's store." He shook his head. "Whoever would have thought such a thing would come about. I hardly recognized him, he looks so happy and well."

"Ben is a very proud little boy and wanted to earn his keep. We let him think he is doing that." She glanced toward the kitchen, then drew her gaze back to Samuel Benton. "It was James's idea that he work for Mr. Simpson." A smile played at her lips. "I thought it was poetic justice."

He chuckled, and her stomach did that funny little flutter.

"It's good for a boy to feel he's helping out. From what I see, Ben looks pretty busy. Maybe this new boy can carry groceries at Simpson's, too."

So she was right. He had brought her the boy instead of arresting him. And he intended the boy would stay in her care. Happiness bubbled. She tamped it down. What had brought about this change in him? Was it real?

The captain slid his hat around in his hand, glancing around. "Where is Katy? Is she doing well?"

Mary nodded, as she brushed at her hair. "Katy is much better. But she still needs rest. She is upstairs napping." She glanced up. He was staring at her again. She stiffened. "Is something wrong?"

He shook his head, reached toward her hair, then drew his hand back and made an awkward little gesture. "Chalk."

Oh, no! Mary turned her hands palms up. The finger and thumb of her right hand were covered with the white powder. *That* would never happen to the elegant and beautiful Miss Stewart. But what did it matter? The captain was here on business. She brushed her hands together and forced a laugh. "We were having school."

He nodded. "I saw the slate in Ben's

hand." He took a step toward the door. "Well . . . I have to get back to my patrol. Thank you for taking the boy, Miss Randolph. Good afternoon."

She pressed back against the wall to let him pass. "Good afternoon, Captain Benton." She watched him tug his hat on and walk down the porch steps, then closed the door, squared her shoulders and headed for the kitchen ignoring the wobble in her legs. She had a young boy to take care of.

Now what did the mayor want? Why had he sent for him this time? What couldn't wait until morning? Sam climbed the steps to the Stewarts' porch, knocked on the door and stepped back as it opened.

"Captain Benton, how nice to see you again. It has been awhile." Levinia stepped out onto the porch, dimpled up at him. "I have been waiting for you. I am afraid Father had to leave suddenly."

"The mayor is gone?"

"Yes." She pouted up at him. "Are you not going to greet me, Captain?"

"Yes, of course, Miss Stewart. Forgive my bad manners." He made her a slight bow.

She smiled up at him. "You are forgiven." She drifted toward the railing, glanced up at the sky. "What a lovely evening."

Sam braced himself. He was beginning to recognize Levinia's smiles. This one meant she was after something. No doubt another compliment. He was beginning to tire of the demand. The woman's vanity was never sated. He searched around in his head and mustered something appropriate. "The beauty of the evening cannot compare to your loveliness, Miss Stewart."

"You flatter me, Captain." Another dimpled smile, followed by a pretty little pout. "But you seem . . . quiet. Father said you had a little disagreement this morning. Is it troubling you?"

Ah! So *that* was what she was after. The mayor had set Levinia to bring him to his knees. And arranged this meeting to bring that about, no doubt. Was the man inside waiting to hear if Levinia made him change his mind? "Disagreement?" Sam reached up and adjusted his hat to hide his irritation at being "handled."

"Why, yes." A wide-eyed look of innocence. "That is what Father called it. He felt you were . . . annoyed . . . with his refusal to spend city funds on an orphanage for those horrible street urchins. Naturally, he is upset by your stance." She moved back to stand close to him. "He thinks so highly of you, and feels he could help groom you to take his place as mayor when he leaves office."

Was that a threat? Sam looked down at Levinia, tried to discern what was behind her smile.

"Now truly, Captain —" This time the dimpled smile was accompanied by a slight pressure on his arm from her dainty hand. "Do you not agree the money would be better spent in completing the water works for the comfort of St. Louis's finer citizens, and building a lovely new courthouse with a beautiful park where . . ." a demure lowering of her eyes ". . . a lady and her *beau* could stroll and enjoy each other's company?" She lifted a coy gaze to him. "Or perhaps attend outdoor concerts together? And even plays?" A long sigh. "I would so enjoy such evenings."

She seemed so guileless. Could he be wrong about her intentions? Perhaps her lack of concern for the children was because she heard only her father's opinion of the situation. "I'm afraid the pleasure of such an evening would be marred for me by the knowledge of the children who would be sitting in jail weary and sore from being forced to work on those public buildings and parks."

Anger flashed across her face, quickly hidden by a flirtatious smile. But not quickly enough. He had been right. Her purpose for the tantalizing promises was to bring him into agreement with her father. Though perhaps that wasn't her only purpose. An odd stillness came over him. Sam tried to close his mind, to reject the thought, but it persisted. Perhaps Levinia was grooming him into what she considered to be a worthy husband for her. Perhaps she didn't consider him good enough as he was.

"How can you feel thus, Captain? Those lowborn urchins are accustomed to working for their food. After all, they are the spawn of the filthy poor who swarm into our city from those horrible wagon trains." Her voice coaxed, cajoled. "Why, you would be doing them a favor by arresting them. A bed in jail would no doubt be a *luxury* to them. And at least they would be under a roof that does not leak."

The words speared straight into his memories. Sam clenched his jaw so tight the muscles along it throbbed. He had spent many a night cold and shivering in a bed soaked with rain or covered with snow. But at least the bed had been *his,* and he had been free to leave it whenever he chose. He took a breath, reminded himself it could be she simply did not understand. "The children would have the same sound roof over them in an orphanage, Miss Stewart. And in an orphanage they would not be forced to perform hard labor. Nor would they be under lock and key. They would be free to go outside into the sunshine and fresh air."

She looked up, shaking her curls in a sad little way. "I believe you err in your loyalties, Captain. An orphanage would be a tremendous drain on the city's coffers. And what of the children of the better citizens who may have to give up a park to fund such an institution?" She dimpled up at him, though he noted that it looked slightly forced. "Do you not agree you would do well to save your sympathy for those who are worthy of it?"

Worthy. There it was, bald and bare. Insults, slights, sneers from his childhood flooded his head. Sam stared down at Levinia, and for the first time, he fully and truly saw beyond her surface beauty to the utter selfishness and meanness of her nature that mirrored her father's. He felt a chasm opening between them that he was not sure he could bridge.

"I do indeed, Miss Stewart." The ambiguous answer was the best he could offer, but it was clear it only angered her further. There was a sudden glitter in her eyes, a straight, hard-pressed line where her coaxing pout had thrust her lip outward.

She removed her hand from his arm and stepped to the door. "Perhaps you need to think the situation over, Captain. I am certain, when you have done so, you will reconsider your position concerning these urchins. When you have, I will be pleased to have you call on me again. Good evening." She opened the door and went inside without a backward look.

Sam strode across the porch and down the steps, Levinia's threats ringing in his ears, anger percolating. She had made herself clear. Either agree and support her father's plans or lose her father's backing for his political future, and his chance to win her hand. He had to choose. The Stewarts or the orphans.

Sam sucked in a deep breath of the cool evening air and stepped through the gate. Why had this situation with the orphans arisen, anyway? It made him see truths he did not want to see. Now he was forced to make a decision he did not want to make.

He traveled down the road toward the jail, the sound of his footsteps echoing in his head, dissolving into the night. He was so close to attaining all he had dreamed of. To achieving the purpose that had kept him alive and fighting through all the shame and degradation and poverty and hardship of his childhood — to fulfilling the vow he had made all those years ago. How could he throw away his goals he had worked toward all these years? How could he give them up now that they were within his reach?

How could he not?

The thought brought him to a dead halt. What had he become? Was he a man willing to sell his conscience to pay for his dreams? Sam clenched his hands at his sides, fought the inner stirring, the awakening of truth that made the wall he had so carefully erected around his heart crumble into useless rubble. His face tightened. He stared up at the darkening sky, the knots in his stomach as hard as the clenched fists at his sides, the pain, the longing for love and acceptance that had become the driving purpose of his heart bared. Anger ripped through him. *Why now, God? Why now?*

Mary tiptoed across the bedroom and opened the window. Katy was so much improved, surely the night air would not harm her. A breeze flowed in the window, warm, and so slight she could barely feel it on her bare arms.

She sighed and tiptoed back to bed. There

was little hope the room would cool off, but at least the air was fresh. She plumped her pillow and rested against it, then pulled up the long skirt of her nightgown to her knees and wiggled her bare toes. Did Levinia Stewart perspire? Probably not. She seemed impervious to the heat. At least, she had looked cool enough that day on the courthouse portico.

A mosquito buzzed around her ear. She swatted it away and reached for the bed curtains, then remembered Katy. She could not let the little girl be eaten alive so she could have fresh air. She slipped back out of bed and hurried over to close the window. The corner of the roof of the small shed out back caught her eye. What was in there? Could it be cleaned out and made suitable to sleep the boys? She would look tomorrow.

Ben had pleaded with Ivy to let the new boy, Will, come home with him and sleep on a pallet on the floor in his room. But if the captain brought another child . . . And she was quite certain he would. Gracious, that was clever of him to bring up a possible quarantine! And then, when that . . . that *heartless* mayor declared they simply were not to arrest any sick children, to use the declaration to keep the children out of jail. . . .

He had looked so different — so tender and caring while reasoning with Will — talking him into staying with her. Anger spurted through her. Why did he have to do that? It was easier to deny her . . . her *attraction* to him, when she believed him heartless. But when he had squatted down and taken hold of Will's arms, the look on his face . . .

Oh, how had this happened? She did not even like the man! Mary wrapped her arms about her chest, holding in the hurt. Yes. Yes, she did. That was the problem. There was no use denying it. She had been attracted to him before he had been concerned over Katy. Before he had brought Will to her. She had been attracted to him from the moment he had grinned and took hold of her shopping basket that first day. But now . . . now she *liked* him. What a fool she was, to allow herself to become attracted to a man like Samuel Benton. A man who courted a beautiful woman like Levinia Stewart.

Mary wiped a spate of tears from her cheeks, crossed the room and climbed back into bed. She had tried not to care about the captain. She had truly tried. But it seemed her heart had a mind of its own.

Chapter Fourteen

"Oh, James!" Mary clutched the letter in her hand to her chest, jumped out of her chair and whirled about the room, the long skirt of her blue gown ballooning out around her. "Father says he will not increase my allowance, but he will send an *equal* allowance for the support of the children! Oh, how wonderful! Now I shall have *double* the funds to spend on them."

James laughed and shook his head. "I do not believe that was Father's intent, Mary."

She stopped whirling and dropped back into her chair. "I know, but they have so many needs and I want for nothing. Oh, my. Only think, James! I shall be able to buy new shoes for Will — he does not say so, but I know his are too small and hurt his feet. And another dress and nightclothes each for Callie and Katy. And Ben needs a new shirt. And they *all* must have good clothes to wear to church. And then, of course, more school supplies. I shall go shopping tomorrow!"

She looked over at him. "But I do not mean to ignore your news. What do Mother and Father say in your letter? I mean beyond Mother's avowal to pray and their declarations of love. Did you tell them of your growing interest in Rebecca Green?"

"I mentioned it . . . casually."

She wrinkled her nose at him. "That will not fool Mother. She will know you are more than 'casually' interested in Miss Green."

"I know." He shot her a suspicious look. "Have you mentioned my interest in Miss Green in your letters home?"

She laughed and leaned back in her chair. "I may have *casually* mentioned that I spend quite a few evenings home alone when you call on Miss Green."

"Mary . . ."

"It is only the truth, James." She waved her hand toward the letter he held. "What does Father have to say?"

He gave her a last exasperated look and glanced down at the letter. "He speaks about business, of course. He agrees with my opinion that it would be more profitable to scrap the *Journey's End* —" He glanced over at her. "That is one of our steamboats.

An old stern-wheeler that is small and in very poor condition. Stern-wheelers are harder to maneuver, and her small size is not conducive to high profits per run. So, as I was saying, Father agrees it would be more profitable to scrap the *Journey's End* and build a new, large and luxurious side-wheeler, rather than to invest money in repairs. I estimate a new ship such as I envision will pay for herself in four runs."

"You did not tell me of that, James." She pursed her lips, nodded her head. "It sounds very sensible. You are turning into quite the businessman. You are certainly learning about steamboats. *And* you caught the man who was stealing the profits from the line — though he escaped the law. Wait until Father and Mother learn of that! They will be even more proud of you — as am I. Truly." She smiled at him. "You will have this line turned around and making huge profits in no time."

He laughed and tapped his letter. "I had better. That is what Father sent me here to do. And speaking of profits . . . I need your help, Mary."

"*My* help? Whatever for?"

"The line has been so neglected, we have to do something to improve our reputation. You have excellent taste, and I want your advice on decorating the main hall and passenger cabins of this new luxury steamboat I picture. I want this steamer to be the very best boat on the river!" He frowned and leaned forward. "I have been trying to think of ways to make it different — better than the competition, so people will swarm to book passage with us."

"That is easy." Mary laughed and smoothed the wrinkles from the letter she had crushed in her excitement. "All I have to do is remember our journey here to St. Louis. I was longing for a well-prepared meal. And a greater selection. I became very tired of the fare offered. And those narrow beds! Why, I almost rolled out of mine every time I turned over. You should put regular double beds in each cabin. *That* is luxury! And —"

She stopped fiddling with the letter and stared up at him.

He waved a hand. "Go on, Mary. Those are excellent ideas. What else have you to suggest?"

She shook her head, trying not to be too excited by the thought that had occurred to her. "James . . . you said you were going to 'scrap' the *Journey's End.* Does that mean you are going to . . . to *discard* it?"

"Yes, of course. Why?"

"And everything on it?"

His gaze sharpened at her eager tone. He nodded his head. "Yes, everything is old and, as I said, has been neglected. Why?"

"Then I can have the cots for the children!" Mary jumped to her feet again, too excited to remain seated. "I have been wondering where we can sleep any more children — I am certain there will be more now that — well . . . now. And I thought perhaps we could make use of the shed out back. But, of course, we had no beds. And —"

"And now we have them."

"Yes."

"And you have been praying for beds?"

"Yes, but it is only a coincidence, James." *Was it?* She folded her letter. "I should like to accompany you the next time you go to the levee. I would like to see the *Journey's End.* I may find other useful items aboard."

"Very well. We shall go tonight, directly after dinner. Before nightfall, but after the heat of the day has begun to wane. But now, I must return to the office. I have hired a new bookkeeper to take Goodwin's place and I am keeping a sharp eye on his accounting!"

"It is such a pleasure to have your company,

Miss Randolph."

"Please, call me Mary, Mrs. Lucas."

The elderly woman beamed a smile at her, then went back to pouring their tea. "Thank you, I shall. Cream, dear?"

"A little. No sugar." Mary accepted her cup and placed it on the table in front of her. "I am sorry it has taken me so long to pay my promised call. But I have been so busy I find it difficult to find time for social calls."

"Yes, I can imagine." Mrs. Lucas added sugar to her tea and stirred. "How many children have you taken in now, dear?"

Mary gaped. "You know of the children?"

"Oh, yes. Ben keeps me informed. But my lumbago is acting up again, so I have not been to Simpson's in a few days." Mrs. Lucas made a face that caused her wrinkles to deepen. "A nasty inconvenience, lumbago. It interferes with my gathering of the latest news." She gave a hearty chuckle.

Mary's own lips curled in a wide responsive grin. "How many of the children do you know of?"

"Hmm, let me think. There is Ben, of course. And a young girl of eight years named Callie —" her face squinched in thought "— and another little girl named Katy, who, I believe, was ill. How is she doing?" Mrs. Lucas picked up a tray and held it out to her. "Cookie, dear? There are ginger and plain sugar ones."

Mary smiled and put a ginger cookie on her plate. "Katy is doing fine. Her sore throat is healed, she is able to eat and is putting on some weight. But you are behind one child. We — my brother James and I —"

"Yes, I know about James. I believe he is courting Levinia Stewart's cousin, Rebecca Green." The faded blue eyes brightened with interest. "I also know about your cook, Ivy. And your maid, Edda. But you were saying . . . ?"

Mary choked back laughter. "Our newest child is a young boy of ten, named Will. You may, perhaps, see him the next time you go to the store. He, like Ben, wants to earn his way. And I thought perhaps he could join Ben in carrying baskets for Mr. Simpson's customers. Actually, it was Captain Benton that suggested he do so."

"Ah, Captain Benton." Mrs. Lucas's wrinkled face flooded with satisfaction. She placed a cookie onto her plate, set the tray down and smiled. "And is this Will of yours a nice, handsome, blond young lad like Ben?"

Mary jerked her thoughts back to the

children. "No. I mean, he is very nice, but there is no physical resemblance between Will and Ben. Will has dark eyes and brown, rather curly hair, a long nose and a wide mouth." She watched in fascination as Mrs. Lucas broke off a piece of ginger cookie, placed it on her spoon and lowered it into her cup of tea. A moment later the woman lifted the spoon to her mouth and ate the bite of cookie.

"The boy sounds a mite homely."

There was nothing mean about the words, only factual. But still, Mary bristled. She knew how it felt to be unfavorably compared to others. She took a sip of tea, put down her cup and broke off a piece of cookie, giving herself time to form a calm response. "I suppose some would see Will that way. But that is only his outward appearance. He has a wonderful, kind heart. And a gentle manner with the girls, who absolutely *plague* his steps. And when he laughs, you cannot help but laugh with him. Everyone in our home adores Will. I find him quite beautiful." She put the bite of cookie in her mouth to keep from saying more.

"He sounds right pleasant to be around." Mrs. Lucas soaked another bite of cookie in her tea. "Do you suppose he would be willing to do some chores for me? Nothing too hard, mind you. Only fetching in stove wood and such like. I'd pay him well."

There was a wistful quality in Isobel Lucas's voice. Mary peered more closely at her smiling eyes. There was a shadow of loneliness in them. Her heart swelled. "I am sure Will would be pleased to come and help you. Would it suit if I send him around tomorrow morning? We have school in the late afternoon — before supper."

"Morning will be fine." The old woman's eyes sparkled across the table at her. "And if there is anything I can do to help you with these children you take in, you let me know."

Mary peered at her, remembering her influence with Mr. Simpson. "Can you get this ridiculous law about arresting orphans under the age of twelve revoked?"

Mrs. Lucas shook her head, fluttering the gray wisps of hair escaping from the knot on her head. "I'm afraid not. Nobody can change Simon Stewart's mind when he gets ahold of an idea. But what won't go in a front door can be carried in the back. An' I know most everybody in this town — an' all their secrets, too. So if you have a problem . . . you come see me. I'll be pleased to help. It'll give me somethin' to do."

"It is kind of you to offer, Mrs. Lucas." Mary finished her cup of tea. "I am afraid I must be leaving. I am going with James this evening to see a steamboat that is being scrapped. I hope to salvage a few of the beds." She sighed and ran her hands over her hair. "We are running out of space to sleep the children, and I am considering turning the shed in our backyard into a dormitory of sorts for any more boys that come our way. It is very small, but it shall have to do as the mayor will not consider establishing a city-funded orphanage."

"You asked Simon Stewart to build an orphanage?" The elderly woman chuckled. "I can imagine his answer." She shook her head. "Simon's nose is so high in the air he can't even see the ground. He's plumb lost his way. Still . . . there's always that back door." She brightened again. "If you need some help with supplying the needs of those orphans . . . you know . . . blankets, clothes, shoes an' such, you let me know."

The sun was still shining, the golden rays bathing the *Journey's End.* But nothing on the steamboat reflected the bright light.

Mary lifted the front of her long skirt and walked up the gangway onto the scarred deck. The white paint of the railing was chipped and peeling, and the paint on the sides of the boat was little better. Everywhere she looked there was dirt or soot. The cabin windows were dulled with dust.

"This way, Mary."

She turned and followed James to the stairs that led to the boiler deck. He stood back and let her precede him. The steps were worn, but sound, the railing firm. She stepped off the stairs into the main cabin and looked around. There were four round, wood tables, each with six chairs, clustered about a heating stove with a round chimney pipe that rose straight through the ceiling. At the far end was a similar heating stove in the middle of a grouping of furniture — a couch and two chairs with dirty, torn fabric — sitting on a threadbare carpet.

"Goodness, James. I thought the *Fair Weather* was in poor condition. Has this boat been running in this state?"

"Until a few weeks ago, yes." He looked around and shook his head. "I told you that we needed a truly luxurious steamboat to repair our reputation."

"My, yes!" She turned and opened the door to one of the passenger staterooms that lined both side walls. The room was small, narrow and deep, with a single bed covered with a faded woven coverlet, a stand beneath the window in the outside wall and a horizontal board, with double hooks every few inches along its length, spanning the wall opposite the bed. Everything looked dusty and dingy. She could not decide if the paint on the walls was faded and dirty, or if it was the quality of light coming through the thick dust on the window. But that did not matter. It was the bed she wanted.

She lifted the hem of her gown clear of the door sill and turned. "James, how will — Oh!" She pressed her hand to her chest and stared at the figure at the top of the stairs.

James pivoted — smiled. "Good evening, Captain."

Samuel Benton nodded, then looked her way. "I did not mean to startle you. I thought I saw movement through the windows and came to investigate." He strode toward them.

Mary glanced down at her gown, brushed at a spot of dust clinging to it. Was there any on her bonnet? She glanced back over her shoulder, but it was impossible to see her reflection in the filthy window.

"As long as I am here, may I have a word with you, Mr. Randolph? About that business you told me of this morning."

Mary shot a glance at the captain, then looked at James.

"You may speak freely in front of Mary,

Captain. I discuss these things with her. She knows the M and M line lost three steamboats to questionable 'accidents' shortly before the line was purchased and I took over as manager."

"Very well." The captain glanced at her. "The buyer kept his name a secret, and for a while I suspected him of arranging the 'accidents,' but —"

Mary jolted. "You thought m— the new owner arranged to have the steamboats destroyed?" She caught the captain's quizzical look at her and hastened to cover her shocked slip of the tongue. "Gracious! Why would anyone do such a thing?"

"There are a lot of reasons. But none of them matter for your brother proved me wrong." The captain smiled. "He would make a good policeman."

She looked at James. "What did you do?"

He shrugged. "When the captain told me his suspicions about the 'accidents' to the steamers, I searched back through the company books and found there was insurance purchased by the line for the cargos that were lost, as well as insurance on the steamers, but there was no record of any payments received. I showed the captain what I found this morning."

"And I went to talk with the manager of

the insurance company."

"And . . ."

James's word hung in the air. She looked at the captain.

"And they paid the claims to Mr. Thomas, the former manager. The new owner and . . . anyone else new to the company . . . is cleared of any complicity in the staged accidents. If you press charges, I'll fill out warrants for his arrest and send them around to the towns downriver."

Anyone else new to the company? Mary stiffened. Did he mean James? *How dare he!* She drew breath. James touched her shoulder. She glanced at his face and held her tongue.

"I will come to your office and do that tomorrow, Captain. I am glad that mystery is solved and I can now expend all my efforts in improving the line." James smiled. "And it is good to know you are quick to check into possible trouble — though I am surprised you bother with a steamboat that is about to be scrapped."

Mary stared at James. How like their father he was, so calm and controlled. Pride coursed through her.

"I've chased many a drunken mountain man or idle laborer — even Indians — from abandoned boats, Mr. Randolph. Fire is always a threat, and they treat them like a boardinghouse. Figure they can sleep in one of the cabins and no harm done. But —"

"A *boardinghouse!*" Mary stared at the captain, looked at James and laughed. "A *boardinghouse.* Of course!" She whirled around, marched to the center of the room and turned in a slow circle, counting.

"What are you doing, Mary?"

"There are twenty-four staterooms, James."

"Yes . . ."

She hurried back to his side. "Oh, James, do you not see? It is perfect!" She looked up at Samuel Benton, saw understanding flash in his eyes. And doubt. She lifted her chin. "How many children have you in jail, now, Captain?"

"Children in — Mary! Have you gone *mad?*" It was a roar of disbelief.

She reached out and gave James's arm a soothing pat. "How many, Captain?" He grinned — that slow, lopsided grin that did queer things to her stomach.

"Six boys and two girls, Miss Randolph."

Sam strolled down the street letting his presence keep things on the levee under control. A smile tugged at his lips, which broke into a full-blown grin. He couldn't help it. He had been grinning all night. Every time he thought of Mary Randolph standing in the middle of the *Journey's End* main cabin, jabbing the air with her finger and counting staterooms.

He detoured toward the river to check on the activity at the various warehouses. He couldn't help thinking about her, either. That woman could out stubborn a mule! There was no give in her. At least, not where the orphans were concerned. The mayor had refused her request that the city fund an orphanage, now here she was, figuring on turning that scrapped boat into one. But how would she manage it? Even a scrapped boat was worth something. Of course, with her brother as manager of the line . . .

How many children have you in jail?

Sam shook his head, watched some laborers loading up their ship with wood. He had been stunned by her question. Still was. Even more by the determined look in her eyes when she had lifted that little square chin of hers. No, she was not giving up. She was going to get those children out of jail and make a home for them on top of it. Quite a difference between Levinia Stewart and Mary Randolph. One was determined to keep the orphans in jail, and the other was determined to get them out.

"One o'clock, the weather is fair, and all is well."

The words sounded clear as he scaled the incline back to the street. Time to go home. Sam frowned. All was not well in his life. There was no open friction with the mayor, but it was obvious he was no longer in favor. And Levinia had turned her back and walked away when he had seen her in front of the dressmakers this afternoon.

His frown deepened. He lifted his hand and massaged the taut muscles in his neck and shoulders. The message sent by Levinia's behavior was clear. Either change his stance on the orphans and support her father, or any hope of a future between them would be gone. It did not disturb him as much now. He was growing to accept the demise of his goal for a future in politics with Levinia at his side. In truth, he was beginning to look on it as a fortunate escape. Levinia was not the person he had thought her to be. The woman had no heart to her. And he would not accept her terms. Not even to have his dreams. A man didn't amount to anything if he didn't have his self-respect.

He yawned, then turned onto Walnut Street. *Don't you worry, Ma. You sit tight, Danny. I will keep my promise. I'll be some-*

body. You have my word on it. Sam set his jaw. He would gain his goal without the Stewarts' help. He would do it the same way he had achieved all he had so far accomplished — by honest effort and hard work. And all was not lost. He still had his plans for his showcase house.

He tried to summon the vision, but for some reason it would not appear. All he saw was the knoll, the grassy fields around it and the river. He must be too tired. It had been a long night. Three drunks jailed. He hated putting them in the cell beside the boys, but he had no choice. It was a good thing Miss Randolph didn't know about that. A smile curved his lips. Mary Randolph. She sure had a cute little chin.

CHAPTER FIFTEEN

"Mary, I understand your desire to help these children. *I* want to help them! But this . . . this *plan* of yours is . . . is . . ."

"I believe *ludicrous,* or perhaps *preposterous,* is the word you are searching for, James."

He scowled down at her. "They are both apt! And I should add *costly!*" He snatched his hat from the hat tree and slapped it on his head. "And I am not speaking only of money. You are investing too much of your heart into these children."

Mary nodded. "Perhaps. But someone has to care about them, James. And I have no husband or children of my own to spend my love and care on."

James's face softened. He stepped toward her. Mary frowned and turned away. She had not meant to let that bit of bitterness be bared.

His hands gripped her upper arms. "Forgive me, Mary. You hide your feelings so well, I forget about your pain over Winston's betrayal. But, please, do not be discouraged. The Lord will send you a man who will love and cherish you as you deserve. One whom you will love with your whole heart. And you will have children of your own. As many as you wish."

Mary sighed. If God wanted her to have a husband who would love and cherish her, He would have made her beautiful and gentle-natured and appealing. But dear James would never admit that. He was such a wonderful, caring brother. And he meant well. It was not his fault the words he spoke to encourage her only deepened her sadness. His vision of her future would not come true. She had accepted that. But she would have to do a better job of guarding her tongue, to protect her brother's tender heart. And she would have to pretend she believed what he said was possible. She forced a bright smile and turned to look up at him. "You may be right, James. But, meanwhile, there are hungry, hurting children who need care."

"I know. But you give your heart so freely, and I do not want to see you hurt or disappointed, Mary."

He did not add the word *again,* but she

heard it in his voice. She swallowed back tears and kept the smile pasted on her face.

"Please, do not become too excited about this plan to turn the steamboat into an orphanage. There are so many obstacles." He frowned and shook his head. "The boat has to be renovated — which is expensive and time-consuming. And even should you, by some miracle, accomplish that, you have no land to place it on. And then there is the cost of maintenance. And of feeding, clothing and —"

She touched his lips with her fingertips, unable to listen to more without breaking down. "I know, James. Truly. I know. But, for some reason, I feel . . . compelled . . . to save these children. I know what it feels like to . . . to receive scorn." She blinked away tears. "I cannot give less than my best for them, James. And if that means my heart gets bruised — well —" she gave a small shrug "— it has been bruised before." She forced another smile and gave him a little push toward the door. "Be off to work, now. I have a full morning with lists to make and shopping to do."

"All right, Mary. But we will talk more tonight about this plan of yours for salvaging the *Journey's End* to use as an orphanage."

She stood in the door until he reached the gate, then gave a final wave, closed the door and leaned back against it. If only James's wishes for her would come true. But they would not. Not for someone as plain and *angular* as she. Those dreams were for the Sarahs and Veronicas and Miss Stewarts of the world.

Poor little Miss Mary. She'll have a hard time findin' herself a husband, bein' plain like she is.

Mary lifted her chin and shoved the memory of her nanny's voice back into the dark recesses of her mind where she had carried it since she was five years old. She pushed away from the door and squared her shoulders. That was enough of feeling pity for herself. She may never have a husband who loved her, but she had children to care for.

"Don't forget now — slow down when you are in town. You don't want to run someone over and hurt them." Sam fastened a stern gaze on the boys sitting astride their restless mounts. "You save your racing for out on the plains — hear?"

"Yes, sir, Captain Benton."

"All right. If I have to speak to you again, I'll get your fathers to sit in on our conversation. Now, be on your way. And give your parents my best."

"Yes, sir."

The boys rode off at a fast walk. Sam grinned and shook his head. That would probably last until they turned the corner. He started back up the street, then halted. Levinia Stewart was coming out of Sanderson's Hats and Gloves. She was garbed in an expensive gown that flattered her petite form, and a hat that revealed her blond curls and the beauty of her face. Her pink cheeks were dimpled, her mouth curved into a smile as she chatted with her friend. He watched her, waited for the disappointment, the sense of loss to hit him. But there was nothing. Not one little stirring. No desire to go and speak to her. Only an irritation that he had succumbed to the beauty she used as a weapon to win her way.

He moved forward again, saw when she spotted him. Watched the beguiling smile she put on, as other people would don their clothes. Using it as an instrument to win him over. He touched his hat brim in polite greeting as he approached. "Good morning, Miss Stewart . . . Miss Weller."

Levinia started to turn her back. He did not pause or slow his pace. Shock swept over both women's faces. Levinia's smile died. A glitter appeared in her blue eyes, which sharpened her gaze as he continued his purposeful stride. The lovely features contorted into an expression of fury at his lack of submission. Levinia Stewart did not like to lose. The woman was spoiled, pampered and willful. How had he ever thought her beautiful?

Excited chatter drew his attention. Sam glanced ahead. A young boy and two smaller girls, all carrying paper-wrapped packages tied with string, stood around the doorway of Nicholson's Shoes and Boots. He took in their clean, smiling faces and shining hair and smiled. All that remained of the gaunt, filthy, fearful children Mary Randolph had taken under her care were the neat patches applied to the boy's clean dungarees, which sported new suspenders. The girls both wore new dresses, one in yellow and brown checks, the other in blue. And the boy had on a pair of shiny, new work boots.

His heart jolted. How he had yearned for a pair of boots when he was a barefoot kid.

"Children, do not block the door, it is impolite." Mary Randolph stepped out of the store and moved to the side. The children crowded around her. "Do you all have your packages?" Wind gusted off the river, flipped her bonnet backward. She grabbed for it, dropping one of the packages she carried. She leaned down to pick it up, and banged heads with the boy who had done the same. Laughter bubbled out of her, echoed by the children's giggles.

Sam rushed forward and scooped up the package. "You seem to have your hands full, Miss Randolph." Brown eyes with honey-colored specks aglow with laughter looked up at him. The laughing lips whispered a soft "Oh," and a deep rose color crept along delicate high cheekbones. He stared. The rose color grew deeper. Long, thick, black lashes swept down over the brown eyes, and a narrow hand raised to pull the bonnet forward.

"Thank you, Captain Benton."

Her voice was softer, huskier than he remembered. He filled his suddenly air-starved lungs, became aware of the children's silence and looked down. They had all taken a step back — moved a bit closer to her. Shame hit him. These children thought he was some sort of ogre. So did Mary Randolph.

He smiled and dipped his head at the girls. "You young ladies are looking pretty today." That won him a timid smile from each of them. He glanced at the smaller of the two. "It is good to see you well and able to enjoy such an outing, Katy."

He shifted his gaze to the boy and held out the paper-wrapped parcel to him. "You look a good strong boy, and a gentleman always carries a lady's packages."

The boy's eyes flashed with pride at the compliment. He took the package, tucked it under his arm, then reached out for the two smaller ones Mary Randolph still held.

She inhaled to speak, glancing up at him. He gave a very small shake of his head. She exhaled and handed the boy her packages.

Sam smiled down at him. "Good man."

The boy grinned.

He heard a softly indrawn breath, looked back at Mary Randolph and read the approval in her eyes. And something more. But before he could identify it, she looked away.

"Thank you again, Captain. It was kind of you to help us. Now, we must be on our way. It is almost time for dinner." She smiled at the children. "Please lead the way, Will."

He watched them walk away, Will and the older girl in front, Miss Randolph and Katy behind. A hunger grew in his heart, spread to every part of him. They looked like a family. And he didn't even know how to be a part of a family. But he wanted one.

The thought jolted him.

He stepped to the side, out of the flow of shoppers and stared after Mary Randolph and the children. He hadn't thought much about it before. He'd been too busy planning his road to financial and social success, but he wanted a family. A whole houseful of healthy, noisy kids. Maybe he'd even have one that looked like Danny.

The yearning deepened, followed by hard, swift relief — the kind he felt when he had evaded a mountain man's knife or a laborer's hard fists. He shot a quick glance up the street the other direction. Levinia Stewart was entering Miss Mayfield's Emporium. The relief hit him again. If she had not given him that ultimatum over the orphans . . . If he had not been forced to face his own heart . . .

Sam returned his gaze to Mary Randolph and the children. She was holding Katy's hand and laughing. He could not fit Levinia Stewart into that picture. He could not imagine her as a mother, holding a baby in her arms, wiping away a toddler's tears. Levinia would have a nanny to care for her children. He frowned and shook his head, remembering the night of his parting from her. He had blamed God for it. If that was true, he owed God his gratitude, not his anger.

Sam snorted and turned to cross the street. That was a new thought. One foreign to everything he had believed all these years. But he could not shake his feeling of relief. And if God had saved him from making a mistake in marrying Levinia, perhaps — No. That was going a stretch too far. He'd give it some thought later.

Right now he needed to visit the *Golden Fleece.* He had heard two of the furnace stokers were there who had been part of the crews of two of the M and M steamboats that sank due to explosions. They might know something about Duffy or Thomas and those "accidents." And if he could get them to tell him what they knew —

"Captain!"

Sam spun back, saw Will running empty-handed toward him and jerked his gaze down the street. Mary Randolph was standing, packages in hand, girls beside her, looking his way. *What* — He looked down as Will skidded to a stop in front of him. "What is it, Will? What's wrong?"

"Ain't nothin' wrong, Captain. Miss Mary sent me back to ask if you ain't patrolin', would ya like to come . . . er . . . join 'em . . . fer supper tonight? She said t'tell ya they eat shortly after Mr. James comes home — 'bout seven o'clock. And she apologizes fer the short notice."

It took him a moment. He looked back at Mary Randolph, saw her smile and give a single nod. What had prompted her invitation? He looked back down at Will and nodded. "Please tell Miss Randolph I will be pleased to accept her gracious invitation. And don't forget to carry those packages for her."

"Come in, Mary, come in!" Mrs. Lucas beamed a smile at her. "I did not expect to see you again so soon. Have you come for tea?"

"No, I truly do not have time for tea, Mrs. Lucas. I have a very busy afternoon ahead, and a guest coming for supper." Mary stepped inside and closed the door. "But you asked me to tell you about the children, and I am so excited I wanted to share my news with you."

The elderly woman's eyes lit with interest. "Well, come in and sit down."

Mary followed her into a lovely parlor. A large floor clock ticked off the minutes, making her even more aware of the pressing time. Mrs. Lucas took a seat in a chair covered with tapestry and indicated the one facing her. "Now tell me your news. Have you another child?"

Mary took her seat and shook her head. "No. But I believe I have discovered the answer to providing a home for them all." She removed her bonnet and smoothed her hands over her hair. "You know my brother, James, is the manager of the Mississippi and Missouri steamer line?"

"Yes. And I hear he discovered Eli Goodwin had been cheating the company and set the law on him. Everyone speaks most highly of your brother. But what has that to do with an orphanage for the children?"

"James has recommended that one of the older steamboats be scrapped —"

"The *Journey's End.*"

Mary laughed. "Yes. Truly, Mrs. Lucas, I am astounded by how much you know about what goes on in St. Louis!" She leaned forward. "Do you already know what I am about to tell you?"

The elderly woman's face crinkled with laughter. "I promise you, I do not. But if you give me a day or two, I will."

Mary grinned. "Very well. Here is my news. I am going to renovate the *Journey's End* and turn it into a home for the children!"

Mrs. Lucas's eyes went wide, her mouth

opened — closed — then turned up into a wide grin. "Why, what a . . . a . . . simply perfect idea! You are truly an astonishing young woman."

"Oh, it was not my idea — well, it was — but only after Captain Benton mentioned that mountain men and idle laborers often use abandoned steamboats as boarding-houses. When he said that, it suddenly seemed the perfect answer for the children's needs."

"Captain Benton?" The faded blue eyes sharpened.

"Yes. He happened by as James and I were looking over the steamer. He thought we were mountain men or something."

"I see." The older woman's lips twitched.

Mary frowned. "What is it?"

Mrs. Lucas waved a hand through the air and shook her head. "Nothing at all, dear. When you mentioned the captain, it made me remember he and Levinia have hit a rocky patch is all."

Her heart lurched. "A rocky patch?"

Mrs. Lucas nodded. "Yes. But you were telling me about your idea."

"What? Oh. Yes, of course." She rose and began to walk about the room. Mrs. Lucas was studying her face far too closely. "There are twenty-four staterooms on the steamer

— each quite small, but more than adequate for a child. And the beds are there, though they will need painting and new bedding. And the main cabin will do wonderfully well for a school *and* a play area." She made her way back to her chair. "Of course, everything is dreadfully dusty and dingy. The entire boat needs a good cleaning and painting. And the curtains must be replaced. And —"

"And have you funds to do all of this?"

Mary sighed and resumed her seat. "Not yet." She squared her shoulders. "But I will *find* a way. I simply have to get those children out of jail."

"I'm sure you will, dear." Mrs. Lucas leaned forward and patted her hand. "And I will think about what I can do to help."

Mary rose, then leaned down to give the elderly woman a hug. "Thank you, Mrs. Lucas. Now, I must be going." She picked up her bonnet, put it on and began to tie the ribbons. "If I am too busy to come myself, I will send news of my progress by Ben."

"You do that, dear. And may the Lord bless you. This is truly a wonderful, charitable thing you are doing, and —"

Mary stayed her hands, looked down at Mrs. Lucas. "And what?"

"Oh, nothing, dear. Nothing." She started to rise.

"Please, Mrs. Lucas. Do not trouble yourself. I can see myself out."

"All right, dear." The woman relaxed back in her chair. "Come again, Mary. I shall look forward to your next visit."

Mary walked to the door and glanced back. Mrs. Lucas was sitting in the chair with a wide smile on her face, looking very pleased.

Chapter Sixteen

He was coming to supper. Oh, why had she extended that invitation? When would she learn not to be so *impulsive?* Mary pulled her ecru pongee from the cupboard, then put it back again. The captain was not coming to call on her, and that was her best gown. She certainly did not want to give him the impression that she had meant more by her invitation than — Than what?

Mary shut the door on the cupboard *and* her thoughts and walked away. She would not treat this supper differently than any other. Her green gown was good enough. She marched to the dressing room, peered into the mirror, smoothing the lace collar and straightening the cameo pin at its juncture.

Against her will her gaze lifted to her face. She could not wear a hat or bonnet in the house. He would see her as she was, in all her plainness. Of course, he had seen her that way before, on the day he had escorted her to the courthouse, and again the day he had brought Will to her.

The argument did not help. None of it helped. Not the sensible reasoning, or the foolish reassurances. She had asked the captain to supper because of the children. Because he had treated them so kindly and made them smile. Because he had made Will feel so proud and fine. She had wanted to thank him in a way that would let him know she recognized his change of heart toward the orphans. But now *her* heart — her foolish, *foolish* heart — wanted to make something of this supper that it was not.

Mary lifted her chin and tucked away the locks of hair that had, once again, fallen from her knot. Plain brown hair. And plain brown eyes. And those horrible high cheekbones!

She sighed and turned from the mirror. She hated mirrors. Had hated them since she was five years old. Every time she looked in one she heard again Nanny Marlow's words and realized she was one of the unlovely of this world. Not ugly, but not beautiful like Sarah, or Veronica, or — *Veronica, my beloved, what man would not choose your petite, blond beauty and sweet nature over Mary's dark, angular plainness and bold, forthright ways?*

Mary clenched her hands. What was she thinking? Why did she allow her heart to even pretend there might be something more to this supper than appeared? Because she *wished* it to be so? Winston's words and actions proved the folly of such a desire. And her appearance mattered not a fig's worth! The captain was courting the beautiful Miss Stewart — even if they had hit a . . . a rocky patch!

The thought crushed the last of her resistance. Tears welled into her eyes. Mary whirled and rushed out of the dressing room, away from the mirror that stole all her hopes and dreams.

Sam stopped short of the gate, straightened the cravat at his throat, tugged his vest in place and shrugged his shoulders to loosen the constricting feel of his coat. He had worn his good clothes for the children's sake. They would be more comfortable with him out of his uniform. His lips twitched. "You keep telling yourself that long enough, you might come to believe it, Sam."

He frowned and shrugged. He might as well admit it. He wanted Mary Randolph's approval. He held the woman in high esteem. And he had been the object of her challenging looks and words long enough. He wanted her to know he had risen to her challenges. And —

Sam stiffened, stared at the cottage as if he could see through the walls. Mary Randolph was the one who made him examine his own heart concerning the children. It was *her* challenges that made him realize he could not comply with the mayor's plans. And today, it was the sight of her with the children that made him realize how much he wanted a family of his own. How much he wanted —

The truth slammed into him. He stood there, astounded, *dumbfounded* and not a little disgusted by his own stupidity. Why had he wasted time courting Levinia? He was in love with Mary Randolph.

A steamboat whistled. A dog barked. Sam shook his head, pulled himself together and pushed open the gate. Mary Randolph considered him a cruel, heartless ogre. How would he ever prove himself worthy of her love? The cannonball on the end of the chain rose, then fell again, closing the gate when he stepped through. He strode up the brick path, climbed the porch steps and paused with his fisted hand ready to knock on the door.

Peals of laughter sounded from inside the

house, Mary's low, musical laugh among them. It was the most wonderful, the most inviting, the most terrifying sound he had ever heard. He was twenty-seven years old and had never in his life, since he was seven years old, been around a family. And never a happy one. And that was what was inside that house. A family. Perhaps not of blood, but a family, nonetheless. And Mary was its heart.

He took a deep breath, reaching to knock. The door burst open and a laughing boy crashed into him, followed by two giggling girls. "Ugh!" Sam staggered back a couple steps, instinctively closed his arms about the children to keep them from falling and grinned at Will, who skidded to a halt, went up on his toes and wildly circled his arms like a windmill to keep from pitching forward onto the others. He opened his arms. "You want in, too? I am strong enough to hold all four of you."

There was a chorus of giggles and laughter. The children righted themselves. Katy reached out and snatched the bonnet Ben clutched in his hand. "Told you I could catch you!"

"You didn't catch me, *he* did!" Sam found himself the target of Ben's pointing finger.

"Well, I *would* have!" Katy yanked on the

bonnet so hard it came down over her face, which set off another gale of laughter.

Sam chuckled, then raised his face to the tall thin woman who appeared in the open door. "I'm sorry, sir. They didn't know you were here." The woman wiped the smile from her face. "Children, apologize to Captain Benton and we'll be off for home."

There was a flurry of apologies. Sam acknowledged them with a smile as the children filed off the porch. At least he thought he did. He couldn't be sure. His attention was riveted on Mary, who now stood at the open door, laughter lighting her face and warming her eyes.

"I apologize for the overly exuberant welcome, Captain. Please come in." She stepped back.

Sam removed his hat and crossed the threshold, his palms moist, his mouth suddenly dry as dust. If God *was* involved in all that had thus far happened, may He grant that the invitation would be into Mary's heart.

"Oh, what a lovely cool breeze." Mary stepped through the door the captain held open for her onto the porch, and fought back a rising disappointment. Supper was over. The captain would make his excuses and leave now. And James —

Was standing before her putting his hat on. "If you will excuse me, Mary . . . Captain Benton. I have an engagement."

"With Rebecca Green?"

James grinned at her teasing. "No other. Well, I am off. Enjoy your evening."

Heat rushed into her cheeks. She could have shaken him. He made it sound as if the captain were courting her!

James's grin widened. He gave her a wink, tipped his hat to a jaunty angle and then trotted down the steps to the road. His merry whistle floated back to them as he hurried away.

Mary stared after him, vowing to make him pay for that bit of embarrassment. She sucked in a breath, lifted her hands and smoothed back her hair. She might as well give the captain his opening to leave, then go and help Edda with the dishes. "Would you care to relax here on the porch a moment, Captain Benton?"

"That would be pleasant. After you, Miss Randolph." He bowed her toward the porch furniture.

Was he not leaving? Mary masked her surprise, stepped over to the new porch swing James had hung and seated herself. She watched from under her lowered lashes as the captain propped his shoulder against one of the roof support posts and crossed one ankle over the other. He certainly did not look as if he were in any hurry to leave. Her heart thudded. She plucked an imaginary piece of lint from her skirt to gain time to compose herself.

"I know you have not had much time, Miss Randolph, but have you thought over your original intent? Do you still plan to use the *Journey's End* for the orphans?"

"I do indeed, Captain. Though I have not as yet determined how I shall accomplish my goal." Is that why he stayed? Was he trying to discover her plans for some reason? Perhaps for the mayor? Her stomach twisted with disappointment. Were his acts of kindness toward the children for a nefarious purpose? *Oh, God, if You care for these children, please, please, let it not be so.* She pushed her toes against the floor and set the swing in motion.

"I have been giving the matter some thought."

"Oh?" Her disappointment swelled. She braced herself to argue her position.

"Yes. The steamer can stay in the dock while it is being renovated, but, of course, it cannot remain there permanently." His gaze fastened on hers. "Have you any notion where you will locate the boat when the work is finished?"

"No." Her mind raced. Why was he asking? "I know only the land shall have to front on the water. I should imagine it would be very difficult to move the boat inland any distance."

He nodded. "It can be done. But it would be costly. As will any land on the river. Those parcels are highly sought after by men of business. Millers and such. And you won't want the children close to the levee area." He stared off into the distance, the hat in his hand tapping against his thigh. "There is talk of expanding the levee both up and down river."

Her heart sank. If she could not use the steamboat, what would she do? She looked down at her lap. Smoothed a wrinkle in her skirt. So much for prayers.

"Still, there are a few possibilities . . ."

She lifted her head and stared up at him, trying not to show her confusion at the statement. "Possibilities?" Was this some sort of snare she could not perceive? Perhaps she should make him give her facts. "If you would be so kind as to tell me the location of those possibilities, I shall look into them immediately." She lifted her chin. "And perhaps you could draw me a *map* so I might find my way? Oh! And — forgive my ignorance, but I have never been involved in these sort of transactions before. Where does one go to find the cost of these land parcels?"

He grinned.

She stiffened. "May I ask what it is you find amusing, Captain? Is it my questions, or my behavior? I realize it is unseemly for a woman to be so bold in her requests, but —"

"I do not find it unseemly, Miss Randolph. I find it delightful. That is the reason for my smile." He sobered and his gaze fastened on hers. "I applaud your enthusiasm in your quest to help these orphaned children. And I hope you will accept any help I am able to offer you."

Her mind stalled on the word *delightful.* It took her a moment to accept the term as a politeness. She was not accustomed to the captain in a social capacity. He was quite good at turning a polite compliment, for whatever his purpose. She composed herself and looked at him. The time had come to stop this charade. "You wish to help?"

"I do."

He sounded so earnest. "Truly?"

He nodded.

Mary stared, then looked down at her

hands. She wanted so much to believe him but she dare not trust her judgment.

"I know we have crossed swords over the children in the past, Miss Randolph. But I am the captain of the police and it is my job to uphold the law. I hope, however, that I have demonstrated to you, by calling upon you for help when Katy took ill, and by bringing Will to you, that I am not heartless or uncaring of these orphans' needs. And that I do not agree with the mayor's plan to use them as free labor on city projects." His voice was deep, quiet, persuasive. "And, while I still must do my job, I will continue to do my best for all of these children, and to prove myself honorable to you. I only ask you grant me the opportunity to do so."

Mary looked up at him, her head cautioning her to be careful, her heart telling her to trust him. She wanted to. With her whole being she longed to trust him. But Winston had seemed honest and sincere, also. He had looked straight into her eyes and made his declarations — and every word he had said to her had been a lie. And this time, it was not only her heart that could be hurt. It was the children, as well. She took a deep breath. *Almighty God, please, if I err in my judgment, do not let the children suffer for it.* "I will be glad of your help for the children,

Captain."

He nodded. "Thank you for your trust, Miss Randolph." He shifted his position as he sat on the railing. "Have you made plans beyond housing the orphans on the steamboat?"

"What sort of plans?" She flushed at her skeptical tone, but he seemed not to notice it.

"Well, for instance, who will be with them to watch over them? Do you plan to hire someone to oversee the orphanage? And where will they live on the boat?"

Mary rose, walked to the railing and stared out at the twilight sky. "I have not had time to consider all you ask, Captain. But I believe I can answer your queries." She gave him a sidelong glance as he rose and stood beside her. "James has grown fond of Miss Green, and I believe she feels the same fondness for him. Therefore, as James is quite persuasive and disinclined to tarry once he makes a decision — *and* as this cottage is very small — I am quite certain I shall, at some time in the not-too-distant future, need to find another place of residence. In a way, I shall be orphaned, too." She gave a small laugh and smoothed her hands over her hair. "Therefore *I* shall be with the children, and, of course, live in one of the staterooms." *How would she ever manage?*

"Housing for the children's caretaker is one of the things I have been pondering, Miss Randolph. And I believe you may find my suggestion acceptable, even favorable. But the hour is late. May I call again? To go over my thoughts about the renovation of the steamboat with you?"

Mary looked down at her hands gripping the railing and tamped down the tingle of excitement caused by the thought of spending more time in his company. He was not asking permission to make a social call. It was for the orphans. She looked up at him and smiled. "I shall look forward to hearing your suggestions, Captain."

"And I to the pleasure of your company, Miss Randolph. Perhaps I could escort you to the *Journey's End* Sunday afternoon, around two o'clock? It may be easier to explain my ideas there."

"Very sensible, Captain."

He made a slight bow. "Until Sunday, Miss Randolph."

She smiled and nodded, then made herself turn and go into the house. She did not want him to look back and find her watching him walk away. All the same, when she reached the door, she could not resist one quick look over her shoulder.

He was standing at the gate watching her.

Her cheeks flamed. But he could not see from that distance. She dipped her head in a polite farewell, thrust open the door and hurried inside.

Sam strode up Market Street, cut across Fourth Street and headed along Walnut toward the boardinghouse, his long strides eating up the distance. What did that little glance Mary Randolph had stolen mean? Dare he hope it meant the same as the look he had stolen at her? How could it be? She was so cool, and defensive and . . . and prickly around him.

And why wouldn't she be? They had clashed so often over the children, how could he even expect her to trust him or hold him in any sort of respectful regard? He was a fool! Why had he taken so long to see the truth?

Sam pivoted, crossed back over to Market and headed for the stables behind the jail. Forget the suit! Forget the dark! The moon was out. The road out of town hard-packed and free of holes. And he needed a ride. An all-out, no-holding-back, ground-eating, hoof-pounding ride!

Chapter Seventeen

Sam stared up at his deputy. "So Goodwin is dead?"

Jenkins nodded. "The New Orleans police got a record of it. He was cut up and robbed outside of a gamblin' hall. They found his body the day before I got to New Orleans with the warrant for his arrest."

"And Thomas got away."

Jenkins nodded. "The police found the boardinghouse he was living in, but he was gone when they got there. He left the same night Goodwin was killed, on a ship for London."

"Probably with Goodwin's money on him. All right, Jenkins. There's nothing more we can do now. But we'll be waiting when he comes back. Go home and get some sleep."

"Yes, sir."

A murmur, low and restrained, ebbed and flowed from pew to pew. Glances, surreptitious and angry, rode its crest, broke over Mary, drowned the pleasure of bringing the children to church for the first time. It had started from the pew occupied by the mayor, his wife and his daughter, swelled to include the front section on the left side of the aisle and rippled through the rest of the congregation.

Mary stared at the vacant pew in front of them, could feel the emptiness of the one behind. She glanced at James, read the message of support in his eyes and sat straighter. She lifted her chin higher and smiled at the children lined up in the pew, though anger tingled from her head to her toes. How could people be so cruel? Had the children noticed? Did they realize the looks and the mutterings were about them? They were so quiet and still, only their gazes moving across the congregation then returning to her.

She touched Callie's shoulder, received a soft smile that made the girl's rather plain face a thing of beauty. Gave Ben and Will smiles of reassurance, got a cheeky grin from handsome, blond, blue-eyed Ben, and a wink from the irresistible, dark-haired, dark-eyed Will in return, and patted Katy's hand. Timid Katy, who nonetheless had a quick temper. The boys delighted in teasing her. And she gave back in kind, her blue eyes snapping, her black curls trembling, and more often than not, her small finger shaking in her tormentor's face as she corrected them. She was a beautiful child. They all were beautiful, in their own way. And so well-behaved on their first time in church. Goodness, she was proud of them!

Tears stung the backs of her eyes. Had she done wrong by bringing the children to church? She had expected a few shocked looks, but she had not anticipated such ostracism and anger. The children had already been hurt by people on the streets and she did not want them suffering rejection again.

She listened to the church filling, all but the pews in front and back of them, and blinked back tears. Should they leave? *Almighty God, please, please, do not let these children be hurt by my decision to bring them here today. Please. Amen.* A calm settled over her. It was odd how often she prayed these days. She had not prayed for years. But while she still questioned God's love for her, she was quite certain God cared about these orphans.

The door opened at the back of the church. A woman's soft footsteps came down the center aisle. Mary heard Ben whisper to Will, "It's Mrs. Lucas." She lifted her head to look. The elderly woman passed by two partially empty pews on the left and turned toward the pew in front of them.

A woman on the left aisle seat whispered something. Mrs. Lucas turned back, nodded and smiled. "Yes, I know, Rose. Miss Randolph and the children are friends of mine." The elderly voice broke the silence. Drew glances. The woman snapped upright, gave a toss of her head and faced the front.

Mrs. Lucas smiled and stepped toward their pew. James rose, motioning for the boys to do the same. Mrs. Lucas's faded blue eyes twinkled up at him. "My! You are a handsome lad."

Color rushed into James's face. It was the first time Mary had seen him blush in years. But he rose to the occasion. He smiled and winked at the elderly woman. "And you, madam, are a lovely woman of impeccable taste."

Mrs. Lucas laughed and motioned for him to lean down. "Rebecca Green is a very lucky young lady." Mary heard the whisper, had to clamp down on her lip to keep from laughing at James's shocked expression. "Now take your seat, young man. I shall sit up here." Mrs. Lucas turned toward the pew in front of them, then looked back. "With your permission, I should like these two young gentleman to sit with me." She beamed at Ben and Will.

"Of course." James stepped aside, and the boys filed out and into the other pew, one on either side of the small, elderly woman.

James took his seat and they all slid closer together. Closing ranks. The thought was not a happy one.

The murmuring began anew.

Please, God, do not let Mrs. Lucas be hurt because she has befriended us.

The organist struck a chord. Mary rose with the congregation to sing the opening hymn, swelling with pride at the sight of Will and Ben rising to stand straight and tall beside Mrs. Lucas. The singing started and the children joined in. She glanced down at the girls, then exchanged a smile with James. Callie had a beautiful voice, true and clear. Katy was not as fortunate, but sang with great enthusiasm, all the same.

There was a general rustle and stir as people resumed their seats when the singing was over. The pastor strode to the pulpit, looked down and gave a small nod. Mary watched as Mrs. Lucas gave one in return. She frowned and took her seat. That was more than a casual greeting. It was a bit of silent communication. And the elderly woman's face now bore that same pleased expression she had worn at the end of their visit.

Silence settled.

"Almighty God, bless these Your people with 'ears to hear' and open hearts to receive Your message of truth this day. Amen." The pastor opened his Bible. "I take my text today from the book of James, chapter two. 'My brethren, have not the faith of our Lord Jesus Christ, the Lord of glory, with respect to persons.' "

Mary smoothed a wrinkle from her skirt and settled herself to listen.

" 'For if there come unto your assembly a man with a gold ring, in goodly apparel, and there come in also a poor man in vile raiment; and ye have respect to him that weareth the gay clothing . . .' "

Mary snapped her attention to Pastor Thornton, looked at Mrs. Lucas, who was sitting, gaze fixed forward, hands folded in her lap, a beatific smile on her face. Is that what — Had she —

Mary darted a look across the aisle at the Stewart family. The mayor was scowling, Mrs. Stewart was looking at her husband, and Miss Stewart was staring at the pastor, looking displeased.

" 'But ye have despised the poor.' And in

doing so, you commit sin." The words rang out.

The mayor went rigid. His face turned a frightening shade of purple. He turned his head her way.

Mary stared at him, alarmed for his health. He seemed to be having trouble breathing. Mrs. Stewart said something and patted his arm. And Miss Stewart — Mary stiffened. Miss Stewart, like the mayor, was glaring at her. She stared at the woman's face, at the features suffused with anger, at the glinting blue eyes, the lips curled with disgust and felt the animosity aimed their way.

She reached her arm around Katy, pulled her close, then looked down to reassure Callie. Her breath caught. Plain little Callie sat listening to the sermon, a soft glow warming her brown eyes, a small, gentle smile on her mouth. Tears filmed her eyes. Callie was not plain. The child was beautiful. Truly beautiful.

"In the book of Samuel, it says . . . 'For the Lord seeth not as man seeth; for man looketh on the outward appearance, but the Lord looketh on the heart.' "

Mary looked from Callie to Miss Stewart and the truth, bright and glimmering, shining in all its glory, burst upon her. To God, Callie was truly beautiful. As beautiful as anyone. Because God did not look at golden curls or dimpled cheeks — God looked at a person's heart. And if that was true, then — Tears welled into her eyes. *Oh, God, I have been so wrong! Forgive me, for doubting Your love for me. And please let my heart be pleasing unto Thee.* She blinked hard, reached for the embroidered, linen handkerchief she carried in her reticule and dabbed her eyes.

The pastor stepped out from behind the pulpit, looked out across the congregation. "My brethren, in light of this message, I urge each of you to examine your hearts today. Do you value others because of outward appearances and worldly successes? Do you 'despise the poor,' to your discredit? Or do you, as does the Lord, look upon a person's heart and character? May the almighty God help us all to follow as He leads."

At the last amen, the mayor rose and stormed up the aisle, his wife in tow, his daughter at his side. Several others rose and followed them. Mary clutched her handkerchief and watched them go. Miss Stewart turned her head, shot them all a venomous look, then stuck her nose into the air and swept on by.

For the first time in her life, Mary looked at a petite, beautiful, blond woman, not with envy, but with compassion. She turned and gave Mrs. Lucas a hug. "Would it be possible for you to join us for dinner, Mrs. Lucas? The children and I would be delighted with your company. James has other plans."

"Yes, I see." Mrs. Lucas twinkled up at him. "I believe your 'other plan' is dawdling by the door, Mr. Randolph. I suggest you hurry to her before Rebecca runs out of reasons to tarry."

James chuckled. "I believe I am going to enjoy getting to know you better, Mrs. Lucas." He leaned down, gave her a peck on the cheek, then waved a hand to the children and rushed off up the aisle.

Mrs. Lucas smiled and looked up at her. "Your brother is a delightful young man, Mary. The two of you are a wonderful testimony to your parents. As these children will one day be to you. Now, let us depart. I am afraid I am too weary to accept your kind invitation, but you all may see me home."

The sun beamed down on the *Journey's End,* its brightness creating the contrast of deep shade. Mary welcomed the coolness of the shadows, the slight breeze coming off the river. She raised her hand and lifted a strand of hair off the nape of her moist neck, and tried not to think how every suggestion the captain offered made more clear the enormity of the task she had set for herself.

"And now about the kitchen."

Mary nodded and followed him into a dismal room, took one quick look around and gasped. The place was a disaster. "Oh, my." She closed her eyes, took a deep breath and opened them again.

The captain grinned. "Cooks on steamboats are not known for cleanliness. But if you look beyond the dirt and grime . . ."

"Yes." She took a closer look. Iron pots and pans littered a brick hearth along the far wall. Large, long-handled spoons and two-pronged iron forks, along with other implements, hung from cut nails pounded into the rough beam mantel and in the brick beside the bake ovens. Pewter trenchers and goblets marched in broken formation down the length of the mantel, and porringers formed piles at the end.

Overhead, sooty oil lamps hung from a joining of two long iron hooks. Along the wall to her right was a large dry sink holding a copper basin full of pots and pans, and a tall cupboard — one door hanging askew from its hinges — full of crockery and pewter dishes. The wall on her left was formed by a deep pantry she assumed held the food stores. Nothing could have induced her to open one of the doors to see if she was correct.

A long table with a thick, scarred top, stained with something she did not want to examine too closely, marched down the center of the room. And behind her, on both sides of the arched opening through which they had entered were barred cages. Feathers mixed with dried dung in the bottom told of their purpose. She took a breath, albeit a shallow one, and shrugged. "It seems to be well supplied. And, I suppose it . . . has possibilities . . ."

The captain threw back his head and laughed, a deep-chested, full-throated laugh.

She stared at him.

He shook his head, knuckled tears from his eyes. "I apologize, Miss Randolph. But if you could see your face . . ."

Her own lips twitched. "I suppose I do look rather undone. I confess, I am feeling a bit overwhelmed by the vastness of this undertaking. I did not realize . . ." She shook dust from the hem of her old blue gown and squared her shoulders. "Nonetheless, I shall manage. Somehow. What is next, Captain?"

"The cargo storage area of the main deck. That is the open area we walked through to reach the kitchen." He led her back through the arched opening. "As you can see, there is a wall at the outer edge of the boat opposite the kitchen. That was meant to keep perishable cargo dry." He stepped to the end of the long wall, then walked toward the center of the boat at a right angle, drawing the toe of his boot along the floor to make a line through the dust. He strode to the other end of the wall and did the same, then made another line connecting them. In the middle of the long rectangle, he drew two more lines, stopped and faced her. "I told you the other night that I had a suggestion for where the overseer of the children can live. This is it. If we build walls where I have indicated, there will be a dressing room —" he pointed to the square he had drawn in the center "— and two spacious bedrooms. One for the overseer and, I thought, perhaps one for the cook." He indicated the two large rectangles on either end.

Mary studied the lines, nibbling at the corner of her upper lip. "Yes. I can see that. What an excellent suggestion, Captain!"

"Wait. I'm not finished. If we build a wall across this end from here —" he hurried down to the far end of the line, placed the toe of his boot on the corner and drew another line in the dust to the corner of the kitchen wall "— to here, it will make this entire area in between these rooms and the kitchen into a comfortable sitting area, and large dining room, heated by one of the furnaces. That will free the main room on the boiler deck for the schoolroom and play area you want for the children. And here, in the center of this end wall, we can build a staircase that leads to the play area on the deck where the children's bedrooms are located, and place the door to go out onto the remaining portion of the main deck. A sort of porch." He came back and stood looking down at her. "What do you think?"

She could not speak. Her heart was too full. Her throat too tight. He had said *we.* Not once but several times. It was not a mistaken slip of his tongue. She lifted the hem of her gown, turned and walked to the bow of the boat to look down at the new lines he had drawn in the dust so he could not see the folly of her heart reflected in her eyes. "I think it is a *wonderful* plan, Captain. I should not have thought of anything like it."

She heard him come toward her and moved to the gangway. He held her elbow to help her down the ramp. She thought of Miss Stewart's soft roundness and longed to pull her thin arm out of his grip. "With your plan in mind, I am most eager to begin work. I shall start with the cleaning tomorrow."

"I am certain your brother knows of those who make their living renovating steamboats, Miss Randolph. But if you should need any advice as to who would perform best —"

She shook her head, followed his guidance around a pile of firewood, and continued walking beside him up the levee, acutely aware of the warmth where his hand still held her arm. "I do not have funds to hire the work done, Captain. At least, not yet."

The din and buzz of activity fell behind them. They crossed Front Street and, at last, he released his hold on her elbow. Disappointment warred with relief. They strolled up Market Street side by side, his long-legged strides making her hurry her steps. "But, as the children in jail cannot wait until I have the funds, I shall begin the work myself — in the morning, before the heat becomes oppressive."

His steps slowed. "Miss Randolph, that is not wise."

"But necessary."

He gripped her elbow again and drew her to a halt. She looked up at him.

"Forgive me." He released her. "But I do

not believe you understand the risk involved. You should not go alone to the steamboat. There are —"

"Unsavory elements on the levee. Yes, I know, Captain. You told me of them that first day." She resumed walking. They turned the corner and strolled toward her gate. "And, as you also explained that first day, I realize it is your duty to be concerned over the safety of the citizens of St. Louis, but you need have no concern for me. I shall not go to the *Journey's End* alone. I shall have James escort me there when he goes to the office — and escort me home at dinnertime. And I will stay out of sight in the staterooms while I am working."

"Miss Randolph —"

"I shall take every precaution, Captain." She stepped through the gate he opened for her, turned and smiled up at him. She should invite him in — it was only right after all his trouble, but she could not do so. She wanted it too much. "Thank you for your excellent suggestions. I truly do appreciate your help, Captain. Good evening."

"All right it's settled then, Jackson. But you and Harmon do not get your money until the job is finished."

"Ah, Captain, that ain't right." The short,

wiry man lounging on a cot in the cell hopped to his feet and came to the stand, holding on to the bars beside his friend. "Half now, half when the job is done."

Sam shook his head. "No. I'll pay for your meals at the Cock's Crow while you are renovating the *Journey's End,* but not one coin in your hand. I'll not have you drinking up the money — leaving Miss Randolph unprotected and the work undone."

Sam jiggled the keys in his hand. "And she is not to know I am paying you. You will offer to do the work for the privilege of sleeping on the boat. That will allow you to stay there all night and protect it from looters. Understood?" He jiggled the keys again.

The men looked down at the ring of keys, looked back at him and nodded.

"One more thing."

Their gazes sharpened.

"You eat your meals at different times. I want one of you on that boat at all times. And if either one of you gets drunk, I'll throw you back in jail and you will finish out this sentence, as well as serving a new one. Understood?"

"Yeah, we understand. Open the door."

"In the morning. That's when the deal starts."

Sam stepped down the dark hall and

glanced at the children sleeping in the last four cells. He had managed to delay things so far, but the mayor had sent word that the children were to be taken to the courthouse tomorrow morning. Work had started on the additions to the building, and the children were to clear away unearthed stones.

Sam turned and headed back for his desk in the other room. It wasn't that clearing off stones was so hard. There were a lot of farm children who did much heavier work. But they did it because they were part of a family. And he had done much harder work himself when he was these children's ages. But he had been free. It had been his choice. And he had been paid for his labor. It was not right to make slaves out of these kids.

Sam scowled, stepped through the barred door, then plunked down in his desk chair and threw the key ring in the drawer. Turning that steamboat into an orphanage was a clever idea. Once he had gotten over his shock and started thinking about it, it made good sense. Renovating that boat would cost much less than buying or erecting a building of comparable size, and it could be ready quickly.

The big problem would be a plot of land

to settle it on. He laced his fingers behind his head and tilted back on the chair's hind legs. That could be expensive. And, it appeared Mary Randolph dreamed beyond her means. Nothing wrong with that. He had done that all his life. And he had worked to make those dreams come true. Now . . .

He rose, stood again in the barred doorway and looked down the hall toward the children's cells. Now it seemed his dreams would have to wait a little longer — these children couldn't. Preparing this orphanage could get expensive, and Mary needed money now. There was no hurry for his showcase house. A year or so delay wouldn't matter. He had to wait on the property anyway.

And he had to convince the spunky Miss Mary Randolph to share it with him.

Mary stared out at the starry sky and reminded herself for the hundredth time since coming home to keep her head about her. To keep the wall in place around her heart. But the truth was, the captain had already breached that wall.

We. If we *build . . . If* we *move . . .* Her heart pounded. It did not matter how often she told herself that his only reason was to help the children. He had still said "we." He would be working with her.

How would she ever be able to hide her growing feelings for him, from him?

Chapter Eighteen

Sam fought back a smile. Mary was standing against the railing of the main deck of the *Journey's End* wearing a long white apron over her dress, a large handkerchief tied over her hair. A bucket of water sat at her feet, and she gripped a broom in her hands. But it was not her costume that made him want to grin. It was the wary, combative look in her eyes as she faced Harmon, perched on an upturned wooden barrel. What a woman! But that spunk and that broom wouldn't hold off anyone set to do her harm.

The smile died. Dealing with a woman as determined as Mary Randolph had its drawbacks when you didn't have the right to protect her. Sam frowned and trotted up the gangplank, Jackson at his heels. "Is there a problem, Miss Randolph? Jackson said you wanted to see me."

Her gaze shot to his and for a moment he

read the relief, the trust in her eyes. It was so intense, it was almost as if she ran to him. His heart thudded. *God help me never to do anything that will destroy her trust in me again.*

"Yes, Captain, I do. It is good of you to come." Her death grip on the broom relaxed. "These men want to help with the renovation of the boat in exchange for the privilege of sleeping on it. They said you would recommend them as good and honest workers."

Sam read the doubt in her eyes. He turned to the man beside him. "Run up against some hard times, Jackson?"

"*That's* the truth, Captain."

Harmon shook his head. "Yeah, me an' Jackson are havin' a *dry* time right now."

Sam shot him a warning look. "I do know these men to be good workers, Miss Randolph. They know how to get a boat back into shape, and they are quick about doing it. And it is more than a fair deal. Have you cleaning tools and supplies enough for them?"

Mary looked down at her bucket and broom, the pile of rags she had brought from home. "I have only these, but —"

He held up his hand and turned to Jackson. "You and Harmon go to Gardner's and get what you need for the cleaning. Tell Jim

I'll stand good for it. And see you come straight back. I'll be waiting here with Miss Randolph."

He turned back. She was staring at him, her eyes wide. He fastened his gaze on hers and got lost in her eyes. Those brown eyes with tiny, honey-colored specks glowing with approval, warmth . . . He stepped closer. A deep-rose blush spread over her cheekbones. His heart kicked. She stepped back, groped behind her for the railing and lowered her eyelashes. They rested like an inky smudge on the crest of her cheekbones.

"Y-you are most kind to —" a quick little breath "— to offer to purchase the cleaning supplies, Captain." Hands rose to fuss with the handkerchief, lowered to grip and ungrip the railing. "But —" a quick glance up at him from under her lashes "— I do not know when I shall be able to —" a hand rose to pull at the knot of the handkerchief again "— to repay you." Soft, husky, *quavering* voice.

He made her nervous.

So she was not as cool toward him as she portrayed. The knowledge sent joy surging through him. His heart hammered. He wanted to whoop! To turn cartwheels. To show off for her like a ten-year-old. To take her in his arms and kiss her until —

"Capt'n Benton!"

Sam sucked in a breath, blew it out and turned. "What is it?"

"It's yer man, Buckles. He's got two mean drunks cornered at the Broken Barge, an' they done pulled knives. He told me t' see could I find you."

Sam braced his hand on the railing and leaped from the deck — "Stay here with Miss Randolph until Jackson comes back!" — and took off at a dead run.

Knives.

Mary shuddered, dipped her cloth in the bucket of vinegar water and scrubbed at the dirty corners of the small panes of glass. On tiptoe, she leaned her head against the window, trying to see through the dirt on the outside to the gangplank. Why did he not return? Of course, he did not say he would. And there was no reason he should. He did not know how she felt about him. How concerned she was about his welfare. Yet, there had been that moment when he had looked at her as if . . . as if . . .

"Cease that foolish dreaming this instant, Mary Randolph!" She glared at her dim, blurry reflection in the window. "You have far too much imagination. Captain Benton is courting the beautiful Miss Stewart. Why would he have any interest in the likes of you? You are only placing yourself in danger of being hurt again. Do you never learn?"

She grabbed a cloth from her dwindling pile and swiped the window dry, studying it as if cleanliness were the most important thing in the world. It was difficult to tell if it was clean. She would have to do the windows again when the men had washed the outside. At least most of the grime was gone.

The rag twisted in her hands. She threw it back on the pile, sank down on the edge of the narrow bed and covered her face with her hands. What if he was hurt? Or . . . or worse. *Oh, please, God, do not let him be hurt. Please, do not let him be hurt.*

The worrisome thoughts nagged at her, knotted her stomach. She rose, picked up the bucket and the rags and moved on to the next stateroom. The men had said they would wash the walls and scrub the floors. All she should do was the windows. Thank goodness for the training to be a wife and run a household that she had received from her mother. She was not entirely unequal to the tasks she had taken upon herself.

She sighed, squeezed the extra vinegar water from the rag and swished it over the windowpanes in a first pass. She had to wash each window at least three times to get it clean. She had finished four. That left twenty more to do. On this deck.

"Mary?"

She started, then rushed to the stateroom door. "Here I am, James. Is it dinnertime so soon?"

"Yes." He frowned, looking over his shoulder toward the stairway. "Who are those men scrubbing down walls?"

"That is Jackson and Harmon." The vinegar water splashed against the bucket as she dropped in the rag she was using. She looked over her shoulder at the sound of James's footsteps. He was in the doorway. Grinning.

"What?"

"You look like Edda or Ivy. Only they are cleaner."

The words pierced the ache inside. The captain had seen her looking like a *maid.* She stuck out her tongue at James so he would not guess how his innocent teasing had hurt her, and took off the apron and handkerchief. "I will tell you all about the men on the way home." She smoothed her hands over her hair and walked with him to the stairway, forcing one foot to move in front of the other. She did not want to leave. How would she learn if the captain had been wounded? What if he needed care?

Would Miss Stewart nurse him back to health?

"Mary?"

She looked up. They were already halfway up the levee.

"You were going to tell me about those men."

"Oh, yes. Of course." She shoved her anxieties away once more and smiled up at James. "The most amazing thing happened this morning . . ."

It was good to feel clean again. Mary picked up the green cording that matched the trim on her dress, wrapped it around the loose knot on the crown of her head and tied it in a bow at the back. There. All finished. And she had time to write a letter home before she began the children's schooling. It would help keep her mind occupied so she wouldn't worry about the captain.

She closed the dressing-room door and stepped to her desk, forcing herself to concentrate. There was so much she wanted to tell her parents. She would start with the events in church and —

"Miss Mary?"

Her heart stopped at the hail. For one wild moment she thought someone had brought her news of the captain. Perhaps Will had heard something. Her skirts billowed out as she turned and hurried to the top of the stairs. “Yes, Will. What is it?”

The boy charged halfway up the stairs. “Mrs. Lucas says, beggin’ yer pardon for the short invitation, but would you please accompany her to the Ladies’ Be— bene—”

“Benevolent?” She made the suggestion absently, still adjusting to the rapid change of subject.

A grin split his face. “Yeah, that’s it. The Ladies’ Benevolent Society meeting this afternoon. She said I was to tell you she wants to carry things in through the back door.”

“Carry things in the back door?”

He shrugged his shoulders. “Yeah. That’s what she said. I’m to take you, or your answer, to her.”

She did not want to leave the house — in case. But she owed Mrs. Lucas so much . . . *Carry things in through* — Oh! What had Mrs. Lucas said that day? *But what won’t go in a front door can be carried in the back.* Yes. That was it. But whatever could she mean? Mary sighed. This day was full of surprises. “All right, Will. Go to the kitchen and tell Ivy I will be leaving for the afternoon. I will be down as soon as I fetch my bonnet.”

She hurried to the cupboard, found her green bonnet with the shirred brim and settled it on her head. *Carry things in the back door.* Well that certainly gave her something to think of besides the captain. She pulled the bonnet's ties into place and knotted them under her chin as she hurried downstairs.

"This here's the place. She said you was to go on in and ask fer her."

Mary swept her gaze over the stone house, grander than any she had thus far seen in St. Louis. "All right, Will. Thank you for bringing me. Now go straight home, please."

She smiled at his nod, opened the gate, walked up to the porch and knocked. The door opened.

"Yes?"

Mary took in the black dress, the white apron and cap. "I was told to meet Mrs. Lucas here for the Ladies' Benevolent Society meeting."

"Of course, miss. Right this way."

Mary stepped into the entrance hall and followed the maid to a room on her right. Muted women's voices flowed out into the hall.

"The meeting has already started. You can go in, miss."

Mary stepped through the door that the maid opened. Talk ceased. Heads turned her direction. She smiled, then froze — stared at Levinia Stewart . . . Levinia's mother . . . read their shock. Will had brought her to the wrong —

"Ah, there you are, Mary!"

Mrs. Lucas. She shifted her gaze. The elderly woman smiled and patted the empty space beside her on a linen-covered settee.

"Come sit beside me, dear. And don't bother to apologize for being a little tardy. I have already told the ladies it was my fault for issuing my invitation so late in the day. And the meeting has only begun."

The shock on several of the faces turned to anger. Heads swiveled back toward Mrs. Lucas. The elderly lady seemed not to notice. She merely smiled wider and patted the cushion again.

Mary lifted her chin. Everything in her wanted to leave, but she could not disappoint Mrs. Lucas no matter how uncomfortable she was. She pasted on a smile and made her way to the settee.

Mrs. Lucas beamed up at her. "My, you look lovely today, Mary. The green of your gown suits your vibrant coloring."

"Isobel, speaking as president of this

organization, I would like an explanation, please."

The frost in the voice could have frozen the river. Mary glanced to identify the speaker. It was Mrs. Stewart. Her dander rose. It was one thing for the woman to freeze her out — it was quite another for her to be disrespectful to Mrs. Lucas.

"Why, I told you I had invited a guest with a worthy project for our society, Margaret."

What? Mary jerked her gaze back to Mrs. Lucas, and her shock dissolved into amusement. She had never seen anyone look so sweetly innocent. Clearly, Mrs. Lucas was not disturbed by the glares of outrage aimed at her.

"It is customary to discuss a proposed project with the officers of the society in advance of the meeting, Isobel. And you know it!"

"I do indeed, Margaret. But there simply wasn't time. You see, the idea came on me suddenly — while I was examining my heart in view of Sunday's sermon. You know, the way the pastor urged us all to do." Mrs. Lucas shed her beatific smile over everyone. "Anyway, helping Miss Randolph provide a home for orphaned children would be a very worthwhile project. And fully in keeping with the pastor's message. And I know it says in the Bible — though I cannot quote it exactly — that pure and undefiled religion has something to do with our treatment of the fatherless."

Mary scanned the faces of the ladies from beneath her lowered lashes. Some looked abashed, others — including Levinia — seemed as if they would choke on their anger. She looked at Mrs. Lucas in awe. The woman had placed them all in a position where they dare not protest her idea for fear of seeming to lack a Christian attitude.

"Now, as I said, my friend, Mary Randolph —" Mrs. Lucas reached over and patted her hand "— has a perfectly wonderful plan for providing a home for the orphans that presently roam our streets. Of course it is costly to provide for children. But with our help —"

"Mrs. Lucas, I believe this project is unnecessary." Mary watched as Levinia Stewart turned a dimpled smile on the elderly woman. The smile did not reach her eyes, which continued to glitter with anger. "Father has already put a plan in motion to rid our streets of those fil— fatherless children. And the city of St. Louis will bear the cost of housing them."

Mary stiffened. Mrs. Lucas squeezed her hand. She took a breath and sat back to let the elderly woman handle Levinia Stewart.

"You are young and without husband or child, Levinia. But, speaking as a mother, I do not consider a jail to be proper housing for a child. Especially one who has done no wrong save the misfortune of losing his or her parents to death. Nor do I believe it is right to force them to labor on city projects to earn their board of scanty meals and hard cots behind bars. And I am certain every mother here would agree with me. Now this is my idea . . ."

Mary shoved her toe against the porch floor and set the swing moving. Her head was still reeling. She longed to go for a brisk walk, but it was improper — and unsafe — for a young lady to do so in the evening without an escort.

She frowned and pushed with her toes again. Without James home to accompany her, she was confined to the porch and small yard.

Despite her restlessness, excitement bubbled through her. So much had happened today. Jackson and Harmon had offered to renovate the boat at no cost to her — for only the privilege of sleeping on it — which would keep it safe from vandals! And the captain had paid for the supplies they needed. And now — she shook her head in pure amazement — now the Ladies' Benevolent Society was going to provide all that was needed for the children's bedrooms! Mrs. Lucas had proposed the idea that each lady provide the accoutrements — window curtains, bedsheets, pillow and quilt or coverlet — for one stateroom and they had agreed! Why, once Mrs. Lucas had finished with them, some of the ladies were even eager and excited about the project.

Mary laughed and pushed the swing faster. The woman was a genius. Wait until the captain heard — Her laughter died. The swing slowed, the creaking of the chains a lonely sound in the twilight. If only she knew the captain was well, the day would be perfect. Oh, of course he was! He was probably this minute sitting on Miss Stewart's porch and —

"Good evening."

"Oh!" She jammed her toes against the floor, to stop the swing.

"Excuse me. I guess you did not hear me approach on the grass." The captain folded his arms on the porch railing and smiled up at her. "My patrol is over and I was on my way home when I heard you laughing. I couldn't resist coming over. Care to share what has made you so happy?"

She looked at the captain's blue eyes, his smiling lips, his strong arms. He was well. And he was here. She smiled and let the words come out, soft and full of joy. "A perfect day."

Chapter Nineteen

Mary glanced at the paper in her hand — fourth house on the right-hand side. This was the place. She nodded to James and squared her shoulders. They marched up the walk and knocked on the door — exchanged glances and stepped back as it was opened.

A gray-haired, plump woman peered out at them. "Yes?"

Mary smiled, waited for James to speak. "I should like to speak with Mr. Monroe, please. About the Spruce Street property he has for sale."

"Come in." The woman stepped aside. "Wait here, please." She disappeared into the dim interior.

Mary closed her eyes. *Please, Lord, this is the last name on the list the captain gave me. Please, let this man be willing to sell the land to us.*

A well-dressed, prosperous-looking man

came striding into the hall. He looked them both over, addressing James. "You are interested in my Spruce Street property, young man?"

James smiled, held out his hand. "I am if you are Wilfred Monroe."

"I am." The man grasped James's hand. "And you are . . . ?"

"I am James Randolph, Mr. Monroe. And this is my sister —"

"Randolph!" A scowl darkened the man's features. "I have heard about your sister. Making an *orphanage* out of a steamboat." He gave a disdainful snort. "A ridiculous idea. And I have been warned you are now coming around to decent people and trying to buy land from them to hold that disgrace." He pulled the door open. "You will get no land from me. No, nor from anyone I know, for I will tell them all of your scheme. You will devalue all the properties around your ridiculous steamboat orphanage. Good day to you!" He rattled the doorknob.

"And to you, sir." James took Mary's elbow and together they walked out the door. It slammed shut behind them.

"Is that the last of them?"

"Yes." Mary looked up at him, tears in her eyes, though from anger or defeat she could not say. "What are we to do, James? The *Journey's End* will soon be ready for the children, but we have no land to put it on. And none of these people will even talk to us."

"There is more property for sale than this small list, Mary." James smiled down at her. "The captain gave us a list of the best properties for our purpose. And the ones we might be able to afford. We shall simply have to expand our search, and extend ourselves more. I believe you should write Mother and Father of this problem. They are so proud of what you are doing for these children, I am sure Father will increase the amount he will pay for the land."

The thought cheered her. She smiled up at him. "Perhaps you are right. I shall write Mother and Father this evening." She sighed and glanced back at the house. "Sometimes it is very hard to maintain a Christian tongue."

He laughed. "I saw you swallowing your words. The truth is, I swallowed a few of my own." He sobered. "But I truly believe God has been blessing your efforts, and I am certain you will have your land when you need it."

"You are right, of course." She slanted a wry look at him. "I am new at trusting God, but I am learning. Thank you for coming with me today, James. I would not even have been received had I approached these people on my own."

"My pleasure, Mary. With all that has happened at the steamer line, I have had little time to help with your endeavors. But I am happy to do all I can. And now, my dear sister, you may help me in return."

"Oh? In what way? What do you wish?"

"Come with me to the office. Our new luxury steamboat is well under way and there are final decorating decisions to be made. I need your advice on carpet and paint and chandeliers."

"Goodness, Miss Mary!" Ivy stopped and shook her head. "I've been admiring the boat from afar, but it looks even better when you get near."

Mary laughed and swept her gaze over the *Journey's End.* The steamboat gleamed. The fresh white paint was so bright it hurt your eyes to look fully at it when the sun was high. The boat's name, which she had kept, deeming it so appropriate for the orphanage, was emblazoned on the side in the dark blue paint that also graced the window frames, the two tall stacks and the paddle wheel at the stern. The deck glistened. The windows shone. The outside of the boat was finished.

Her heart swelled. She was so proud of the steamboat orphanage, and so grateful to everyone who had helped make the dream come true. Her mother was right. God truly did work through His children. Why had she resisted that truth so long? She smiled at Ivy. "I agree. I cannot simply go aboard. Every time I come, I stop here by the gangplank to admire the steamer. And to remember how many people have helped along the way." She smiled at her cook. "You were the first, Ivy. You opened your heart and your home to help the children, and I am very grateful."

Mary shook her head. "I always scorned my mother's insistence that God watches over His children, and that the things that happen in our lives are not coincidences but God's blessings. Now I know that is true. The way the steamboat orphanage has come about in the face of the city fathers' opposition has proved that beyond any doubt. But there is more to be done. We need land." She looked down at the children fidgeting with impatience. "And you must all help by praying every day. Now, go ahead."

She laughed as the children rushed, sure-footed and fearless, up the bright red gangplank. But her heart ached for the children still in jail. *Almighty God, please, provide land so we may free those children.*

"Katy, please stay back from the rail. And, all of you, do not pester Jackson and Harmon while they are working!" She watched the children run inside chattering about their new home and glanced at Ivy. Her cook was gazing at the steamboat and seemed undisturbed by the children's remarks about their new home. Perhaps she hadn't heard them.

"Shall we go inside, Ivy? I cannot wait to show you around." She led the way up the gangplank and through the door in the new end wall. "The children's quarters on the boiler deck are all completed. But work continues here on the main deck. However, the kitchen is finished." She laughed at the sudden gleam in Ivy's eyes. "I will show it to you first. Come this way."

She swept her arm in an arc. "This large area will be the dining room. The tables and chairs are from the old dining room above. And here is a sitting room. Those rooms on either side will be for the headmistress — me —" she laughed and made a small curtsy "— and the cook. Who at present is unknown. And this is the kitchen." She led them through the archway, now boasting cupboards where the open crates had been, and stopped.

"Oh, my . . ." Ivy moved into the room, running her hand over the scrubbed-clean table.

Mary watched her and laughed. "Your reaction is very different than mine when I first saw this room." She looked around with a little thrill of pride. "It is much the same as it was, except now everything is repaired and clean and polished and in its proper place. And we have a new iron cookstove."

Ivy nodded, then began exploring the kitchen — opening the pantry doors and peering inside, moved on to the cupboard full of dishes, the dry sink with a new wide shelf above it, then turned and fastened her gaze on her. "Miss Mary, I want to be the cook. That's why I asked to come with you today and see the steamboat."

Mary stared, taken aback by the sudden pronouncement.

"I've given it lots of thought. I like helping these kids. But my place isn't any bigger than a mouse's squeak, and I can't take in any more. But here, I could be doing for all of them."

"But —"

"And, it appears to me, Mister James will be marrying soon. His bride will want her own help and her own ways. And nothing makes me happier than baking up a batch of cookies and seeing those children's happy grins."

"Well . . ."

"Thank you, Miss Mary."

Mary lifted her hands in a gesture of surrender and laughed. "You are welcome, Ivy. But *you* get the honor of telling James!"

"Come in, Captain Benton. Have a seat." The mayor gestured to the chair at the end of the long table.

Sam removed his hat and moved toward the chair. Unease, that policeman's instinct that warned him of danger, rose. Something was in the wind. And it wasn't good. He could feel it. He took a quick scan of the aldermen seated around the table. They all looked tense but pleased. He gave a polite nod as a covering reason for his look and took his seat.

The mayor cleared his throat. "I have asked you to join this meeting, Captain, because I believe you are quite familiar with the person and the subject it concerns."

Sam's unease doubled. The mayor was seething under that polite mask he wore. Still, pleasure over what was to come lurked in the depth of his eyes, easy to read as an item in a newspaper. This was about Mary and the orphans. He placed his hat on his knee, leaned back in his chair and affected a guise of relaxed ease. No sense in giving the man the satisfaction of a response. He already looked too smug.

The mayor frowned. "I am, of course, speaking of Miss Randolph and this ludicrous steamboat orphanage she thinks she is creating."

Stay in control, Sam. He wants you angry. Defensive. He gave a short nod. "I know Miss Randolph. And I am familiar with the orphanage she *has* created out of a steamboat, yes." He couldn't resist the slight emphasis.

The mayor's eyes narrowed. "Oh, I know of all the renovation that has taken place, Captain. *And* that the Ladies' Benevolent Society has contributed generously to bring it about. Also that they intend to continue that philanthropy."

There was a general muttering and nodding of heads around the table.

Ah, so that was it. These men's pocketbooks were involved. No doubt Levinia —

"But all that has been accomplished is a useless, renovated steamboat, Captain. The orphans will stay in jail. And they will continue to work for their keep." The mayor looked straight at him and smiled. "And, of course, more will join them as you and your men continue to arrest them. You see no one can *live* on that piece of folly. Miss Randolph has no land to situate it on. Though it has come to my attention that she is trying to purchase land for that purpose." The mayor's eyes glittered. "I intend to see that she will *never* do so. *That* is what this meeting is about. And that, as an officer of the law, is the message you will convey to Miss Randolph when we adjourn."

Sam gripped the chair arms. It took all of his control to stay in his seat, to keep from rushing around the table to pummel the man more senseless than he already was. His jaw muscles twitched. His hands clenched and unclenched on the chair arms. The orphans did not deserve this. *Mary* did not deserve this. She was the most wonderful, the most beautiful, the most —

"And I assure you, Captain, that was *not* an idle threat."

The words shot out like bullets from a gun — fast and deadly.

Sam jerked his attention back to the mayor. The man grabbed the gavel by his hand and crashed it down on the table.

"*Gentlemen,* I am proposing a new law. From this day forth, there will be no steamboats or other river vessels permitted to be permanently situated or used as a residence on land in St. Louis. No matter what changes or renovations have been made to them! All in favor, acknowledge by saying aye."

One by one, clockwise around the table, each alderman spoke aye.

"Let the record show the new law was passed by unanimous vote." The mayor leaned back in his chair and smiled. "And that, Captain, puts an end to your Miss Randolph's steamboat orphanage."

Sam wanted to rip the smirking lips off the man's face. He took a breath, let it out slow and even. "*My* Miss Randolph?"

"Why, yes." The mayor's gaze bored into his. "Did I forget to mention I am also aware that you have been spending a great deal of time with the woman? Of course, that could change . . ."

So this was about Levinia, also. Spoiled Levinia who did not like to lose. Sam shoved back his chair and rose. "You are correct, Mr. Mayor. That could change." He smiled inwardly at the flash of victory in the mayor's eyes and drove home his killing thrust. "And I hope it does — to courtship and marriage."

He swept his glance over the men around

the table, letting his contempt for their high-handed, unjust tactics show. "Good day to you all. I will deliver your message to Miss Randolph." He yanked his hat on his head, spun on his heel and strode from the room.

"Excuse me. Are you Miss Randolph?"

Mary turned at the soft query and looked over the pile of bedding in her arms at a young, thin woman with red hair and green eyes. "Yes, I'm Mary Randolph." She lowered her burden to a game table and smoothed the front of her skirt. "How may I help you?"

The young woman stepped forward from her position at the top of the stairs, her eyes rounding as she glanced around. "My. This is . . . this is . . . lovely."

"Thank you, Miss . . ."

"Oh. I am sorry." A blush swept over the pale skin, making the freckles stand out even more. "Please forgive my rudeness. I was not prepared for such a . . . a wonderful place." The blush deepened. "I am Jane Withers, and I —" She stopped and drew her shoulders back. "I have heard that you are making this steamboat into an orphanage. I wondered if, perhaps, you were looking for a teacher for the children who will live here?"

Mary smiled and shook her head. "I would very much like to have a teacher, Miss Withers. But at present, I will be teaching the children. I am afraid I do not have the funds to pay another."

"Oh." The young woman looked absolutely crestfallen. "I understand. Forgive me for interrupting your work, Miss Randolph." She turned to leave.

Mary scanned her clothes. The gown was neat and clean, but not of rich fabric or style. And the heels of the shoes peeking out from under the long gingham skirt were worn. "Miss Withers?"

The young woman turned back.

"Who told you about *Journey's End*?"

"A Captain Benton. He said he thought perhaps you would want a teacher when there are more children."

"I see." Mary's heart swelled. "I do not wish to pry, but . . . have you, perhaps, fallen on hard times?"

The shoulders firmed. "I have. Through no fault of my own. I was to marry and travel west with my new husband, and so journeyed here to St. Louis in the company of friends who were also going west. But when John saw me again, after two years apart, he decided I was too frail — not sickly, but *frail* —to be of much help to him on the trail or in settling on a new place. He chose another to be his bride."

Hurt flashed in Jane Withers's green eyes, but was quickly masked. The remembered pain and humiliation of being cast aside because of one's appearance spiraled through Mary.

"And so, Miss Randolph, I am here in St. Louis. I was a teacher back home in Pittsburgh, but I have been unable to find a position here. I have found employment as a seamstress." A wry smile touched her pink lips. "I am not very good at sewing."

Mary laughed. "And I am not very good at teaching, Miss Withers. Would you be interested in the position though I cannot pay much wage? Room and board aboard the *Journey's End* would be included, of course."

"Oh, I should be very interested, Miss Randolph!" The young woman cast another glance around. "And where would the schoolroom be?"

"In the captain's and pilot's cabin above. There are tables and stools, and cabinets for supplies. It would be most helpful if you would make a list of needed supplies." Mary frowned. "I cannot say for certain when we shall be needing your teaching services. We are still looking for land to place the boat on. Will you be able to manage until then?"

"Yes, I will manage. Thank you so very much, Miss Randolph. I am most grateful for the opportunity to teach children again. But I have taken enough of your time. I shall make the list immediately. And should you need me for anything else . . . to help prepare the schoolroom or such . . . you have only to ask. Captain Benton knows where to reach me. I shall look forward to your summons to my duties as teacher aboard the *Journey's End.* Good day."

"Good day, Miss Withers." Mary watched the woman walk away knowing full well her heart had once again run away with her head. How would she manage a wage for a teacher? She could not ask her father for another increase in her allowance. He was already doing so much to help these orphans. And her personal monies were quickly dwindling. Well . . . she would simply have to find a way. And, with God's help, she would.

Mary smiled and turned to put the bedding, now lying on the table, into a cupboard. God's ways were indeed mysterious. Who ever would have thought stopping Ben from being jailed that day would lead to all that had happened? Or that helping the orphans would teach her of God's love for her. *And* teach her to trust Him. Though she was still learning to do that.

Her lips quirked. She put the last of the sheets on the cupboard shelf and reached for the pillow slips. Was this another lesson? It seemed so. Her mother said there was always a blessing in God's teaching. And though the finances would be difficult, one more problem was solved. A definite blessing. She had been concerned about teaching so many children. It was limiting enough to teach four of them. Now she would be free to concentrate on all the other matters concerning the running of an orphanage.

Mary laughed and put the last of the bedding away. How happy her mother and father would be to know of the change God had wrought in her heart. It was as if she had been blind and could now see His blessings in every area of her life . . . save one. Her laughter died. She pushed away the sudden surge of self-pity. Perhaps one day God would see fit to bless her with a husband who loved her and children of her own. Until then, she would busy herself with the orphans. Her life was full with helping them.

Captain Benton's image burst upon her. The image that constantly hovered at the edge of her thoughts. She tried to shut it out, but it refused to go away. But now there was something else. Something gnawing at the fringe of her mind, wispy yet determined to be remembered.

She sank onto a chair by the game table and sat quietly waiting. Finally, her father's favorite saying floated into her mind. *Not even God can fill a hand or heart that is already full.* Was that what she was supposed to hear? Tears welled into her eyes. A sob broke from her throat. How could God bless her with a husband and children of her own when her heart was full of love for Samuel Benton? Captain Benton — a man who belonged to another.

Guilt smote her. She closed her eyes, forced words from her aching throat. "Forgive me, Lord, for coveting a man who belongs to another. I confess my love for Captain Benton to You, and I ask Your help in purging this love from my heart and opening it to only the love You have for me. Please help me to accept with joy whatever future You have chosen for me. Be it unto me according to Thy will. Amen."

She waited for a calmness, a peace to flow over her. But all she felt was the pain of her breaking heart.

Mary paused, nibbled at her upper lip.

Wrote a bit more about James being serious about Rebecca Green, sent her love and signed her name. She put down the pen, stopped the ink well and stared off into the distance. Sarah was married and expecting her first child. James was in love, and would soon be married if she knew her little brother. And she — She would mail the letter in the morning.

Knuckles rapped against the front door. The sharp, staccato sound echoed throughout the house.

She pushed back her chair, then hurried down the stairs and opened the door a slit to peer out.

"Good evening, Miss Randolph. Might I have a word with you?"

A test of my sincerity so soon, Lord? Mary stared up at the captain, then nodded. "Of course, Captain. James is not home, but I will join you on the porch." She glanced at his face again in the lamplight, then stepped outside and closed the door. "Is something wrong?"

"A difficulty has arisen, yes." He smiled down at her and gestured toward the swing. "Why don't you have a seat and I will tell you about it."

She studied his face in the fading light and shook her head. "No, I prefer to stand."

She moved to the railing and turned to face him. "I assume this is about the orphans?"

"Yes." He came to stand with her by the railing. "The mayor has learned you are turning the *Journey's End* into an orphanage. He also knows about the Ladies' Benevolent Society's ongoing efforts to help you."

Misgiving skittered along her nerves. "And what has that to do with the mayor? The city is not involved."

"True. But he has also learned of your efforts to purchase land to place the orphanage on."

She studied his face. He was very angry. Her misgiving blossomed into concern. "I do not follow you, Captain. How does that present a difficulty?" The small muscle along his jaw twitched. So did her fingers. She wanted to touch it — to calm him. He took a deep breath, and she knew he dreaded whatever he was about to say.

"The mayor is determined you will not be successful in your efforts. He called a meeting of the aldermen today and they passed a new law stating that no steamboat or other river craft can be permanently located or lived in on land in St. Louis."

The air rushed from her lungs. She stared at him, unable to speak, to even think. When she returned to awareness, she shook her head to rid herself of the numbness that had seized her. "I see." She lifted her hand and rubbed at the spot over her aching heart. Managed a small smile. "You are right, Captain. That is a . . . difficulty."

She turned toward the railing and stared at the orange, purple and pink twilight sky. "How shall I tell all of those who have trusted me? Who have given so generously of their time and talents and money to help make a home for these children? How can I tell them that it is over? That in spite of all they have done and given, the children will stay in —" Her voice broke. She forced a little laugh. "How shall I tell them, indeed? I cannot even say the word."

"You don't have to, Mar — Miss Randolph. All is not lost."

His deep voice flowed over her like a soothing balm. He was so kind. How could she ever have thought him heartless? She turned to look at him. "Please, Captain. Do not encourage me further in my foolishness. It is clear I am defeated. No one would sell me land. And now, even if I could buy land, it would do me no profit. You said the law states that no one is allowed to live on a steamboat on land."

"Exactly."

He grinned, that slow, breath-stealing grin, and leaned toward her. She looked at the excitement dancing in his blue eyes, caught her breath and waited.

"But there is no law against living aboard a steamboat on the *river.* And there never can be — unless they want to destroy St. Louis."

Mary stared up at Samuel Benton, memorizing the way he looked, the excitement and compassion burning in his eyes, the joy on his face. How had she ever thought him heartless and cruel? For one timeless, breathless moment, she allowed her love for him to swell her heart, to fill her soul, and then she tucked it away and gave him a polite smile. "Thank you, Captain. You have given me renewed hope. With your help, and the help of all the others, I will not fail those children."

Chapter Twenty

Mary pulled her lace-edged handkerchief from her pocket, dabbed the moisture from her brow, then put it back and adjusted the brim of her straw hat to shield her face from the sun. There was nothing she could do about the waves of heat shimmering off the cobblestones. At least she was almost there.

She shifted the basket she carried into her other hand and hurried across the street to stop beneath the shade of the large elm on the corner of the courthouse property. Lovely, wonderful shade!

Mary put the basket down, massaged her tired hand and searched for the children. They were spread in a line across the furrowed soil at the far end of the lot picking up stones and dropping them in the buckets they carried. Her heart ached for them. She had hoped they would not be put to work in this heat. Thankfully, Ivy had packed double the usual amount of cold mint tea.

Would the foreman let the children come now? Or would he make them work their way to her? She scanned the area, spotted him standing in the shade of the building talking with two of the workers. Of course he would be in the shade — he was the boss. A boss who resented her interrupting the children's work by bringing them something to eat and drink.

She looked back to the children, squinted her eyes against the sun's glare and frowned. Was Tommy staggering? She watched him a moment, lifted her skirts clear of her shoe tops and broke into a run, her gaze fastened on Tommy now down on his hands and knees with his head pressed against the earth. *Please, God, let him be all right.*

From the corner of her eye she saw the men in the shade look her way, then turn and look the direction she was running. She dropped to her knees beside the boy, now prostate on the ground.

She rolled him over, shaded his face with her body. "What is wrong, Tommy?" No answer, only a dull look in his eyes. Sweat sheeted off his forehead, soaked the hair at his temples, dripped to the ground. "Tommy?" *Dear God, let him be all right.*

The children clustered around, silent and staring.

Mary put her hand on his forehead. It was cool. How could that be in this heat? Footsteps thudded to a stop beside her. She looked up to see the foreman, the two workers behind him. Rage shook her. "This boy is ill. One of you men go for a doctor!"

One of the workers turned.

The boss grabbed his arm and halted him. He looked down at her. "There ain't no call to go fetching a doctor, miss. The boy's only had a mite too much sun. Some can't take the heat like others. He can rest a few minutes. He'll be all right."

"Rest a few —" Mary rose, lifted her chin and fastened her most aristocratic look on one of the workers. "You — carry Tommy to the shade of the elm!" The man didn't even look at his boss. He stooped, picked up Tommy and started toward the tree.

"And you —" she pinned the other worker with another look "— go find Captain Benton and bring him back here immediately!" The man wheeled and hurried off.

"Now see here, miss —"

Mary spun to face the foreman. "And you, sir — *you* may come out of the shade and pick up your own stones." Her voice was low, quiet and cold as ice. She turned and held out her hands. "Come with me, children. There will be no more work for you today."

Sam opened the stable door and stepped out into the heat. Of all the days for Judge Simmons to order Seth Parker served with an eviction notice. It had to be over a hundred degrees. Good thing he had started for the Parker place early. He trotted across the lot, shoved open the door and stepped into the jail's dim interior. It felt good. The small windows and thick stone walls kept the place somewhat cool.

He tugged off his hat, threw it on a hook, then swiped his forearm across his moist forehead and looked over at Jenkins. "Parker's not happy. Made quite a fuss about that notice. But I got him calmed down some." He stretched and motioned the man out of his chair. "Thanks for holding down the fort. I'll take over now. You go get your dinner."

Jenkins grinned and pulled on his hat. "Y'don't have to tell me twice. I'm feeling kind of hollow." He strode to the door, looked back over his shoulder. "We got a new prisoner. The report is on the desk."

"Right. I'll look it over." Sam tipped back in his chair, laced his hands across his abdomen and closed his eyes, letting the coolness seep into his overheated body. A nap would sure feel good right about now. But first he'd better read that report. He stretched out his hand and picked up the paper.

Mary Randolph!

The front chair legs crashed to the floor. Sam lunged to his feet, scanning the report while he snatched the key ring from the drawer. His lips twitched. By the time he reached her cell, he was chuckling. He unlocked the door, leaned his shoulder against the framing bars and grinned down at her. She was seated all prim and proper on the edge of the cot, looking very composed despite the dirt and grass stains on the skirt of her gown. "Good afternoon, Miss Randolph. What brings you here to enjoy our hospitality?"

Those brown eyes of hers flashed up at him. "Good afternoon, Captain. I am here because one of your policeman invited me."

"I see." His grin widened. She was not as unruffled as she pretended. Underneath all that poise, she was mad as a wet hen. "Would that be the one who found you at the courthouse ordering the laborers and foreman about, and refusing to allow the children to go back to work when they were told to do so?"

Another flash of those incredible eyes. "He

did not *find* me. I sent one of the workers for you and he brought the other policeman in your stead. The rest of your statement is correct." She looked down and brushed at a spot of dirt on her skirt.

"And what did you hope to gain by such behavior?"

Her head lifted. "Medical treatment for Tommy. And a doctor's orders that the children were not to work in such heat. Which I accomplished." A look of pure satisfaction spread across her face.

His heart bucked. "And landed yourself in jail in the process."

She nodded, gave him a smug little smile. "Yes. And the children, also — where they are out of the sun."

Sam's heart thudded. He shook his head, gave her a mock stern look. "Miss Randolph, what am I to do with you?"

She slanted a look up at him from under her lashes and flashed him a cheeky grin. "Pay my bail?"

He had never wanted to kiss anyone so much in his life.

"In *jail,* Mary? You spent the afternoon in *jail!* I thought you were at the *Journey's End.*" James lifted his hands and raked his fingers through his hair.

"I intended to be, James. But . . . well . . . I was waylaid as I explained." She smiled up at him. "You look exactly like Father when you do that."

He rounded on her. "Do not try to distract me, Mary. It will not work. What were you thinking of?"

Her chin lifted. "I was *thinking* of getting those children out of the sun before they all sickened . . . or worse." She tried another smile. "As you would have, had you been in my place."

James stopped pacing and looked down at her. "That is different! Forgive me, Mary, but you have got to stop being so — so bold! What would have happened to you if Captain Benton were not a friend?"

"He is. And he is also *present,* James." Heat climbed into her cheeks. She turned so the captain could not see. "Perhaps we could delay this discussion until later?"

James spun around, lifted his hands in surrender. "*You* talk to her, Captain. She will not listen to me." He stormed off the porch and strode up the road.

"Well, gracious! I am glad I did not tell him before we had supper. It would have quite ruined his meal. And ours. If it has not done so anyway." Mary turned from watching James to look up at the captain.

He was half sitting on the railing, leaning back against the corner post with his long legs stretched out in front of him, looking at her. Her heart fluttered. She frowned and looked away. "I apologize for that unseemly display, Captain. James sometimes becomes protective of me. I wanted this to be a pleasant meal, to thank you for bailing me out of jail."

"No thanks were necessary, Miss Randolph. But it was a very pleasant supper. I enjoyed the company."

She could not sit there with him so close any longer. She rose and walked to the top of the steps. Light flickered across the southern sky. "James is very entertaining."

"I wasn't speaking only of James."

The soft words sent a delicious little shiver rippling through her. Foolish woman! She forced a laugh. "I suppose I am entertaining, too. At least, my escapades must seem so."

"I wasn't speaking only of entertainment, either."

She scowled. Why did he talk like that? So soft and deep. It was like . . . like dark, warm syrup. And it seemed fraught with meaning. Of course it was not. It only seemed that way to her feckless heart. *Help me, Lord.* She wiped her hands down the long skirt of her yellow cotton gown and stole a sidelong glance at him. He had not moved. It only felt as if he had drawn nearer. She wished he would go. Prayed he would stay. And was disgusted with herself for caring either way. He was another woman's beau.

Silence reigned.

She tried desperately to think of something clever or amusing to say, but all she could think of was him. How compassionate he was. How handsome and strong and kind and gentle and utterly special he was. Miss Stewart was a very fortunate woman.

A steamboat whistled. Another answered. A horse's hooves clopped against the cobblestones of Market Street.

"James is right, you know. I understand his concern over you."

The syrup again. Warm and sweet. She would probably dream about it tonight.

He moved, and every fiber of her being tensed, aware of each whisper of cloth as he rose — every tap of his boot heel against the wood porch floor as he came to stand beside her. Her lungs strained to fill. How foolish, foolish, *foolish* she was!

"You should be more careful of yourself. It will do the orphans no good should you come to harm."

The orphans. Yes. Of course. The orphans.

She braced against the disappointment, swift and hurtful, that rose to dash the tiny bit of pleasure she had felt at the thought that he cared what happened to her. Why would he care? He belonged to another. She must keep reminding herself of that. Not that a man like Samuel Benton would be interested in her anyway.

Lightning glinted across the distant sky. Thunder rumbled. Perhaps it would cool off tonight. She brushed back her hair and nodded. "I know you and James are right, Captain. I am far too impulsive and bold for my own good. But . . . well . . . I had to help the children." She looked up. He was gazing down at her.

"I was not aware that you took food to the children every day."

She gave a tiny wave of her hand. "It is not much. Some biscuits and jam. A cold drink. Sometimes a pickle. They like pickles." Why did he not look away? She ran her hands down the sides of her long skirt again. Spoke to fill the silence. "It is to help strengthen them. And it gives them something to look forward to. I thought it would make their days a little better — for now, I mean. Until I can get them out of jail." She clamped her mouth shut to stop her chattering.

He nodded, but still his gaze held hers.

Heat crawled into her cheeks. "Is there something wrong, Captain? You are staring." She lifted a hand to her face. "Have I a smudge, or —"

"No. There is nothing wrong, Miss Randolph. Nothing at all." His eyes darkened. "You have very expressive eyes. The tiny honey-colored specks throughout the brown shine when you are happy and flash when you are angry. Your eyes glow with warmth when your emotions are touched."

The words flowed into her heart, settled there though the warmth she felt at them was unwelcome. She raised her chin. "I will thank you to not make such remarks to me, Captain. I find them inappropriate from a man who is courting another woman."

"My remarks stand as spoken, Miss Randolph. I am not courting another woman."

Disappointment flooded her. She had never known the captain to lie to her. "I *know* of Miss Stewart, Captain."

"What of her?" He leaned a shoulder against the post beside him and looked straight into her eyes. "I have not seen Miss Stewart on a personal basis for some time. A fact you can easily verify to be true or false."

A rocky patch, Mrs. Lucas had said. Could

it be there was a rift they had not mended? Would he be that relaxed if there was no substance or truth to his words? She *could* easily find out if what he said was true.

He was not lying. And she was too quick to believe all men were like Winston Blackstone. Remorse for her accusation brought an apology rising to her lips. "Please forgive me, Captain. I did not realize you were no longer courting Miss Stewart. I — I hope the loss of her companionship was not too painful for you."

He straightened to his full height and stepped close to her. "In truth, Miss Randolph, it was not. I discovered some time ago that Levinia Stewart is not the woman for me." He moved closer, locked his gaze on hers. "Would you like to know how I made that discovery?"

She nodded, held her breath.

"I looked into a pair of beautiful, honey-flecked brown eyes."

CHAPTER TWENTY-ONE

Mary leaned forward, studied her reflection in the mirror and frowned. The captain could not have meant what she thought he had meant. It had *seemed* he said he . . . favored . . . *her* over Levinia Stewart.

She straightened and finished tying the ribbon encircling the thick fall of long hair at her nape. It was clear she had misunderstood. For such a thing was not possible. It was only her silly heart wanting its dream to come true.

Still . . . he was no longer courting Miss Stewart. Had Levinia perhaps refused his suit? She snorted. Now that was another ridiculous notion. And it would not explain his remarks about her eyes. . . .

She stole another quick look in the mirror. No, they were still the same. Perhaps a little . . . dreamier. Oh, she was being utterly ridiculous!

She spun about, left the dressing room

and walked to her bedroom window. The rain was falling in earnest now. It drummed on the roof, splatted against the window and sheeted down the small panes to splash against the sill and run down the brick walls of the house.

Sulfurous yellow streaked from the black sky to the earth with a wicked snap. She flinched, listened to the thunder crack and grumble away and wished she could open the window to the welcome coolness of the outside air.

Outside.

She smiled, hurried to the cupboard and shrugged into her dressing gown and slippers. Light flickered throughout the room as she ran on tiptoe for the stairs.

"Ah-ha! I see we both have the same intention."

She jolted to a halt, looking up at James. "The porch?"

He nodded and stepped back to let her precede him down the stairs. She went down two steps, looked back over her shoulder and laughed. "I call dibs on the swing!"

"Oh, no. You will not pull that old trick on me." He leaped down the two steps.

Mary yelped, whirled, lifted the front of her nightgown and raced down the stairs,

James's footsteps thundering behind her. She giggled and sprinted for the door, grabbing the knob.

Strong hands grasped her waist. Lifted her off her feet.

She squealed and pushed at his hands. "James, *no!*"

He gave an evil little laugh, set her down behind him, then opened the door and shot across the porch to plop down dead center in the swing.

Mary marched over, fisted her hands on her hips and stood in front of him so he could not swing. "Move over." She struggled to keep the laughter from her voice. "You have to share."

Lightning flashed and gleamed on the white teeth exposed by his grin. "Uh-uh. It was a race. I won."

"You cheated!"

"So did you."

She snorted.

They both burst out laughing.

James scooched over and patted the seat beside him.

"*Thank* you." Mary turned and smoothed her skirts forward to sit down, heard a creak and tensed to jump out of the way. She was too late. The forward edge of the swing caught her behind the knees and her legs buckled. She fell backward onto the slatted seat, bumped against the arm he held across the back to cushion her landing. She joined his laughter, waited for the right moment then pushed her toes against the porch floor in rhythm with his to keep the swing from wobbling.

He nudged her with his shoulder. "That felt like we were ten years old again."

"I know." She looked over at him and grinned. "We should do that more often. But not in front of the children."

The swing creaked. They pushed their toes against the floor in unison, maintaining the gentle to-and-fro motion. Rain beat against the shingles, sluiced off the roof and landed with a splash on the ground. Lightning sizzled from the sky, grounded with a sharp crack. She looked at him and they shared another grin. She jabbed him with her elbow. "You flinched."

"So did you."

Their laughter blended with the rumble of the thunder.

"The cool air feels good. Almost like back home."

She nodded, reached forward and pulled her dressing gown closed over her knees. Her nightgown was becoming damp from the rain spatters when they swung forward.

"James?"

"Yes?"

"Are you in love with Rebecca?"

He leaned to his side, turned his head to look at her. "That is quite a jump from 'you flinched — so did you.' Where did that question come from?"

She shrugged, rubbed at the sudden coolness where the warmth of his arm had been. "I was only wondering."

He relaxed back into their former shoulder-to-shoulder position. "Rebecca and I are in love with one another."

She felt his smile. "That makes it perfect." She looked up at him. "I am so happy for you, James. I want you to be happy always."

"Thank you, Mary. I want the same for you."

"I know." She looked down, fiddled with a button on her dressing gown. "How — I mean, *when* did you first know you loved Rebecca?" She glanced up, saw him smile into the distance.

"Remember that day we met her outside the church, when I helped her into her father's farm wagon? That was it. When she looked down at me and our gazes met — I knew."

I looked into a pair of beautiful, honey-flecked brown eyes. Her pulse skipped a beat. Could it possibly be that simple? Or was it only the longing of her heart? *Poor little Miss Mary. She'll have a hard time findin' herself a husband, bein' plain like she is.*

The swing wobbled. James glanced at her. "Sorry." She waited for the right moment and shoved her toes against the porch again. The swing evened out.

Veronica, my beloved, what man would not choose your petite, blond beauty and sweet nature over Mary's dark, angular plainness and bold, forthright ways? The memory still hurt . . . but not as much as it had. *I discovered some time ago that Levinia Stewart is not the woman for me. Would you like to know how I made that discovery?* Her breath snagged. *I looked into a pair of beautiful, honey-flecked brown eyes.* What was she to believe?

"James? If you were not my brother — I mean, if you were another man. Would you think me . . . attractive?"

"No. I would think you beautiful."

"Truly? If you were another man?" She looked over at him. "Heart's promise truly?" She held her breath. You could not lie when you said "heart's promise."

"Heart's promise truly." He turned his head to look at her. "You have never been vain, Mary. Quite the opposite. So I know you are not simply questing after a compliment. Why are you asking?"

She shook her head. "No reason. I was only wondering. James, that day after church — when you were talking about how beautiful Rebecca was — I thought you were talking about Miss Stewart."

"Not likely."

"Do you not find her very beautiful?"

"I do not." He gave her a look as though she had lost her mind. "Men look at women differently than other women do. Not that we do not appreciate a beautiful face and form. But there is much more to beauty than dimples and curls, Mary. And the first time I looked into Miss Stewart's eyes, that day we met her and the captain on the portico at the courthouse, I knew how shallow and vapid her beauty was. The woman has no heart. When you look in Miss Stewart's eyes, all you see is Miss Stewart. There is nothing beautiful about a woman in love with herself. Does that answer your question?"

"Yes. I think I am beginning to understand. Thank you, James." *I discovered some time ago that Levinia Stewart is not the woman for me. Would you like to know how I made that discovery? I looked into a pair of beautiful, honey-flecked brown eyes.* She sighed. Perhaps her heart had read too much into the captain's words. Most likely he had only meant that when he had compared her eyes with Miss Stewart's eyes, he had discovered Miss Stewart's vanity.

At least the captain did not consider her shallow or vain. That was something.

But how lovely it would be if she had not misunderstood him after all.

Had he said too much? Too little? Should he have stayed instead of walking away? No. He had said enough. Sam frowned and pulled off his boots. If he had stayed he would have asked Mary to marry him. And he could not do that. Not yet. He did not want to scare her away by saying too much too soon. Not that Mary frightened easily.

His lips twitched. He would have liked to have seen her ordering that foreman and those workers around. Standing there with those children gathered around her and defying the order that would have sent them back to work. He could imagine how her eyes had flashed, and how that little chin of hers had jutted into the air. She was a fighter. No doubt about that. But fighters sometimes got wounded. And above all he wanted Mary safe. Especially her heart. And the mayor was a formidable foe.

Light flickered throughout the room. Thunder clapped and boomed. The rain poured off the roof in a wide, shimmering waterfall. Sam walked to the window and tugged it open. Fresh, cool air flowed in. One good thing about this room — the storms came from the other direction. He could always open the window.

How did Mary feel about him? Would she welcome his suit? There were moments — like when she was perched on the cot in that cell and looked up at him — when he thought she might. Then the next minute she went all cool and prickly on him and he was unsure again.

Sam huffed, yanked off his shirt and tossed it over the back of the only chair in the room. That moment in the cell had been hard! He'd had to hold on to the bars of the cell to keep from charging over there and taking Mary in his arms. But he wanted it to be right, with everything proper and settled, before that happened. Because once he held her, he didn't intend to let go.

He turned at another flicker of lightning and walked back to the window. He loved her. Above and beyond anything he had ever known, thought, imagined or dreamed. And he'd give his life to have her love him, too. He might as well, because without her in it, his life would not be worth living.

He shook his head, leaned down and peeled off his socks. If he ever ran across Thomas, he was going to shake his hand. He'd arrest him first, but *then* he would shake his hand. If it hadn't been for Thomas's scheme of stealing the insurance money, he never would have looked into those steamboat mishaps. And if he hadn't been investigating them, he would not have met the Randolphs. Strange how that all worked out. It had sure saved him from making a costly mistake. He snorted. Costly was right! Levinia Stewart would most likely have gone through his money smooth as a canoe glides through water. But the real cost would have been all he would have lost. He never would have known love.

Sam tossed the socks at the foot of the chair and flopped down on the bed, staring up at the soot smudge on the ceiling and listening to the rain. It always made him think of a woman's tears. His mother's tears. But he didn't feel as if his mother was crying tonight. For some reason, it felt as if she was smiling. And Danny, too.

Poor Danny and Ma . . . Knots twisted in his stomach. He had a promise to keep to them. The old bitterness rose and twisted the knots tighter. He had heard James Randolph say that the Lord was blessing the orphans. That it was evident in the way things were working out in spite of the mayor and aldermen and other spiteful folks in St. Louis. Randolph said that God often worked His blessings through people — like him and Mrs. Lucas and the Ladies' Benevolent Society.

He couldn't go along with that. God wouldn't use a sinner like him. And while Mrs. Lucas had a good heart — she was lonely and helping these orphans gave her something to do. As for the Ladies' Benevolent Society, most of them seemed to want to help now, but they got into it because Mrs. Lucas shamed them into it. Still . . . things were working out. The orphans were being helped. Was Randolph right? Was it God?

Sam rose up on one elbow, pounded his pillow into shape and turned over onto his side. Mary had told him about the mayor's reaction to the pastor's sermon on God loving everyone equally and being no respecter of persons. But he didn't believe what the pastor said either. If it was true, why hadn't God sent someone to care for Danny and his ma and him?

His face tightened. He flopped onto his other side and stared at the plaster wall.

One of those chips in the paint looked like a rooster . . .

Lightning flashed. Thunder rolled. Something flickered before him — like a picture against the wall. More of an impression really. Two women, each holding an umbrella and basket, standing outside a door with the lightning flashing behind them.

Sam rubbed his forehead, blinked and closed his eyes. There was something about those women . . .

Lightning flickered against his eyelids. Thunder crashed.

The images came again and memory broke through the walls of years of denial. More images flashed. The women standing outside their house, begging to be let in. His father drunk, shouting at them to go away, that Ruben Benton's family didn't need anybody's charity. His mother, sick in bed, holding Danny next to her. And him, huddled in the corner, crying and bleeding from the beating his father had given him for going to the church to ask for help.

Sam opened his eyes and stared at the wall. He had blamed God for not helping his mother and Danny and him. All these years he had blamed God for not answering his prayers, and for the beating he had received for turning to the church for help that never came. But help *had* come. God *had* sent someone to help them. And his father had sent them away. God didn't kill his mother and Danny. His father had.

Sam swallowed hard, all the hurt and sorrow and guilt swamping him as he faced the truth. He had known it when it happened. When he was only seven years old, he had known it was his father's fault that his mother and Danny had died. But no matter how terribly his father had treated them all — he was still his father. And he had not wanted his father to be guilty. So he had blamed God. And he had run away so he would not have to look at his father and remember.

And he hadn't.

Until now.

Sam scrubbed his hard, callused hand over his squeezed-shut eyes and cleared the lump from his throat. He was tired of harboring bitterness. It was time to be free of it.

He turned on his back, opened his eyes and stared up at the ceiling. "God, I was wrong to blame You for Ma and Danny dying. I ask You to forgive me. And I ask You to help me never to run from the truth again."

He listened to the rain, watched the

lightning glint across the ceiling. And his dream house came to him, more clear than he had ever seen it. His showcase house sitting on the grassy knoll in all its splendor. And then it crumbled and disappeared. There was nothing left. Only the grassy knoll. And Mary. And behind her . . .

Sam smiled, snapped a salute toward the ceiling. "I hear You, God. I'll start out tomorrow."

Chapter Twenty-Two

Sam slipped his rifle into its scabbard, gave his bedroll a jiggle to be sure it was secure and led Attila out of the stables. The air was fresh and sweet after last night's rain. He took a deep breath of the invigorating coolness and scanned the sky. It was clear and blue, but the sun was already giving off shimmering waves of heat as it climbed. It was going to be another hot one.

He checked the knife at his belt, made sure his Colt Paterson was ready to hand and mounted. Too bad he could not have started earlier. But he had to get things set up so his men could cover his patrols and the jail while he was gone. And he had to wait till James Randolph was at his office. He tilted his felt hat forward so the wide brim would shade his eyes, gave Attila a pat on the neck and settled in the saddle. "All right, boy. Let's go."

He walked him out to Pine Street, reined

left and urged him into an easy lope when they reached the road out of town. He scanned the area ahead, alert for any sign of trouble, but his thoughts traveled backward toward town, toward Mary. A smile touched his lips. It was a new, not unpleasant, sensation for him, missing someone.

Mary put the maps Miss Withers had requested on the highest shelf and aligned the edges. "Where did he go?"

James shrugged and looked around. "He only said to tell you he had something to take care of out of town. And that he did not know how long it would take him."

"Oh. I see." What of the children in jail? She knew the captain protected them as much as he was able. And what of the land she needed to purchase to have a permanent dock for the orphanage? Who would tell her where to locate it? And what of her? She smoothed her hands over her hair, then lowered them to dangle idle at her sides, aware of an empty feeling deep inside. How could she miss him already?

"I think this may be a mistake, Mary."

"What is a mistake?" She turned. James was standing at the huge wheel, his hands on the protruding pegs the pilot grasped to turn it, staring out the windows at the river.

She smiled. In spite of his business garb, he looked like a little boy with a new toy.

"Putting the schoolroom up here." He swung his arm in a wide arc that encompassed the entire wheelhouse. "There are no walls up here, only windows. How are these young boys, and girls for that matter, to pay attention to their schoolwork?" He looked at her and grinned. "They will all be sailing the rivers and oceans playing 'pirates' in their minds."

She could not resist. "Is that what you are doing?"

He slewed his mouth to one side and squinted an eye at her. "Aaarrgh! Guilty, mate!"

Laughter bubbled up, burst out. She turned in a circle. The view *was* magnificent. "I fear you may be right, my dear brother. I believe some curtains forward of the worktables may be in order. Now get away from that wheel before I make you walk the plank. I am finished here and have work to do on the main deck." She started down the stairs.

He fell into step behind her. "You are a cruel and heartless captain, my dear sister."

"Headmistress, James." She smiled over her shoulder at him. "Headmistress of the Journey's End Orphanage . . . almost."

"Is that doubt I hear?"

"It is fear." She stopped in the play area of the main cabin on the boiler deck and faced him. "So many people have helped to make this orphanage possible, James. Look . . ." She walked to one of the bedrooms for the children and opened the door. There was a cream-colored quilted coverlet embroidered with trailing vines of small pink roses, and matching curtains at the window. A small, flower-patterned rug laid on the polished wood floor. "Mrs. Shields of the Ladies' Benevolent Society paid for this room. And she did the embroidery work herself. She said it gave her pleasure because she never had a daughter of her own."

Tears flooded her eyes. She spread her arms and spun in a circle. "All of these bedrooms are like that, James. And look at this playroom! A lovely new rug, and game tables and toys and —"

She stopped, clenched her hands and stared at him. It was too much. It was suddenly all too much. He rushed over and put his arms around her, tugged her close. She burrowed her head under his chin. "Oh, James. How can I tell all those lovely people the orphanage may come to naught because of that *mean-natured* —" she thumped his chest with her fisted hand "*— heartless —*"

thump "— *cruel* —" thump "— *miserly mayor!*"

She lifted her head, looked at him through her streaming eyes. "I hope all of his mean acts toward those children are multiplied to him a thousand times!" She swiped at the tears on her cheeks. "And I am sorry if that is not a Christian attitude, and I disappoint you. But I cannot help it! I do not have any land. And no one will sell me any. And now the captain is gone and I do not know what to do!"

She burrowed her head back under his chin and sobbed out all the hurts she had held for so long.

"Shh, easy now, boy. Easy now." Sam drew Attila's head close to his chest and placed his hand over his muzzle. These Indians weren't of the friendly tribes from around the St. Louis area, and though it was likely safe, he would as soon not test that theory. It was too easy for a man to disappear in the unsettled lands of the frontier. Fortunate for him, he had heard them coming.

He scanned the area as best he could from behind the screen of vine-draped branches and frowned. The Indians were coming from the direction he was traveling and there was no telling how many more might be following in their path. Should he need to make a run for it, his best chance would be back across the river and into the woods on the other side.

He took another quick glance at the Indians, dropped his gaze to the path in front of them. Staring would draw their attention. The vines were thick and the air still. There was no breeze to betray his presence to them. Luck was with him today. Or maybe it was something more than luck. Maybe God had taken a hand. He'd give that some thought when he had time.

The Indians rode by, bare legs gripping their ponies, folded blankets for their saddles. Sam tensed, barely breathing as they passed, then thundered off down the trail.

He waited, straining to hear and identify every sound. A fish jumped. Birds flew over the water, the snap of their beaks as they caught their food on the fly loud in the silence. Squirrels ran along branches, jumped from tree to tree. The wilds returned to normal.

Sam released Attila's head, patted his neck. "Good boy." The horse pricked his ears at the whispered words, tossed his head. Sam led him out from under the tree branches and stepped into the saddle. He touched the handle of his knife, rested his hand on his Colt and let out his breath. "All right, boy, let's go find Charlie and Harry. But you warn me if any more Indian ponies come our way."

"All you kids, get back to work!"

Mary looked up at the foreman, but held her tongue. Captain Benton was not around to bail her out of jail. A band of worry clamped around her chest. Where was he? He had been gone four days. Was he all right? She managed a smile. "Goodbye, children. I shall see you tomorrow."

She watched the children hurry off to resume their work, then knelt on the grass to put the quart jars, tin cups and dirty, cloth napkins back in her basket. The unusual heat had ceased and there had been no more sickness among the children, but it still made her ache to look at them. Their thin arms bore bruises, their hands scratches and sores. They were all gaunt, with large eyes full of fear and distrust and pain. Most of them never smiled.

She longed to tell them to be brave, that they would soon have a new home, but, of course, she could not. She did not know if that would come to pass. She had tried, with James's help, to purchase land fronting the river for a permanent docking site, but no one would sell. It was always the same. The property owners would not speak with them once they found out their name. Now they had run out of prospects. And without the captain here —

"Tidying up after your daily charitable duty, Miss Randolph?"

Mary looked up. Levinia Stewart stood in front of her, beautiful in a gold linen gown. Her matching bonnet was a confection of shirred linen and lace rosettes.

But her expression was one of haughty condescension.

Mary's ire stirred. She rose, forcing Levinia to look up at her. And for once she took satisfaction in her height. "It is not a duty, Miss Stewart — it is a pleasure."

The blue eyes narrowed. "Oh, come, Miss Randolph — you may forget your pose as the virtuous woman. The captain is not around to see your performance."

She all but spat the words.

Mary took a breath, held it and counted. "My performance?"

Levinia's eyes narrowed farther. "Do not act the innocent with me, Miss Randolph. My father and I are aware of your little scheme. You forget his office is in the courthouse. He sees you through his window, playing the sweet maiden feeding and caring for the darling, hungry, little street children. It is disgusting!" She reached up and bounced a golden curl.

Mary looked away before she gave in to her desire to reach over and yank it. "And what motive would I have for such playacting, Miss Stewart?"

"Why, to capture Captain Benton's affections, of course. A woman like you would need an excuse to gain his interest." The woman's eyes turned from hot to icy cold. "I do not know how you learned that Father has been grooming Samuel to be the future mayor of St. Louis, Miss Randolph, but that is not of importance."

Mary's mind raced. Captain Benton was to be *mayor?* He had said nothing —

"What *is* important is that you realize your little scheme with the orphans will not work. Captain Benton is also being groomed to be my husband. As his wife, I will continue my mother's role as the head of the women's organizations and charities of St. Louis. It is a position for which I am perfectly suited. Captain Benton realizes that. When the captain returns, I will let it be known to him that I have forgiven him for his small act of rebellion against Father and am willing to accept his suit again. I assure you, he will choose me over you and your pathetic street urchins."

Mary's heart lurched. *Was* it Levinia that had stopped the captain's courtship of her? Her stomach churned. Had he lied to her? What exactly had he said?

Levinia smiled. "You have failed, Miss Randolph. I do not know why you feel someone like you would be a fit wife for the future mayor of St. Louis, but Father has stopped you from opening that ridiculous steamboat orphanage, and that will end Captain Benton's little rebellion against Father's authority as well. I am planning a December wedding. There is nothing left for you here in St. Louis, Miss Randolph. I suggest you go home to wherever it is you came from. Good day."

"A moment, Miss Stewart." Mary waited until Levinia turned back to face her, drew herself up and looked straight into those blue eyes. "I know nothing of Captain Benton's plans of being the next mayor. Nor am I interested in the position of mayor's wife that you so crave. I am, however, very interested in the children who have no parents to love or care for them, and find no mercy in the hearts of those in authority. And I have *not* failed in my purpose to create a home for them. I *will* do so. You may take that message back to your father, Miss Stewart. Good day."

She turned her back and returned to her task. Not for anything would she let that woman see the doubts her words had raised — the uncertainty only Captain Benton could erase.

"I'm sorry to hear about Harry, Charlie. He was a good man." Sam looked down at his hands. Studied the dark brew in the tin cup he held. It was the most bitter coffee he had ever tasted. But it was nothing like the bitterness that had grabbed hold of his heart. How was he to ask Charlie to sell him the land Harry had prized? And he had thought God had directed him here for that purpose. He held back a snort, took another swallow of the bitterness instead. All that risk. All that way. For nothing.

"Harry thought high of you, too, Captain. He was always talkin' 'bout the chance y'took on us. Riskin' yer money so's we could come out lookin' fer the silver. Nobody else would listen t' us." The old miner stuck a fork in the meat in the frying pan and lifted it onto a tin plate. He added a scoop of beans and a biscuit, slid the plate across the table, then tossed a fork after it and turned to fill another. "Yessir, Harry thought high of y'all right."

And now Harry was dead. Crushed by a collapsed wall of a worthless mine he spent a lifetime searching for. And Mary's dream of an orphanage had died with him. Sam stared down at the plate, his stomach twisted in a knot so tight no food could get through it. Harry and Charlie had laid claim to that parcel of land on the Mississippi way back when they were young. Every time he saw them, Harry talked about living on that land when they were old. It had been their dream. But he had figured, for enough money, they would be willing to change their dream and sell him the property for his showcase house. Now, with Harry gone, that was unlikely.

"Bear meat's best et afore it gets cold, Captain. Mite gamy else."

Sam looked across the table at the old miner, nodded and picked up his fork. If he had to ask the man to part with the last link he had to his dead brother, the least he could do was eat the man's meat. He took his knife from the sheath at his belt and cut off a bite.

"Glad ya come out t'see how we was comin' along with the mine, Captain. Saves me makin' the trip back t' St. Louis." Charlie shoved back from the rough board table, then opened a trunk and rummaged through it. "This here's fer you." He shoved a folded piece of paper at him. "Harry said I was t' give it to ya should anything happen to him."

Sam put down his knife and fork and unfolded the paper. "This is a will." He hadn't even known Harry could read and write.

"Yep. He got that writ up all legal-like 'for we left town t' come out here."

Sam nodded, started reading. Read it again and looked over at Charlie. "It says here Harry leaves the property on the Mississippi to me."

Charlie nodded, broke off a piece of biscuit and mopped up the meat juice on his plate. "Harry had high notions fer that land had he lived t' see 'em out. But he wanted you t' have it if anything happened t' him. Thought high of y' he did."

Sam slipped his rifle into the scabbard, checked his bedroll. "What are you going to do now, Charlie? Are you going to try and open the mine again?"

The old miner glanced at the rubble and shook his head. "Nah, it's a fittin' grave fer Harry. I'm fer the west country. Always did want t' see them high mountains I heard talk about. Now Harry's gone, I'm gonna do it."

Sam nodded and mounted. "Keep a sharp eye out for Indians. I ran into four of them on my way here."

The old man grinned. "If yer gonna go, an arrow's as good a way as any."

"I guess that's right." Sam returned the grin and leaned down to shake the hard hand. "If you ever come back St. Louis way, look me up. I'll be on Harry's land." *By God's grace and with His blessing.*

"He'd be right proud of that, Captain. Luck to y'."

"And to you, Charlie."

Sam reined Attila around and started down the trail, the will in his pocket, a smile in his heart and a new, strong confidence that God might have a plan for him after all.

Chapter Twenty-Three

"The steamboat is finished, Mrs. Lucas. It sits idle in a berth at the Mississippi and Missouri steamer line docks." Mary rose from the settee and walked over to look out the window. Behind her the floor clock ticked off the minutes.

"Everything is prepared for the orphans — the ones I know of. Even clothing." She looked over her shoulder at the elderly woman. "And Ivy has laid in stores enough for an army." She tried for a laugh — could not summon one. "And still I have no land — nowhere to dock the *Journey's End.*"

She turned and made her way back to the settee. "There are orphans in jail — and an empty orphanage. And I have run out of ideas for getting the two together. Without land, it is impossible."

Mrs. Lucas leaned forward and patted her hand. "Nothing is impossible with God, Mary. Trust Him. He will make a way."

"I know, Mrs. Lucas. And I believe His hand has been guiding all that has happened, that He has been blessing our efforts for the orphans' sakes. But now . . . well . . . even you have tried to help us purchase land, to no avail. And I — My faith is failing me."

The faded blue eyes studied her. "This is not like you, Mary. I have never seen you so discouraged. Is there something else troubling you?"

Doubts. Fears. A wounded heart that cannot quite trust, but refuses to forget. "I am tired. Perhaps that is my problem."

"Perhaps." Mrs. Lucas did not look convinced. Mary sighed and rose. "It is getting late. I have to go home. I have already stayed too long." She leaned down and kissed the woman's dry, wrinkled cheek. "Pleasant dreams, Mrs. Lucas."

"And you, Mary. Rest well."

That was not likely. Mary frowned and let herself out of the house — walked to the street. She could not remember the last time she had slept well. Yes, she did. It was the night before Miss Stewart had spoken to her. Since that day, in spite of her best efforts to keep believing her plan for the orphanage would succeed, doubt slipped in. And the captain . . . She did not know what to believe about the captain.

Mary pulled her long skirts to the side and stepped around a small pile of horse droppings as she turned onto Market Street. Had the captain hinted at an . . . interest . . . in her because Levinia had cast him aside? And, if so, now that Levinia wanted him back . . .

Her steps faltered. Mary steadied her pace and walked to the cottage. She must face facts. The captain would return to Levinia. There was no reason why he should not. Why would he, or any other man, choose her — with her bold, stubborn ways and her wild dreams — over a life of privilege and power with Levinia? Unless — her breath left her — unless Captain Benton had discovered who her father was. Justin Randolph was a far wealthier, far more influential man than the mayor. Perhaps —

No! Mary shoved open the gate, ran into the cottage and up the stairs. She removed her bonnet and gloves, put them in the cupboard and sank down onto the bed. She would not entertain such thoughts about Captain Benton — she would *not.* He had proven himself to be an honest and honorable man over and over again.

But Levinia is so beautiful. And you are plain. The hateful words whispered through her mind, insinuating themselves into her spirit. *There has to be a reason. . . .*

The past crowded in on her, undermining the new confidence she had received from the belief that God loved her. God — not Samuel Benton. Mary closed her tearing eyes, struggling to hold on to her fledgling faith — her newfound belief that with God, all things were possible. But the hurt she felt pushed it beyond her grasp. She grabbed a pillow and hugged it tight against her aching heart. "Help me, Heavenly Father. Please help me. I don't know what to think — or who to believe. Please show me the truth. And help me to trust again."

Dawn was breaking. Sam rose, went to the window and looked at the pink and gold streaking the lighter gray of the sky over the river. He had ridden long and far yesterday. But he had never felt more rested and eager for a day to begin. *Please, Lord, bless my efforts today.* He grabbed his shaving gear and strode down the hall to the dressing room. He had a lot to do, though some of what he planned had already been accomplished. He had met James Randolph returning home from Rebecca Green's place last night when he had ridden into town, and they had worked things out between them.

Sam chuckled, looked in the cloudy mirror and ran his hand over the stubble on his chin. James Randolph was fast becoming his best friend. And soon, if things went as planned, he would be a lot more than that. Yes, sir, a *lot* more than that. He grinned, took out his razor strop and started honing the blade. He wanted a good, sharp edge. No chance of skipped whiskers today.

Mary shook out the long skirt of her gown and straightened the lace adorning the collar and the sleeves. She had to hurry. She had promised the children she would take them to the *Journey's End* today. They missed playing on the steamboat. But with the steamer now in a berth at the levee, it was inappropriate for them to stay for very long. And, truth be told, she could not bear to be on the boat. It saddened and infuriated her to see the bedrooms empty and the kitchen, dining room and schoolroom idle when there was such need. But her well was dry — she had been unable to come up with a solution.

Mary sighed, shook off the thoughts as she had shaken out her skirts and crossed to the dresser to search for a matching ribbon to hold her hair. She selected a narrow one of darker rose color, carried it to the mirror, wrapped it around the thick knot of hair at the crown of her head and tied it in a neat bow. Now for her gloves and bonnet, and she would be ready.

She started for the cupboard, paused at the writing desk, staring at the piece of paper resting there.

"Dear Mother and Father."

That is all she had written. There was nothing new to tell them. No good news to impart. But perhaps she would think of something cheering to write them about today. And James had good news to share with them. Rebecca had said yes to his proposal. Also, the new luxury steamboat he had commissioned was almost ready for her maiden voyage, though they had yet to choose her name. It was important to make the right choice.

She smiled and walked to the cupboard to fetch her bonnet and gloves. The *Right Choice* . . . That might do very nicely for the name. She would have to suggest it to James tonight.

A steamboat blew its whistle. She frowned and hurried toward the stairs. James was going to meet her at the dock. He said he had something to show her. If only it were a deed to a piece of land!

■ ■ ■ ■

"Thank you, Judge. I appreciate your hurrying things along for me." Sam tucked the papers in his suit pocket and shook the judge's hand.

"Not at all, Captain Benton. I am pleased to help. That is a fine piece of land — some of the best acreage around. And I was not unaware of what has been happening lately. I think you are both prudent and wise to get the deed secured."

Sam nodded and put on his hat. "All legal and settled, sir. I am taking no risks."

He strode from the judge's office, his long legs making short work of the distance to the jail. The interior was cool and empty. He crossed to his desk and did the necessary paper work. When he finished, he shoved it in the drawer and rose. The papers in his pocket crackled. He grinned, patting it to make sure it was secure, and left the building.

The sun played hide-and-seek with white puffs of cloud. A soft breeze blew off the river. A beautiful day. Sam crossed Chestnut Street and cut across lots to Market Street, every step he took one of pure pleasure.

The children were working the land on

the right side of the courthouse. Some were picking up stones. Some were carrying the buckets to dump in the wagon. Others were raking and leveling the soil. The sight hit him in his gut. He quickened his stride. "Children, come here to me."

They froze in place, stared at him, dread clear to read on their faces. They thought he was taking them back to the jail. "Come on. Leave your tools and come over here." He beckoned. They put down their buckets and rakes and started moving toward him, their steps slow. They preferred the hard work in the outdoors to sitting idle in their dark, dank cells.

"What is the meaning of this, Captain Benton? These kids work until suppertime."

Sam looked down into the foreman's scowling face and shook his head. "Not anymore. These children are no longer prisoners. They are free."

"We'll see about that!"

Sam turned.

One of the workers stepped out of the courthouse and pointed their way. A second — short, portly — figure emerged. The mayor bobbed down the steps, skirted the hole for the foundation of the new north wing and hastened across the broken soil toward them.

Sam could hear his labored breath before he reached them.

The children started backing away.

He looked down, read the wary looks on their faces and remembered the smell and taste of fear. When you were young and on your own, you developed an instinct about trouble. That highly developed instinct was one of the reasons he was a good policeman. "It's all right, stay by me." They obeyed. But he could sense their tension — their readiness to scatter.

The mayor puffed up to him, glared at the idle children and waved his hands. "Get back to work, all of you!"

Sam lifted his hand and stopped their movement. "The children stay with me, Mr. Mayor. They are no longer prisoners. I am taking them to the new home Miss Randolph has provided for them aboard the *Journey's End.*" He felt the children's reactions, knew they were hanging on his every word. "From now on, Mr. Mayor, you will have to hire laborers."

"Nonsense!" The mayor's eyes narrowed. "No one can live on that steamboat. She has no land —" He stopped. Stared at the folded paper Sam held. "What is that?"

Sam smiled. "That, Mr. Mayor, is the deed to the piece of property where the

Journey's End will be permanently docked."

"Impossible!"

"Not with God, Mr. Mayor. Not with God."

The mayor snatched the deed from his hand, reading it.

"All legal — and settled in the city records, Mr. Mayor." How good it felt to speak those words. His only regret was that Mary was not here beside him.

The mayor's face turned purple. He crushed the deed in his fist and shook it in the air. "You are through in this city, Samuel Benton! I will see to it that you never get elected to any office, or position of importance, or —"

"That, too, is in God's hands, Mr. Mayor. And in the hands of the people of St. Louis. Now, I believe we are finished."

He looked down at the children who had crept steadily closer and smiled. "You all heard what I said to the mayor. Miss Randolph has prepared a home for you all — and that fulfills the requirement of the law. You are free. Now, follow me! I am taking you to her."

There was an explosion of shouts and laughter.

Sam grinned and started for the street

with the children in a tight cluster around him.

"What have you to show me, James?" Mary tossed her bonnet on the table and smoothed her hands over her hair. The children had disappeared into the upper decks of the *Journey's End.*

"You will see in a moment, Mary. And then — Ah! There they are now. Come with me." He turned from the window, grasped her by the elbow and tugged her after him out the door. "Look!"

"What?" Mary turned to look the direction of his pointing finger and gasped. "What — How —" She lifted her hands to cup her chin, her fingers covering her mouth while her eyes filled with tears and her heart ricocheted around in her chest. She stared at the cluster of dirty, ragged, bone-skinny children marching toward her, Captain Benton in the lead. She had never seen a more beautiful sight. One of the figures broke free of the pack and ran up the gangplank to stand in front her. The rest halted where they stood.

"Miss Mary, the captain says you made this here boat a house for us. And we don't have to go to jail no more. Is that true?"

Mary swallowed hard, looked at the captain, saw him nod and looked back at the boy. "Yes, Tommy. It is true. This is your home now."

The boy turned, lifted his arm and whipped it forward. "It's true! It's true! We don't have to go to jail no more!"

There was a wild whoop. The children raced for the gangplank, ran up it and slid to a stop. They looked about, stared at the swings, at her, at James, uncertainty in their eyes. She got control of her emotions, smiled down at them. "Welcome home. I am so glad to see you all. Come, I will show you —" She stopped — looked down at James's restraining hand on her arm.

"No, Mary. Miss Withers and Ivy and I will show them around. There is someone waiting for you."

Mary turned, looked at the captain standing at the end of the bright red gangplank and her heart soared — then plummeted. It reached depths she had not known existed. He had stayed away so long. It must be because of Levinia. She brushed her hands down her skirt, pushed her feelings aside and started forward. She had to thank him. No matter how he had trifled with her heart, he had brought the children to her. Perhaps one day she would learn the truth.

She stopped in front of him and looked

up. "I do not have words to thank you for what you have done for these children, Captain. But how did this happen? How is it that they are free to stay here, at last?"

A whistle blasted. Mary nearly jumped out of her skin. She spun toward the boat. Steam was pouring from its stacks. The paddle wheel at the stern was churning. And James, Ivy, Miss Withers and the children stood on the "porch" deck. They grinned and waved. She stared. "Where are they going?"

She whipped back around. "Stop them, Captain! They —"

"Will be fine, Miss Randolph. I give you my word."

He smiled. Her treacherous heart fluttered like a wild bird trapped in her chest.

"Now . . . if you will stop asking questions and come with me, I promise you will have all your answers soon."

He took her elbow and she could not refuse, though the words hovered on her lips. He led her to a chaise, handed her in and climbed beside her. The beat of the horse's hooves on the cobblestones matched the cadence of her heart when he looked at her and smiled.

Mary accepted the captain's hand down

from the chaise, though it cost her a few lost heartbeats to do so. She moved a few steps away from him toward the top of a knoll and looked around while she gathered her frayed emotions. Trees of different varieties were scattered here and there over its surface and on the grassy fields at the bottom of its slope. She could hear the whisper of the river flowing by on the other side. "What is this place? And why have you brought me here?"

"More questions?" The captain smiled.

Mary looked away, lest she lose her train of thought. "Yes. And I believe you promised me answers, Captain Benton."

"So I did." He stepped toward her.

She backed up a step. "You can start by telling me where the *Journey's End* has taken the orphans." She gaped at him, struck by a sudden frightening thought. "Did — did they kidnap them? *Oh, my!* Whatever —"

"The children have not been kidnapped, Miss Randolph. I assure you, everything is perfectly legal. I am an officer of the law, after all. Or at least, I was. I believe I have been let go from my job."

"Let go! But — but —" She bit off the rude question. Made an effort to control her shock.

"But . . . why?"

Heat climbed into her cheeks. "I'm sorry, Captain. That is your personal business. I have no right to pry."

"Oh, but you do, Miss Randolph." He stepped closer. "You are the reason I lost my position."

"*I* am?" Understanding dawned. "The orphans."

The captain nodded. "The orphans, too. Certainly. But it was you personally who turned the mayor against me." His eyes held hers.

"I don't understand. What —"

"Levinia became jealous of you."

"Jealous! Of *me?"* Incredulity swept through her. "Whatever for?"

"Because you changed my dream."

She stared at him, bewildered. At a loss for how to respond. It was just as well. The look in his eyes had robbed her of the ability to speak. He looked away. Waved his hand through the air.

"This spot where we are standing is the place where I intended to build my showplace house."

"Your *showplace* house?"

He nodded. His face taut, his eyes shadowed. "My father was a drunk. Whatever money he earned, which was little enough, he spent on drink. There was seldom food in the house — and never enough of it. We lived in shanties and sheds with holes in the roofs and walls and with broken window-panes."

He stared out into the distance, a faraway look in his eyes, and she knew he was seeing those hovels.

"I had a little brother . . . Danny." He shoved his hands in his pockets, hunched his shoulders. "He was a great kid — always smiling and laughing. Except when he was too hungry or sick." He stopped, took a deep breath.

He *was* a great kid. His brother had died. Her heart ached for him.

"Ma was sick, too. I tried to take care of them as best I knew how, but there wasn't anything to do for them. No food to give them the strength to get better." He glanced her way. "I stole some whenever I could find a way." He looked into the distance again. "There were no dry blankets to put on their bed that had not been wet through from the rain. So I prayed. I asked God to give us food to eat and a house with no holes in the roof so Danny and Ma would get well. That didn't happen, so I snuck out and went to a church and asked for help. Some ladies came. But my pa sent them away. Ma and

Danny . . . died. Danny was four years old. I was seven."

He turned and looked at her. "I promised them before they died that I would be somebody someday. That I would be so rich and important nobody would ever sneer at me again. That's why I wanted a showplace house. Right here on this knoll where everyone would see and admire it."

He shrugged. "I ran away from my pa and I worked at everything I could find to do. I saved my money and invested it to make that dream come true. And Levinia Stewart was part of that dream, too. I was going to have a showplace house and a show-off wife. The mayor's daughter — my guarantee into St. Louis society."

Pain stabbed deep in her heart. She looked down and held herself quiet, waiting for him to finish.

"And then I met you."

The words were soft, deep, husky. She heard him walk to her. Stop inches away from her. She looked up.

"You ruined my dream, Mary Randolph. I looked into those beautiful brown eyes of yours and everything I thought I wanted simply crumbled away. God used you, Mary. He used you to show me what true beauty is. That is why Levinia is jealous. You know what I want now?"

She couldn't be hearing him right. It wasn't possible he found her more beautiful than Levinia.

She could not breathe — or speak. He placed his hands on her shoulders and turned her toward the river. There was a new dock jutting out into the water.

"I want this land used to fulfill your dream. It's perfect for that. There's a dock for the *Journey's End.* And fields to grow vegetable gardens and graze animals on. And plenty of room left over for the kids to run and play."

Something white fluttered at the corner of her eye. She turned. He was holding a piece of folded paper out to her. "It's yours, Mary. All legal and settled. I had the deed recorded this morning. And then I went to get the children and bring them to you. That's when the mayor told me he would see to it that I never held a public position again."

Tears streamed from her eyes. It was selfish of her. So selfish. But, oh, how she wished it wasn't all for the orphans. Oh, how she wished —

"Don't cry, Mary." He took hold of her upper arms, pulled her close. "There's one thing more I want."

The deep, hushed words flowed over her.

She clutched the paper in her hand and made herself look up at him.

"If you agree, I would like to build a house here on the knoll. A home for you and me." He tipped his head down. His blue eyes dark and filled with tiny flames. "I love you, Mary Randolph. I've loved you since I first looked into your beautiful brown eyes. Will you marry me?"

The impossible had happened. Samuel Benton loved her. Mary nodded. Forced her soft answer from her constricted throat. "I will marry you with joy, Samuel Benton. I love you. Now and forever."

"Ah, Mary. My beautiful, beautiful Mary. My love." His arms slipped around her, tightened, his head lowered.

Her breath caught, hung suspended.

His mouth touched hers and her lips opened to the warmth like flower petals open to the sun. She went on tiptoe and slid her arms around his neck, answering his love.

A whistle blew.

On the river below the knoll, the orphans' boat steamed around a bend and nosed its way to the dock that was its *Journey's End.*

Epilogue

Mary took her father's offered arm and stepped to the doorway of the *Journey's End* dining room. Everyone assembled there turned and looked at her.

"She looks like a *princess!*"

Katy's voice, filled with awe, floated to her. Her eyes teared up.

"Uh-uh, she looks like a flower."

That was Ben. Her lips twitched in memory.

"No, she looks like a *bride.*"

And that was Callie. Sensible, wonderful Callie.

Mary swept her gaze to the children grouped together with Miss Withers, Ivy and Edda on the left at the front of the room and smiled. Eighteen children beamed back at her. She glanced to the right, and there was Mrs. Lucas standing beside James and Rebecca — his bride of two days. And her sister Sarah holding her new baby boy, while Sarah's husband, Clayton, held their little girl, Nora. And her aunt Laina and uncle Thad, and her cousins William and Emma and Anne. And her mother —

"Ready, Mary?"

And Pastor Thornton. And Sam, who stood waiting for her with that soft look of love in his eyes that was for her alone. She swallowed back a rush of tears and nodded. "Yes, Father, I am ready."

She smiled and walked toward her love.

Sam stood in the doorway of the main salon of the *Right Choice* and looked down at his bride. His heart thudded. Every time he saw Mary his love grew stronger. And to see her holding her baby nephew did queer things to his stomach. Mary looked up and their gazes met, held.

"All right, you two, stop looking like James and Rebecca!" Sarah laughed and reached for her new son. "Go kiss your husband, Mary, before he bursts or something."

"An excellent idea." Mary laughed and ran to him. He gave her a kiss with a promise attached, which she returned with an equal amount of fervor.

"Did I hear our names mentioned? Move over. Make way for my bride." James laughed, nudged Sam and Mary aside and started into the room with Rebecca beside him.

Mary nudged James right back. "You and Rebecca have been married a whole two days longer than we have. I am the bride here."

"Are not."

"Am, too."

"Children!" Elizabeth Randolph laughed and looked at her husband, Justin. "I despair of our children ever stopping their competitions!"

Justin laughed and lifted little Nora into his arms. "Pray God, you may be right, Elizabeth. Life would be dull without them. Though I do not know where their competitive spirits come from."

"Well, certainly not from me, dearheart!" Laina crinkled her nose at her brother, then smiled at her husband. "Tell them I am very mild of manner, Thad."

Thad grinned and dropped a kiss on the top her head. "And have the good Lord strike me dead?"

All the Randolphs hooted — Laina among them.

The whistle sounded. The paddle wheels churned up water as the *Right Choice* —the new luxury liner of the M and M steamer line — started downriver. Mary and Sam stood alone on the deck and waved to the children and her family on the shore. Their farewell was returned with enthusiasm.

The boat steamed around the bend on the way to St. Louis to pick up passengers for its maiden trip to New Orleans, and the children, running along the riverbank shouting and waving, were lost to sight.

A whole month alone together before they returned. Mary sighed with contentment, leaned back against Sam's broad chest and placed her hands over his hard-callused ones that joined the protective circle of his arms around her.

He bent down and placed his mouth by her ear. "Happy, Mrs. Benton?"

She glanced over her shoulder at him and smiled. "Very happy." Her smile widened into a cheeky grin. "Mother and Sarah both think you are devastatingly handsome!"

He raised his knee and knocked the back of hers. It buckled, and she pressed more closely against him. His arms tightened. She smiled up at him. "And Father thinks you are very intelligent and . . . um . . . intuitive about finances."

He gave her a mock scowl. "You should have told me your father was the owner of the M and M line."

She laughed, twisted around inside the circle of his arms, slid hers up around his neck and gave him a saucy look. “And have you marry me for my money?”

He grinned, that slow, breath-stealing grin that made her heart do all the foolish things a sensible heart would never do, and lowered his lips to hover over hers. “There would be no danger of that, Mrs. Benton. Not once I saw your beautiful, honey-flecked brown eyes.”

Dear Reader,

It has been pure pleasure for me to write this story. I confess, I fell in love with Mary and Sam who had distorted self-images because of the careless, hurtful words of others. It was a joy to open their eyes to the truth.

I have learned it is inevitable that bits and pieces of my life will sneak in when I write a story — and that happened in *The Law and Miss Mary.* Sam is driven by the events of his youth to obtain worldly success. My father was driven to achieve the same goal. I learned from observing his life how important it is that we watch our words when we speak to others — especially children. And, as I have three older, beautiful, intelligent and very talented sisters, I know from experience how Mary can feel "lesser than" her older sister, Sarah. I also know, from experience, how freeing . . . how liberating . . . how utterly wonderful it is to learn that God loves us just as we are.

When we truly understand that God really is no "respecter of persons" — that He judges us not upon our outward appearance or worldly success, but looks upon our hearts through His eyes of love — it casts off the shackles of self-doubt and inferiority and frees us to trust Him. And when we trust in Him, we are free to become all we can be, for in God "all things are possible." That is a truth Mary's cousin Emma Allen learns as she travels west in the wagon train captained by Zachary Thatcher.

I pray that each reader of this book may come to know, in an ever deeper and more meaningful way, the wonderful, warm and secure love of God.

I do enjoy hearing from my readers. If you would care to share your thoughts about this story with me, I may be contacted at dorothyjclark@hotmail.com or www.dorothyjclark.com.

Until next time,
Dorothy Clark

QUESTIONS FOR DISCUSSION

1. Mary believed herself to be "plain" though others found her attractive. What formed Mary's opinion?

2. Sam is driven to be "somebody" — what drives him?

3. Mary did not believe herself favored by God. Why? Do you know others who feel as Mary did?

4. What brings Mary to the realization that she is beautiful to God?

5. How does God work in Sam's life to bring him to the knowledge of His love for him?

6. What is the ultimate truth Sam learns?

7. Mary sets out to care for the orphans —

do you believe God used her acts to bless her? Can you think of a Bible verse that proves your opinion?

8. What is the ultimate lesson Mary learns?

9. The pastor's message of God being no respecter of persons was received in different ways by different people. How did Mary receive it? The mayor and Levinia? Sam? Can you think of a Bible verse that illustrates this?

10. What illustrates Sam's spiritual growth?

11. What illustrates Mary's spiritual growth?

12. Mrs. Lucas played an important role in the story. Do you approve or disapprove of her actions?

13. How do the orphans open Mary's heart to the truth of God's love for her?

14. What opened Sam's eyes to what is truly beautiful?

15. What opened Mary's heart to be able to accept Sam's love?

ABOUT THE AUTHOR

Critically acclaimed, award-winning author **Dorothy Clark** lives in rural New York, in a home she designed and helped her husband build (she swings a mean hammer!) with the able assistance of their three children. When she is not writing, she and her husband enjoy traveling throughout the United States doing research and gaining inspiration for future books. Dorothy believes in God, love, family and happy endings, which explains why she feels so at home writing stories for Steeple Hill Books. Dorothy enjoys hearing from her readers and may be contacted at dorothyjclark@hotmail.com.

The employees of Thorndike Press hope you have enjoyed this Large Print book. All our Thorndike, Wheeler, and Kennebec Large Print titles are designed for easy reading, and all our books are made to last. Other Thorndike Press Large Print books are available at your library, through selected bookstores, or directly from us.

For information about titles, please call:
(800) 223-1244

or visit our Web site at:
http://gale.cengage.com/thorndike

To share your comments, please write:

Publisher
Thorndike Press
295 Kennedy Memorial Drive
Waterville, ME 04901